Thumbelina

Thumbelina

Andrea Koenig

Scribner

First published in the USA by Scribner, 1999
An imprint of Simon & Schuster Inc.
First published in Great Britain by Scribner, 1999
An imprint of Simon & Schuster UK Ltd
A Viacom Company

1 3 5 7 9 10 8 6 4 2

Simon & Schuster UK Ltd
Africa House
64-78 Kingsway
London WC2B 6AH

Simon & Schuster Australia
Sydney

A CIP catalogue record for this book is available from the British Library

ISBN 0-684-85844-4

Printed and bound in Great Britain by
The Bath Press, Bath

in memory of Guthrie House

ACKNOWLEDGMENTS

My wildest, deepest thanks to Gillian Blake, my editor, and Barbara Kouts, my agent. I thank Tobias Wolff, David Shields, Melanie Rae Thon, Michael Martone, Tom Rackmales, Silvia de la Garza-Bassett, and John Randall. Syracuse University's MFA program provided generous support. I thank the Fulbright Commission for a small room in a very wet city.

Tell me whom you love,
and I will tell you who you are.
HOUSSAYE

august

MY MOM ALWAYS SAID NOT TO TELL PERSONAL INFORMATION to strangers. So I'll fix it so I'm not a stranger.

My name is Thumbelina. I am fourteen years old. I used to live across the street from Bean Park on the second floor of those dirty yellow apartment buildings in Tacoma, the state of Washington. We were the orange curtains right above the American flag.

I am pretty normal lookin. I got eyes the color of my mom's turquoise ring that Lester got her from the mall for their anniversary. Anniversary of what's a good question because them two never did get married. I got a big old head that's too far from my feet for a girl my age but there's nothin I can do about it. On my head I got yellow hair that looks like pee and hangs down into the back pockets of my jeans. Me and my mom had identical hair. People used to say to us, You two sisters? Sometimes my mom laughed because she loved flattery like she loved chocolate. Sometimes she poked me in the back which was at her eye level and said, How could this giraffe be my sister?

My mom left me smack in the middle of this month. Fifteen days ago. After three days we buried her because everybody in this world copies Jesus. We tried to find me somethin dignifyin to wear but I don't have nothin in the ballpark, except if you count my jeans which Delores V. didn't. So I ended up wearin one of Delores's dresses that was aggravatingly big around the middle and hung above my knees like a miniskirt, but she said, You can wear a belt, and she gave me one with a buckle you could knock a guy out with. Didn't improve nothin. She didn't notice. Her eyesight's not what it used to be, like a lot of things in life.

Besides Delores there was Betty Fontana and Chee Chee and Daphne from my mom's work and a couple other of my mom's friends. Lester sat alone in the last row with his ponytail tucked down into the suit that his friend let him borrow. His friend wasn't there. When he went up to say good-bye to her his cowboy boots on the linoleum floor got everybody's attention and Delores leaned over and said in my ear, The important thing is that he's here, Thumbelina.

I kept turnin around and lookin, and sure enough, Donny slouched in finally in his black leather coat and slick hair. Everybody said later, How nice of him, considerin the situation, it bein his car. I was plannin on hittin him up for a place to stay, but he left too quick.

I wasn't goin to go up and look at her but Delores said I should out of respect. It was all right. Seein your mom dead don't make you feel like cryin, you just feel pretty normal. The flowers were all wrong though. I told em orange flowers, please. They said we got to take what we can get, long as it's decent. Yellow's hardly what you call decent. As if we want flowers that's the color of our hair.

Her face was as white as those china plates down at the mall that it was her goal in life to buy, even though they tried to make it look alive with Long & Lashy on her eye-lashes (which I've been known to borrow once in a while) and a lot of red stuff on her cheeks and lips. It made her look pretty, but you can't hide the fact of bein dead. They braided her hair around her head with a pink ribbon wove through and put her in her pink dress with the lacy white collar that me and Delores found in the back of her closet. I wanted to put her in her blue jeans and Rollin Stoners T-shirt so she'd be comfortable, but Delores said they needed somethin with long sleeves and a high neck to cover the marks of the steering wheel. She said jeans weren't digni-fyin attire to arrive in heaven in. Specially tight ones, which are all my mom's got. Delores is a Bible thumper. It hadn't occurred to me that my mom was goin there.

I told em to put slippers on her feet because where she was goin in the meantime it's awful damp and chilly. And my mom's little feet *always* get cold.

~ ~ ~

IT'S BEEN a bad summer for me and my mom, and now that I think about it, I might as well say it about the whole year. Some nights she and Lester would be yellin at each other so loud it was like Johnny Cash had backup singers in my headphones. It bugged her that I spent so much time under my bed eatin crackers and drinkin Sprite. Dreamin, basically. What's wrong with the world that the rest of us live in? she'd say. One night last month, a pretty cold night for July, I had to pee so bad. My mom was yellin and Lester was yellin. Somebody kept thumpin on the wall and I had the feelin it wasn't Lester. I knew if I went out there she'd drag me into it. How come you never touch Thumby? she'd say, you let her get away with murder. Finally I just unzipped and bent down over my old church shoes in the back of my closet. They didn't fit no more anyway. Then I poured it out the window, makin sure to miss Delores's flag. It splattered on her back patio. Good thing she didn't come out to check if it was rainin.

A couple nights later my mom knocked on my door. Thumbelina, she said. I crawled out from under my bed and shoved the dresser out of the way. We sat on the bed. We're gonna leave, she said. I blinked. It was my dream in life to get away from him, like some people dream of a pretty house or a horse.

What are you doin, honey?

Gettin dressed, Mom, if we're leavin.

Not *now,* honey, she said. Not this minute.

I shoved my jeans back in the drawer. When, then? I said.

Soon.

How soon?

As soon as we got a plan, honey.

She told me to keep my toothbrush ready but not to pack nothin. She said we didn't want to make him suspicious. She said lie low and wait for a sign. . . .

Which I thought was comin loud and clear a week later. I was under my covers this time. I sat there blinkin and tryin to get my head cleared, but when I reached for my glasses she whacked my hand. Did you tell him? Tell him what, Mom? Did you tell him? You told him. Tryin to get me in trouble! She hauled out a fry pan from behind her back. I shoved her, but it wasn't my fault her head cracked the corner of my dresser, it was the lamp cord that jerked her down. I helped her right up, but she shoved me into the wall, bloody murder in her eyes.

The next day she brought home all this hair dye. I'm tired of you lookin like me. You're a big old giraffe, Thumbelina. She dragged me into the bathroom and made me get down on my knees over the tub and she blasted on the tap and pushed my head under and squirted plum all over my yellow hair. Her fingernails dug into my head.

Ow, Mom.

Thumbelina, I've been thinkin.

Miracles happen, I said.

She pulled my ear. I want you out a my hair for a while. You're always followin me around with your big old eyes. You're creatin problems between Lester and me.

Oh, blame it on me.

What in the hell does that mean?

I didn't say nothin. She got mad. Don't be goin all quiet on me tryin to make me feel guilty, either.

After she went in the kitchen I stuck my head under the tap and washed my head about a hundred times, but I couldn't get it no lighter than strawberry. I got no idea why I let my mom do that.

She turned thirty-three a couple weeks later, on August sixteenth. Just like Jesus, she didn't go no further.

Why didn't she leave him? Daphne Cooper said, who worked next to my mom at Betty's shop and those two didn't ever get along because my mom had everything Daphne wanted, includin the window chair, and Daphne had somethin my mom wanted: a husband. Chee Chee Rodriguez is nineteen and just got one of those, a guy at Fort Lewis, and she got along with Daphne and my mom fine. She chewed bubble gum while my mom did all the talkin, and wore her hair short like a little boy which further helped this friendship between em. She did trims, manicures, and facial massages that were supposed to wipe out a good ten years. Chee Chee talked like a girl who was just married. She said, Daphne, you are wrong, Angelica loved Lester. How can you leave someone you love? Then she put a slice of cantaloupe in her mouth from the fruit tray on Betty Fontana's kitchen table, where this conversation was occurrin.

Why in the sam hell did she have to pick a man that was so complicated? Betty said, who is the owner of Betty's Beauties and never swears except on special occasions, when her best friend drives into the duck pond, which is only eight feet deep.

Angelica was pretty complicated herself, Daphne Cooper said, plonkin her cigarette into the conch shell Betty got at the Oregon coast. (Gave my mom one just like it.) What I want to know is, what's goin to happen to him now?

I never knew people's eyes could weigh so heavy. Man. I sat cross-legged on the door mat with my back against the glass, and the question in all them eyes was clear: *Is he goin to move in with that guy? Is he goin to be all right?* But I had wax in my ears. I just didn't answer.

It sounds kind of serious, if you ask me, Daphne said.

Daphne, honey, nobody is, Chee Chee said, her smile makin it loud and clear: Let's talk about it some other time, huh, Daphne old girl?

She meant me. Sittin there alone. Like if they didn't talk about it, it wouldn't be true.

~ ~ ~

THAT NIGHT saw me layin on Delores's shag carpet because I couldn't fit on her short little couch and I'd like to see who could. I was supposed to be sleepin. I was eyein the headlamp in the sky through the gauzy livin room curtains. She had made me spaghetti and meatballs for a good-bye dinner but I said, No, thanks, Delores, I'm not hungry.

She touched her big cottonball on her head. You aren't goin to make things better by starvin yourself, honey.

I didn't want to hurt her feelings but I wasn't in the mood to eat. So when she went into the livin room to switch the TV, I unlaced my high-tops and shook the plate in and I folded my shoes in my arms. I went into the bathroom and watched my dinner slide into the toilet. I sponged the tomato sauce out with toilet paper. It was a stupid thing to do with my dinner.

I looked at myself in the mirror because it was there. At my skinny face and my thick old glasses and my yellow hair that needed washin bad. When I take off my glasses people say I'm pretty. I'm too blind to know if they are lyin. All of a sudden I started to cry. Mirrors are bad news.

Her fist thumped the door. You OK in there?

Yeah.

You sure?

Yeah.

You know this is the only option we got, Thumbelina.

Silence.

It's goin to be all right, Thumbelina.

Silence.

I listened till she creaked away on her flat old feet and then I turned on the tap full blast and sat down on the tub and let go into my hands till they tasted like my mom's cookin when she was havin a salt cravin. When I was done I put my glasses back on and I went and started makin this list:

SOME STUFF I SHOULD REMEMBER ABOUT MY MOM ANGELICA SKYLER

1. *Men would brake for her even when it said* DON'T WALK, *but the other half gassed it.*
2. *Had weird little knotted feet like she was half tree. She wouldn't ever wear sandals or go barefoot, not even if you paid her.*
3. *Loved to hang things from her ears.*
4. *Orange tulips were her favorite flower.*
5. *Lived to turn the pages of romance books.*
6. *Loved that one song ThenighttheydroveoldDixiedown by Whatsherface.*
7. *Top lip twice as thick as the bottom one. (It worked on her.)*
8. *Loved the sun. (Or the other way around.)*
9. *Eyes the color of her old jeans they wouldn't let me bury her in.*
10. *Loved chocolate. Had a weird way of enjoyin it. Like for instance when Lester was sorry for beatin her up he'd go to Pay 'N Save and buy her a big old box of the good kind and she'd say You're just tryin to make*

me fat, and she'd take them down and give them to
Delores, but Delores never fell for that. She would put
them in her freezer. Then Mom would sure enough
wake up in the middle of the night with a chocolate
cravin and come look for me to go down and get them
for her. That's how me and Delores got to be such
good friends.

11.

12.

13.

14.

15.

16.

17.

18.

~ ~ ~

THE LADY from foster care came by to get me, Mrs. Whatever, didn't catch her name. She was fat and all in red.
That's a color I can't stand. I felt like a bad dog goin to the
pound. I know what that feels like because me and my
mom took three dogs there but not all at the same time.
The lady had a big lump of black hair on top of her head
and a stiff kind of face that didn't smile. I got the feelin that
it could smile if it had to, but it's a lot of work to smile if
you are not in the mood.

Delores brought her into the livin room where I was
watchin *General Hospital* with my paper bag of stuff on my
lap. I had my extra pair of jeans and my sweatshirts and my
horse and my catcher's mask and underwear and socks and
my Walkman and Johnny Cash tapes and my toothbrush

and I had her pair of black high heels wrapped in newspaper. She wore a size five. I'm already in a ten and a half. Course I'm tall don't forget.

That all you got? the lady said.

I showed her my guitar case next to the TV. Inside I had my ballet slippers, which never did see the stage, and a roll of comic books flattened against the fretboard.

That it? she said.

Yep, I said. I wondered if I traveled lighter than other kids. I'm not experienced at leavin home. Only time I ever did was overnight for Cynthia Kazlowski's slumber party last April. We weren't friends. I was on her dad's softball team. I only took clean undies and a toothbrush and Cynthia's present, candy bars I got from 7-Eleven. I bombed at that party pretty bad. I'll get to it.

Delores got the lady from foster care some coffee and I kept my eyes on the soap opera. After Mrs. Whatever had took two sips she got up. Let's go. You could tell she was the kind of lady who had a schedule. So I picked up my paper bag of clothes and the lady took my guitar. I said bye to Delores. She said, Bye, Thumbelina. I followed Mrs. Whatever to the door. Damn red heels clickin on the wood. I said good-bye to Delores again because I've always had a tendency to repeat myself.

Her silver car was in our spot because Lester's van was across town in Marcus's driveway. We put my paper bag of stuff in the trunk but when she reached for my guitar I said, Sorry, Charlie. I got in front and balanced the guitar between my knees. I am a big sucker for lookin back at things so that I will always remember: Delores stood at her kitchen window, between the black curtains with yellow butterflies. Her old, little hand waved. Up in our kitchen window hung the other thing Lester gave my mom

{22}

besides the ring. A papier-mâché clown painted every bright color God made. It smiled out at the ViewCrest parkin lot from under an umbrella. For all the stuff they threw at each other they never did touch that.

We started up Alphabet Hill and before we hit Y Street tears were boilin over like pots on the stove when I was cookin. I always cooked or we wouldn't have eaten and I was always burnin stuff because I was always readin comics and forgettin. I wasn't good at kitchen stuff. My mom wasn't either because she always said what does cookin get a woman in life but a fat husband? But she was better than me. When she put her mind to it she could make pretty good meat loaf off the Quaker Oats box and fish sticks and grilled cheeses in the waffle iron that made you sure to pick off every bit of cheese from your chin. But she hadn't cooked much lately. Mostly at dinnertime she was layin on her bed with her arm over her eyes tryin to block out the world.

But the world is pretty tough to block out. It comes and gets you from every angle. I'd burn dinner and old Lester would go in and whack her for it, because he hated burned food. Especially once he got to know Marcus and realized there was finer things in life. Whack Thumby, why don't you? my mom would holler at him. She burned it. He would just whack her harder. Sometimes in the middle of the night she'd come into my room and haul me in from outer space. Thumby, what's your secret? she'd whisper. How come he treats you so good and me so bad? What am I doin wrong, honey? I'd just tear my covers out of her hands and roll over and say, Whatever, Mom.

~ ~ ~

THE REASON I bombed at Cynthia Kazlowski's birthday party is because I was too good of a catcher. This was before I quit the team which I did because I was tired of usin my butt to warm up the bench. Course not even my big old butt could do much toward warmin up that freezin metal bench at HellyWack Field. All the parents would come and bring blankets and food and cheer us on. My mom couldn't come because she had work and her love life to tend to. I don't know what they would of thought of her in her miniskirts and embarrassin tops. First thing you know she'd be gettin up to cheer and there'd be her rear end hangin out there. All the wives would be hittin their husbands on the head for lookin. I already had a bad enough reputation from bein a little kid under her influence, when she'd do me all up in makeup for kindergarten and make me the laughinstock. There's advantages to bein big. I planted my feet one mornin and said knock it off to the eyeshadow headin my way. And she did.

Cynthia's dad was the coach, that'd be Dr. Kazlowski. He was a doctor. Everybody called him Dr. K. He had all this out-of-control silver and black hair and he wore hikin boots all the time, even in summer, and a red bandanna, and he climbed mountains sometimes. He was tall and had glasses with wire frames and they lived in a house with a pool in the basement. Reason I know is because of the slumber party, which I'm gettin to, when we went swimmin and barbecued hot dogs. Girls were supposed to bring their dads for the food part of it. I told everyone he was out of town on business. That's probably the oldest one in the book. Well, then, bring your mom, Dr. K. said. Oh man. Couldn't say she was out of town on business too. It was hard leadin a double life. She works nights, I said, grittin my teeth and hopin it would fly past him and the Mrs.

who was standin there givin me the eye. I couldn't of brought her anyway without gettin her to redo her wardrobe and come sober and that wouldn't of happened. I always operate best on my own when I'm lyin, which is most of the time.

It was a pretty fun party. All the dads were laughin and jokin around with each other and hittin each other on the shoulder and holdin their girls' hands.

We ate our hot dogs and potato chips and I was probably eatin the most of anybody because it wasn't every day that I got food like that. Then we changed into our swimsuits and we split up into teams for relay races. I never had no swimmin experience but Dr. K. said, You be on my team, Thumbelina, and he took my arm and put me in line behind him. Cynthia smiled at me. She looked good in a pink bikini, her legs were all brown from the tannin machine. All the girls in eighth grade were goin. It was only April. So I got in line, feelin real special. Geena was in line behind her dad, Mr. Delaney, tryin to kill me with her eyes, but I wasn't lookin at her. I figured I could swim all right. All you got to do is jump in and move your body this way and that way, two arms and two legs, what could be so complicated?

So somebody blew a whistle and Mr. Delaney and Dr. K. jumped in. Water splashed our feet and the girls squealed. Not me, I was concentratin. Dr. K. was winnin. All the girls were jumpin up and down and screamin. Geena was yellin at her dad to move his butt faster. She got so excited she fell in and they just got her out in time before Dr. K. smacked the wall. He had ten feet on Mr. Delaney. Nothin on this planet was goin to make me lose his lead. I put my arms up and bent my legs and smashed into the water. I could of made it to China by nightfall. I kicked my legs and moved my arms in that windmill motion. I can fake a lot of things but swimmin is not as easy as it looks. It's one of those things you got to learn young, like small talk and flirtin. I didn't swallow water, I gulped it down like it was on sale. I floated down through seven feet of water, starin up at the blue light. It felt like two hands were inside my head tryin to push my ears to each side of the pool. Oh man. I wasn't thinkin too clearly but I probably knew they weren't goin to let me drown on the bottom of their pool. That'd be bad for morale. Then somebody was in the water beside me and my face was back in the air. I was in Dr. K.'s arms. Mr. Delaney reached down for me, and they both lifted me out of the water. (I guess I'm heavy.) I was sheddin water like a faucet. Dr. K. whacked me over the back and got me breathin again, although it was news to me that I'd stopped.

None of the girls looked at me. I sat on the edge of the pool and Dr. K. wrapped me in a towel, the dads' feet bunched up around me, and I could feel them girls not lookin at me. I couldn't lift my eyes to Cynthia's face. When I finally did stand up it was Geena's brown pair smirkin at me, from the edge of the group.

Dr. K. asked me if I was OK. I said that I was. He asked me if I wanted to phone my mom. I said, Nah. I said, Thanks, I'm OK.

Then the other girls asked me politely if I was OK and I said, Yeah yeah, I'm fine. Cynthia touched my arm. She said I could borrow her hair dryer. The whole thing seemed to drop then as we went off to take showers and get back in our clothes. I liked to think it did, anyway.

Mrs. K. brought out chocolate cake and ice cream and Cynthia opened her presents. The other girls took bites out of their cake and put it down but not me. I peeled the cake away from the icing and let it melt on my tongue. Then I pushed in the ice cream, which was softened just right. Last I scooped up all the icing and sat that on my tongue. It was the best cake I'd ever eaten. Didn't taste like nothin I remembered my mom *tryin* to make. I put down my plate and eyed the other girls' cake goin to waste. Everybody on a diet or somethin? I wondered. Must of showed in my face. Another piece of cake, Thumbelina? Mrs. K. said. She was probably thinkin bad thoughts because her face went pink all of a sudden. You only get embarrassed when you got a reason to be, my mom used to say, right up there with, Whatever you do, put shoes on your feet before you go to 7-Eleven, Thumbelina, you are one poor sucker if you arrive somewhere without shoes. No, thanks, I said to Mrs. K. I didn't want to come across like some pig.

Cynthia got a lot of cool presents. Sherry from first base gave her a box of chocolates with a red ribbon, which is like a warnin bell for fancy. Geena the shortstop gave her a pink lipstick and a matchin nail polish. Mary Anne from right field gave her a red teddy bear with a white stomach holdin a sign that said I NEED LOVE. Leslie from second gave her perfume that made em all go ooh and aah.

Cynthia passed the chocolates around and hugged the bear and sprayed on the perfume. I was dyin to ask her if I could try a little on my wrist, but nobody else asked so I figured they were already wearin their own perfume there. I didn't want to say or do nothin that would embarrass me further. I wanted to get home with a lot of good memories to sort through underneath my bed.

What with all that smellin and cake eatin I forgot she had to open one from me. Hey, where's Thumbelina's present? Geena hollered. You opened everyone's but hers, Cynth.

Thumbelina? Cynthia eyed me with her clear blue eyes that guys in our class were fallin in love with right and left.

Maybe she forgot it, sweetheart, Dr. K. said, givin his daughter the eye.

That's right, dear, Mrs. K. said quickly, her face goin a little red again.

Did you forget Cynthia's present? Geena said loudly.

It was lyin in a paper bag over there under my mom's brown corduroy coat with the black fake fur collar, which she let me borrow for this special occasion. I left the group to get it, and when I turned around none of em were lookin at me again. A bad sign.

Cynthia unrolled the bag and stuck her hand in carefully (least I remembered to take out the sales receipt). She pulled out a Reese's Peanut Butter Cup, with nuts.

Oh, isn't that nice? Mrs. K. said in a voice as sticky as hair spray.

Somebody laughed. I'm not sure who, since I was eyein my hands, which were folded neatly in my lap.

Out came a Mars Bar. Then a couple Milky Ways. Cynthia laid em out in front of her and just stared at em. There's a Three Musketeers too, I said, reachin over and dumpin it out for her. I tried to get you a little of everything.

Say thank you, Mrs. K. said. Say thank you to Thumbelina for her lovely gift.

Thank you, Thumbelina, Cynthia said. She said it polite too. Amazin. I felt relieved. You are welcome, I said back.

Cynthia sort of avoided meetin my eyes for the rest of the night after the dads went home. There were enough girls piled into her bedroom that I got by without sayin much, just laughin along with what other people said. I went into the bathroom to brush my teeth. I left the door open to be polite, in case another girl wanted to come in with me. I guess Geena was waitin for that. She shut the door. She shook a bottle of makeup remover out onto a cottonball and got busy wipin colors off. Her brown eyes met turquoise eyes in the mirror. I am goin to tell you somethin for your own good, Thumbelina. Don't take this wrong, OK?

My eyebrows did her the honor of movin up about a half inch.

For your information, you are not Cynthia's friend. She only invited you because you're on the team and you're only on the team because her dad feels sorry for you. So don't be gettin no ideas that she likes you, because she doesn't particularly. You should hear what she says about your . . . clothes, she snickered, eyein my sweatpants and T-shirt which I had put on for bed.

Cynthia don't say nothin about my clothes, I fired at her.

Not to your *face,* Geena said. Cynthia's got manners, man.

She had rubbed all the colors off her face. Now we were man to man.

I blinked. Well, Geena, thanks for lookin out for me, I said in a voice that sounded stale.

She zinged me a look. I guess your mom was pretty drunk the day she named you.

They don't let you drink in the hospital, I pointed out very reasonably.

Then how'd you get such a stupid name as Thumbelina?

How'd you get such a stupid name as Geena? I fired back at her. And I shoved the toothbrush in my mouth. Pretty soon blood trickled over my bottom lip. I got a strong arm. I wanted to be home right then more than anything in the whole world, under my bed, readin my comics and listenin to my Johnny Cash tapes. But I couldn't do nothin but get in Lester's sleepin bag, which my mom had got out of the storage room downstairs, and zip it up to the top, but that didn't block out the sound of their gigglin and crinklin wrappers of fancy-dance chocolates.

What kind of girl would voluntarily dye her hair that yellow? Geena whispered loudly.

The others giggled a little, wonderin where to go with it.

She doesn't even have a bra, Geena said.

Oh, yeah, she does, somebody said. You got to have one in the eighth grade, it's a rule.

I'll prove it to you, Geena said, and I heard her right by my ear, pawin in my clothes. I tried to breathe evenly, in and out, I knew it would pass like every bad thing does.

Why are you so interested in Thumbelina's business, Geena? Cynthia said in her pretty soft voice.

Because the girl is weird, man.

Leave her stuff alone, Geena.

I'm tellin you, Geena whispered. She does not wear a bra. She likes to tease guys, like her mother. You should see her mother—

Are you still dating that tenth grader? Cynthia said loudly to Leslie, the giver of the perfume.

I got no idea why I didn't get up and knock Geena in the head. Cynthia was pullin for me.

~ ~ ~

So FAR it's turned out all right for me. My foster lady is called Mrs. Leffer. Won't be callin her Mother. She lives in a little house on Heddinger Circle, which is a part of this city that is very far away from ViewCrest Apartments and the duck pond in Bean Park. There are no apartments, just houses, on streets that end in circles. We're the second house from the beginning of the circle. And everybody's got a garbage can and a patch of grass out front to wipe their feet on.

The house has a big kitchen with a linoleum table and a floor that the kid slides on in his socks and a backyard that's mud because of the bad summer we've had and a woodpile under a blue tarp and a Cyclone fence. The front lawn is the color of my hair right now but it's supposed to be somethin pretty great in springtime. I am not plannin on bein here to see it.

Off the kitchen there's a bathroom with two doors that lock from the outside. The other door goes into her bedroom. Totally off-limits. She works in a bank. No sign of a Mister.

I got company. The kid, Roy, who's eight and quiet with black hair and eyes which must of been put in him by mistake because they're so deep and brown you could throw a penny in em and you'd be old before it hit bottom. And this girl, Myrna, who is about five seconds older than me and thinks she is hot stuff, I got no idea why with a stomach that size. She is a pain in my butt already. Always complainin and teasin me like a little orange mosquito buzzin around my head.

Mrs. Leffer put us both out in the backyard with cans of Coke and said, You girls get acquainted. Then she went back inside to the TV. Oh heck. I am not very good at gettin acquainted with girls. This one was a lot different from the softball crowd. She was more dangerous-lookin in black, except for her high heels, which were green. Hunks of silver dangled from her little ears.

I plunked my butt down at the round wood table with the umbrella shut and drippin water. Myrna stood in front of me, hands on her hips. I mean the place they used to be before she got that stomach.

So who are you? Snappin her gum in my face.

Thumbelina.

That's a dumb name.

I didn't say nothin. Wasn't the first time I heard it.

Got a boyfriend?

Naturally.

How come you're here then?

How come you're here? I said, which I've found is a good way to argue.

Because. She snapped her gum. Stan's gone home to the reservation and my dumbass sister don't have a sense of humor.

I got up and went to the door.

I'm talkin to you!

Doesn't look like it.

I slammed the door and went down the hall to my room, which I got to share with her, and started puttin my stuff away. That took about three seconds. I put my other pair of jeans and my cream leggings and my red and blue flannel shirt and my mom's jade blouse, which I plan on growin into, in the second-to-last drawer that was empty for me. I sat down on my bed, which was the bottom bunk, and put my head in my big hands and all this loneliness opened up in my chest.

Pretty soon she came in and sat down on the bed—my bed—and started pickin her hair, which is curly and short and the color of carrots.

You didn't bring any clothes. She unwrapped a new hunk of gum.

You sure did. The floor was covered with tiny tops and socks and skirts I was goin to be gettin the joy of watchin her wear in the days to come.

You poor?

My arm ached to slug her. But I controlled it because my mom always said you shouldn't hit girls, especially when they're half your size. (Always lookin out for herself.)

You deaf, four-eyes?

Shut your trap.

I'm so scared, she said, doin all this fake shiverin. Leffer said your mom is dead.

Myrna knew what she was doin and she was doin it pretty good. I would advise you to shut up, I said.

She drowned in the duck pond. I wish my sister would drown. She's a bitch for kickin me out.

Runs in the family, I said, and I stood up and decked her with the flat of my hand, which I don't need for catchin no more. Her head cracked the bed frame and I grabbed her soft, flimsy arm and jerked her up and plowed her into all that white wall and she rolled over to protect her big stomach and I brought the meat of my fist down on her back. I ripped out carrot hair. She screamed and I said shut up and when she screamed again I kicked the scream back into her.

Then my own hair got yanked. I jerked back into Mrs. Leffer's arms. She seemed to know what she was doin. I was already coolin down or I'd of slugged her too. I let her drag me down the hall by a couple of loops of my hair. I let her shove me in the bathroom. She locked the door from outside. Obviously done this before. I worked my body down between the toilet and the bathtub and dug my chin between my knees. When my mom used to ask Lester how

{33}

come he never hit me Lester would tell her it was because I knew how to keep my mouth shut. It was a lie. I've never kept nothin shut. I opened my mouth and howled.

The TV went up a notch in the livin room. After a while I heard her high heels on the kitchen linoleum. Her little knuckles hit the door. Yoo hoo. You in there?

Silence.

You make plenty of noise till somebody comes to say hi. You're weird.

I've had kind of a long day, Myrna. I would appreciate havin some pleasant silence.

You OK?

Dandy.

You need anything?

Yeah, quite a few things. I doubt you got em.

She won't keep you in long, she's just got to lay down the law. You nearly killed me, you know.

Too bad about that *nearly*.

She said somethin else but I didn't pay no attention because I was cryin. After a while I heard her hummin I'm So Lonesome I Could Cry. I dragged my sweatshirt sleeve across my cheeks. You like Merle Haggard?

No, but I seen the tape in your stuff.

Keep your dumb ass out of my stuff.

Fuck you.

That's original.

Silence for a second, then her high heels went back the way they'd come. Myrna? I hollered after her. Myrna?

Seems like I always want to be left alone until I actually am.

Mrs. Leffer opened the door about midnight and she held the long metal spatula which she also uses for slippin out chunks of cornbread when she's in a cookin mood. I just looked up at her and didn't move.

You done fightin or you want to stay in here all night?

I never was fightin, it was her fault.

Whack! went the spatula on my jeans. Her silver ringlets belly danced above her eyebrows. You got a big mouth, Thumbelina.

Yep. That's what my mom said.

Don't you bring your mother into this.

She's my mother, I can bring her wherever the hell I want.

Whack! went the spatula on my knee.

You must of been a good third baser once, Mrs. Leffer, I said, thunkin my head back against the wall. With an arm like you got.

She dropped the spatula into the sink and sat down on the edge of the bathtub, her big dress came down a second after her. She clamped her fat hand down on my bare knee. You all come to me with so many problems, Thumbelina. I don't know what to do. I didn't do so well with my own kids, either.

That's how we left it between us.

~ ~ ~

I THOUGHT Myrna would get back at me. Maybe grab my glasses like the boys in elementary school used to do. They used to pile on me and swipe em off my face and wave em over my head and say, How much to get em back? I got glasses thicker than a ham sandwich. I'd have paid anything. But I would hold off from sayin so. Finally one of the nicer ones, some Christian type savin up to get into heaven, would bring em back to me. A little scratched or smudged or somethin. I'd wipe em off and shove em on and try to look out more the next time. But I would never see it comin. I was tall but once you had me down I was a goner.

But Myrna didn't do nothin. She was savin it all up, I figured. I'm goin to get you, Thumbelina, just you wait, she passed down in the dark the next night.

I'm holdin my breath, you asshole, I passed back. (You got to give it like you get it in this world, when you are not safe under your bed.)

Her bunk creaked with the effort of her secret plans to get me back.

But after a couple more days it occurred to me that maybe Myrna liked me. And I wondered if I was startin to like her too. We just had to make each other work for it.

~ ~ ~

EVERY FRIDAY it's somebody's turn to choose dinner. This time Roy was in charge. Spaghetti and chocolate ice cream. I sat there starin at the pile of food on my plate.

Thumbelina, are you sick, dear?

No, ma'am.

Myrna snickered into her plate. She's pregnant, ma'am.

I slammed my foot into her knee. She hollered to wake my mom and all the dead. She kicked me!

Damn right, you dumb ass.

Mrs. Leffer's skinny eyebrows shot into her hair. Is that true, Thumbelina?

No, I just hardly tapped her.

No. Are you *preg*nant?

I snorted. No, ma'am. Picked up my fork and started eatin.

Still, I could see the lightbulb click on in her big dumb head.

Got you last, ha ha, said Myrna's green eyes.

Boy, did she.

Over and out, August, you been the worst month of my life.

september

THE FOSTER CARE LADY CAME OVER A COUPLE DAYS before school started, she said I had to repeat eighth grade. She put down her coffee cup. You only attended forty days of school last year, you know.

Since I was aware of this, I didn't say nothin.

You don't like school.

I didn't say nothin.

But you've played extracurricular sports, you liked that.

Sport, I corrected.

Right. Softball last spring. You played on the team.

I warmed the bench.

Well, but you participated.

I shrugged. She was lookin at me expectantly but I couldn't help her out. She sighed. You aren't prepared for high school. I can't advance you. Her big white face looked sad above her black turtleneck.

That's quite all right, ma'am, I said to cheer her up.

I wasn't the only old lady startin eighth grade. Myrna was sharin the honor with me. She didn't seem to mind. Our school is blah blah Middle School just up the street five minutes, goin by my legs. On the first day Myrna said she knew this shortcut. I went along with it but I regretted it right off the bat, because she walks slower than grass growin, especially if she is talkin.

Myrna, if you want to wreck *your* reputation by showin up late, that's fine with me, but I want to keep mine in one piece, OK?

After I have this kid, she said, slowin down another notch in them high heels, I won't have to go to school anymore because I'll get welfare.

They won't let you keep it, I informed her. You're too young.

Look who's talkin.

What do you mean?

You're preggers, dumb shit.

I am not.

Are too.

Am not.

Are too.

Mind tellin me what makes you say that?

She smirked. I got ears. Dumb shit. I hear you in the bathroom.

Maybe I got the flu. I pointed my nose at the sky.

She stopped and bent over her high heels to handle all

the laughs comin out of her. Well that held us up for another fifteen minutes while she laughed her fat old head off. Thumbelina, she said, for your information you're the dumbest dumb shit I ever met, and I've met some. Only so many times I can field that word from her. I slugged her on her fat old arm. I thought for sure she'd whack me back and we could have a real fight and clear things up, but she folded down in the dirt like a cafeteria chair, cryin with all her jewelry clangin, and I took off.

By the time I got to school I was sorry I bopped her because I was lost in swarms of unfamiliar faces. I just tucked my head down and plowed through. The school's a little brown building that's fallin apart. The playground's missin chunks of asphalt, although the basketball rims are nice and orange. Inside the air tastes stale in my mouth and the halls are too little for that many kids.

I had to go to the principal's office for my schedule. They just hand it to you and you leave. It took me a while to find geography. The man with the big old polka-dot bow tie showed me my seat, which I appreciated, so I sat there. Kept my trap shut and nobody noticed me. I was glad I wore jeans and a sweatshirt, nothin flashy like Myrna.

I kept incognito through math. Sat down in my seat where the teacher told me. Where are you from, Thumbelina? the teacher said to me. I smiled and didn't say nothin like I couldn't understand English. For all him and them dumbass kids knew I couldn't. I could of been an immigrant just gotten here. After a while he forgot the question. It's amazin such a stupid man can teach math. He was sittin on a stool in front of the chalkboard makin chalk marks which I didn't even try to pay attention to because the last thing I did in a math class was add numbers with dots in em.

Well of course the day couldn't go that great for me. Not with little Miss Myrna around. I met up with her in the hall after math. She was pinned up behind a bunch of big old football-lookin guys. At first I thought they were flirtin with her and tryin to get a date—yep, I did, which just goes to show I really have been spendin too much of my spare time under my bed—and I was jealous as heck and ready to go on by without givin her a second look. Then I heard the names they were callin her. And the things they were sayin to her.

Whose funeral you goin to in that dress, sweetheart?

That's no dress, that's her Halloween costume.

Who's the big daddy-o of that kid?

They had her squashed up between em and no way out for her with millions of kids swarmin around. I went over and reached between em and grabbed ahold of her because the situation was beggin for it. She looked surprised to see me. She looked kind of dazed actually. Come on, I said, pullin her so her jewelry went clitter clatter. Well that cost me. Who's your four-eyed friend, Myrna? Nothin new. Everyone's a comedian in this world.

~ ~ ~

I THOUGHT Mrs. Leffer would forget. Prayed it, man. Should of saved my breath.

They made me pee in a plastic cup. Luckily I had some available. Who knows what they did with it. When the doctor came in he wasn't smilin. He pushed me back on the table which crinkled the paper under me and he put his hands all over my goddamn stomach. That hurt? he said. Nah, I said. That hurt? he said. Nah, I said. He said hmm over and over. I was dyin to say, Doctor, what's wrong with me? How come I'm so tired all the time? Is this normal? Why did my period dry up? Not that I miss it, but once it starts you're supposed to have it for life, I hear. You got any Drano for human beings, Doctor? But I was too scared to open my mouth. Especially with his fingers up my hole.

Finally he stopped and I sat up and he pushed his glasses up his nose. I pushed my glasses up my nose too. He said, When was your last period? I thought it over. He said, Don't you keep track? I said, I have a lot of things to keep track of in my busy life.

That little bit of smile vanished off his face. Are you more than two or three weeks late?

Oh, man, I sighed.

Could you hazard a guess?

You want me to guess about this?

No, I want accuracy. If you give me the wrong date I could make some incorrect assumptions when we ultrasound you.

Wrong date for what? I wanted him to say it.

He tapped me on the knee and didn't say nothin. I hate it when people don't answer me.

Heaved out another sigh. Had to use fingers on both hands to show him.

Well, he said quietly. Now we're getting somewhere.

How come it's not showin itself? I said, thinkin I had him.

It would be an unusual woman who showed at six weeks, he said. Some women give birth and they don't even

{42}

know they were pregnant. He was lookin at me strangely, I felt.

I'm not a woman, I pointed out. I'm a girl.

You've got something growing inside you, he said, standin firm.

It should of asked permission first, I said.

He smiled. And what would you have said, if it did?

Well, I wouldn't of thrown open my front door.

If that's how you feel, we can do something about it.

I thought about this for a couple seconds. Nah, think I'll pass.

I mean you can have—

Nope, nope, the damage is done, Doctor.

Not necessarily. The guy patted my knee. But I wasn't fallin for his nice-guy act, I had to keep my head clear for decision makin.

Doctor, I said. A fish this stupid is a fish I got a soft spot for. And I slid off the table and crossed my arms over the topic of our conversation.

The doctor blinked at me.

I wasn't born this mornin, Doctor. I pick up a little bit, here and there. I know what you're talkin about. Thanks for lookin out for me. I appreciate it. But I don't want to kill nothin. Maybe she met my mom on her way in. Who knows. I don't even like to kill a goddamn ant, Doctor. And my mom hated em, *hated* em, but she was the one who had to flatten em with her shoe on the kitchen counter. It's the one thing I wouldn't do for her. They came out of the ceiling, you know?

The doctor pushed his glasses in their sturdy frames like good shoes up his short nose. Thum . . . bel . . . i . . . na, he sighed, puttin his weight on each of the four pieces in my name. I think it is dangerous to begin thinking of this . . . to begin assigning a sex and a personality to something you are not even sure you want to keep.

I appreciate your input, Doctor, I said.

You're very young.

I'll do OK.

Where's the father?

I looked down at my big, long toe.

If you don't mind me asking, who is the father, Thumbelina?

Kept lookin.

Do you know the challenge you have ahead of you? It's difficult enough for an adult woman to raise a child alone. You're—

He reached for his clipboard. Fourteen?

Fifteen in ten months.

Argh. He shook his head.

Lighten up, I felt like sayin. Just lighten the hell up. OK?

You're living in a foster home now. Are you all right there?

Great.

Water leaked out of me, down my bare cheeks and onto my paper gown. It was gettin to be a habit, man. This gave him an opportunity to haul out his squarely folded hanky, white as the whites of his eyes, and think to himself, See I'm right, this girl's miserable. I took my glasses off carefully because of the broken nosepiece and dried up my face.

I'll send a social worker out to Mrs. Leffer's to speak to you both about this, if you don't mind. I want you to think over your decision very carefully.

This isn't what it looks like, Doctor, I said. I'm OK. Really. I couldn't be better. I just have too much water in my head and it leaks out once in a while.

But the doctor had a hearin problem. On his clipboard he was writin a story about fourteen-year-old girls who get pregnant and got the nerve to want to keep it. I snagged my cream leggings and when he didn't move I cleared my throat, bringin his eyes over to me, and went hint hint with my eyebrows. He nodded, slapped his clipboard under his arm, and went out. I finished dressing in privacy. Mrs. Leffer's big face stared after me as I tore across the waitin room and down them clinic stairs.

Man it's a drag bein a woman.

~ ~ ~

FOR SOME reason Myrna was happy about the news. You want to get an apartment with me when the brats come?

We were lyin in the dark.

I don't like you, Myrna.

We could take turns babysittin.

No, thanks.

You got to start plannin now for when it comes.

It's not comin.

You're goin to get rid of it?

Don't have to.

Where's it goin then?

Because you're mine, I walk the line, I hummed softly.

Thumby, you are seriously losin it.

I pulled the covers down from my chin and beat my stomach with my big hands to this other, harder Johnny Cash song that ran through my head: *I shot a man in Reno just to watch him die!*

Myrna hit the floor like a sack of potatoes. Christ almighty, you're a riot, and she hit the light. I stopped hit-

{45}

tin my fish to slam my hands over my eyes. You're a retard. You got so much liquid in there you're just makin it dizzy, is all. She went over to the closet and got a hanger. One of the metal ones you hardly ever see anymore. She straightened it with a lot of facial expressions.

If you're serious. If you're not just some kid playin around, I'll help you.

I had my glasses on by now. Her eyes were real green. I didn't move.

Come here.

Make me.

You got to pull down your pants. I got to put this inside you.

He already shoved somethin inside me.

Who. Her eyes were cool.

Who do you think, I replied, just as cool.

Well. We got to bust apart what he started.

Kill it?

That's the idea.

You ever done this before?

I'm about to.

I still didn't move.

I don't got all night, Thumbelina. Come here.

How will you know it's dead?

It'll come drippin down your legs.

I swung my legs over the bed. I put all six feet of me into the shove and her head cracked the desk. You asshole! I hollered.

Fuck you. See if I ever try to help you again!

Help me? You're goin to kill me!

She crouched at my feet. Neither one of us moved. Then I stepped back and said, Get up, man, will you? and I bent down for my guitar. I didn't know what I was in the mood to sing. I just free formed it.

She got her cigarettes out of her orange backpack and went over and reached over my horse and slid open the window, lettin in a blast of freezin fall air.

Your voice isn't too bad.

I didn't say nothin because it wasn't news to me.

She picked up my Appaloosa and turned it over in her hand. I got to introduce you to Todd. He plays guitar in Stan's band. He's the only kid. The rest of them are up there, near Stan's age. Stan has three kids.

Mind puttin that down?

Touchy.

I waited till she put my horse back down then I said, You find it slightly humiliatin bein in junior high still?

Her green eyes socked me in the chops. That'll be our little secret if you ever meet the band. You'll recognize Todd. He's the one losin his hair. Funny, him bein the youngest. Once you get to know me you'll figure out I only hang out with cute guys.

Haven't noticed you hangin out with any guys, Myrna.

She blew smoke out the open window. Look who's talkin.

My boyfriend left town, I informed the back of her carrot head. What am I supposed to do about it.

That's my line, sweetheart.

Yeah, but mine really did. He went to California.

Mine went out to the ocean. He's a Indian.

Must of forgot to take you, I said.

It's business. He didn't take Todd or Mack or Zonskey either. He has to get money for his kids. He has to sort out his business. They give you money for salmon or somethin, if you're a Indian.

I started singin again because she pisses me off, always ready with an excuse, just like my mom, and when I quit I Walk the Line to move on to Hey, Good Lookin What-cha Got Cookin she was sittin quietly beside me, a new cig hangin out of her mouth. She didn't have to ask. I put my guitar on her bare legs (she was in her little blue baby-doll nightgown) and I told her to start with the major chords. You got that finger on the wrong string. You're buzzin the frets. You got to press down harder. You got to lose those fingernails.

Her green eyeballs rolled in her head.

I showed her how to make an A minor. See how sad that sounds? The minors are the heartbreak chords.

I showed her an E major, a C, an F, the G. I told her to fix those down in her head if she wanted to get anywhere, the minors could wait.

How'd you learn to play?

I looked at her. Her eyes had that real green, wet quality to em again. I was born knowin like I was born tall. Got it from my dad.

He plays guitar?

This was his guitar.

If he's so cool, how come you don't live with him?

Well, he's seven feet under, Myrna.

Her eyes were beggin for the story, so I gave her the shortened version. That my dad and mom met at community college in Sacramento and they had a little country band.

She wasn't in the van with him that night because she was in the hospital havin me.

They both died in car accidents?

Suddenly air couldn't pass up my throat. It hadn't occurred to me then, but she was right.

Kind of owed her life to you.

I worked to clear my throat, laughin a little to throw her off the track. It made her grouchy sometimes, bein that much in debt to me.

It would kind of piss me off too, owin you somethin of that size. I bet you're a hard person to owe somethin to.

Scuse me?

She went over to the window that was still open to the night.

Do you have a hearin problem, Myrna? Why'd you say I'm a hard person to owe somethin to?

My mom's in Vegas, she said.

That's not what I asked you.

She's a dancer.

My ears perked up. A *dancer*? I said, figurin this was so juicy I'd get the other out of her later. What kind of dancer?

A real talented, highly paid one. You want to see a picture of my dad? She got her wallet out of her backpack and passed it over.

His skin hung on his face like a bad-fittin jacket, but I kept that observation to myself.

Betty, my mom's old boss, could have given him that haircut. She can't cut hair to save her life.

Myrna rolled her eyes. His new wife cuts his hair. He fixes lightbulb displays in stores in Florida. And here's Dwayne.

Now, Dwayne was cute. He in the army? I said.

Navy. Why?

Well, look at the haircut. I thought Stan was your boyfriend.

Dwayne is my sister's *fiancé*, Thumbelina. She wrinkled her nose. At least I think he is. They were havin some

{49}

trouble, that's why she shipped me off here. Agnes blames me.

Oh, man. What'd you do, Myrna?

Oh, blame it on me.

She turned back to the window. Her shoulders were round and soft and white and her back was completely available for viewin pleasure in her baby-doll. You slept with him, I said, feelin completely convinced.

I love how you at least form that into a question, Thumby.

Did you?

You and Agnes got one and the same mind, Thumby.

You're not answerin the question, Myrna. But Myrna had wax in her ears, miles deep.

october

THE ORANGE MONTH IS MY FAVORITE, NO OFFENSE TO THE other months. You can really feel the earth and sky. You walk outside and the dirt is sad, the clouds are sad, the trees are sad, and the sun, it was in mournin from day one of this month, when it sat in the sky over Bean Park all afternoon waitin for my mom's head. But her head is nowhere in this city. The sun got the message and it never came back. On my way to school leaves were stuck all over the sidewalk like wet paper bags but I did my best to walk around em. I don't like walkin on things that used to be on trees. I don't like eatin birds either. Like on Myrna's night to choose dinner.

I'm a vegathingy, I said, and I put the drumsticks from KFC on Myrna's plate.

A what? Mrs. Leffer said.

Atarian, Myrna said, chowin down a wing. This is not real bird, Thumby.

I held firm.

We had settled into a routine. In the evenings we all sat in the livin room watchin TV, or else I lay on my bed listenin to Johnny Cash on my Walkman or I fooled around on my dad's guitar. Sometimes Myrna and Roy went outside and walked up the street and sometimes I went with em, but usually by the end of the day I was just worn out and I wanted to be alone and I lay on my bed and drifted off to outer space, where it was calm and quiet. If I did go with em we didn't do much. We just wandered around till dark, kickin rocks and runnin into other kids. Myrna talked about the father of her kid constantly and about how she wanted to be a actress after the baby gets old enough to travel to California.

But you ain't pretty, Roy said.

You need all kinds of girls in the movies, Myrna said.

Sometimes at night when we watched TV I'd be sittin there with my can of pop (we each got one for a evening snack, after that if we were thirsty we had to drink water) and some TV commercial or a tune from a show came on that reminded me of her and this feelin came over me. I was so lonely for her. I ached to watch her move. She was right about my big old eyes followin her. They did. Everywhere. So when I started havin this feelin I'd go down to the bathroom and shut the door. I'd sit on the tub and lay my head in my hands.

She was my sister in a lot of ways. She needed me. She

wouldn't ever do the hills downtown without me there to do the parkin brake for her. It wasn't her fault that she wasn't that great with a stick, but over time this flaw worked its way deep under Lester's skin. He was in the army once, but he didn't fight in the war. He fixed trucks. He used to tell my mom that even the army couldn't whip an incompetent like her into shape.

One time I twisted the handle and let her down too soon and we tapped the car behind us. It was a little yellow thing that dented easy, if you ask me. The man in the tie was mad. Lester was mad. Whole world was mad. I thought now was the time for us to make a break for it, leave him and head out into the world, just the two of us, but this was years ago. Back then I had no clue what kind of endurance she had.

One time she got a ticket for runnin a red light at the top of the hill by the library. She told the cop she couldn't stop because she wasn't good with a stick. He said better get a automatic then. That was a tough hill. And we had to go up it a lot, to get to her romance books at the library. We had to park right on that sucker because the library's three parkin spaces always were full. It'd take her about five minutes to parallel park the van in the opening, which believe me never was real big, and all the cars comin by would be honkin and she'd say, Thumby, flip em off for me, willya? while she struggled with the steering wheel, but I wouldn't because I knew she was only sayin that because she was embarrassed.

I say parallel park, but I really mean get the front a couple feet near the curb. Then she'd quit. You got to stay out here, Thumby, and get the license number of anyone who hits us, I'll just be a sec, and she'd go runnin up the front steps in her little skirt and swingin hair and all the men down on the street lookin up at her. They were wastin their time.

A sec my foot. More like two hours. Couldn't get her out of that place quick if your life depended on it. I'd be sittin there goin hum de dum, keepin an eye out in case anyone smacked us. Plenty honked but I'd just pass em a wave. They'd usually wave back but only with one finger. Finally she'd come runnin out all excited with her arms full of romance books.

Well, Mom, it's been mighty entertainin out here.

You didn't have to come.

Didn't have to come? Didn't have to *come*? Course I had to come. Had to help her with the parkin brake on all the hills. But I wouldn't ever use that against her and make her feel like a burden to me.

But on the other hand, if she was mad at Lester she wouldn't need me to do the parkin brake. She'd say leave it, and slam her little foot down on the gas and the engine would scream bloody murder. Then after she cooled down she'd say, You won't tell him how I treat his van, will you?

Aw, for pete's sake, Mom.

Well, you never know, if you get mad at me, you might.

I wouldn't. You know I wouldn't tell him nothin about your drivin. Never.

You never know, Thumby, you're not a saint, honey, and all I'm sayin is if you get the urge to tell him what I did to his van, don't, OK?

I wouldn't get the urge.

You might, she'd say, and we'd battle it out like that, on and on, neither one of us backin down.

I guess sisters can act like that sometimes.

~ ~ ~

HER TWO-MONTH anniversary was October sixteenth.
Myrna lent me three bucks for a flower. Roy gave me all
his change that he picks up here and there because he has
good eyes in his head. I got up early to beat Mrs. Leffer
whose bedroom door was shut. I took her phone book.
Amazin that it wasn't chained down to the hall desk. For
the next kid it probably will be. I didn't have breakfast
because I didn't feel the need but I rinsed water in a bowl,
so it would look like I ate. Roy told me to do that. He said,
Thumby, she's got her eye on you. Those two wanted to
come but I said I needed my privacy. I asked Myrna if I
could borrow her little silver tape recorder on the black
strap that she wears on her wrist all the time, but she said
not unless I let her come.

Didn't know visitin the dead was so high on your social
calendar, Myrna.

Go to hell.

Roy said I could borrow his boom box if I wanted but
it's the size of a bathtub and it would break my shoulder
before I made it out of the turnaround and plus the batter-
ies are the expensive kind and he was in need.

Finally Myrna said, Oh, all right, you can take my stupid tape recorder. So then I got *The Sun Years* tape from my
Walkman and after lookin through the phone book and
tryin to figure out where in the hell I was goin I changed
my mind about privacy. You want to come, Myrn?

We rode the bus to the flower shop. That took a couple
bucks. I wanted to walk and save it but Myrna said, No
way in hell, I'm carryin a baby.

That a fact? I thought you was just fat.

So that was a couple bucks wasted. Course it was her couple bucks.

I swear I wonder sometimes where I've been keepin my head. Because take flowers. In case you don't know they are a rip and a half. A man must really like a girl if he's shellin out cash on flowers. I went up to the counter where the lady was standin. I need some orange tulips, please.

I don't have any.

How come?

We have purple.

I don't want purple.

That's what we have.

What kind a flower store are you that you don't got orange tulips?

You are only the second person that's come in this year asking for them. I have a good memory.

Well, I said because she was lookin pissed off. Give me some of those white thingamajigs in that vase there and I'll get some orange paint. I started diggin out my money.

The roses? That'll run you twenty-five sixty-nine.

My hand stayed in my pocket. Huh? You got anything else?

The lady didn't look too happy. I thought you wanted a bouquet.

I thought I did too. What do you got for four bucks includin tax?

She frowned down her long nose at me. Can't get anything for that. Flowers are not cheap.

You're tellin me.

Who's it for?

My mom.

She smiled and leaned closer. For her birthday?

Naw. For her grave.

The lady looked like she swallowed a worm. Took her a minute to recover. I was patient about waitin. Carnations are good, she said. They're a hardy flower. Three dollars apiece. She slid back the fridge door and pulled one out of its buddies in the white vase.

Thanks, but I want orange tulips.

When I came out Myrna said, Where's the flowers? I filled her in. I was feelin pretty discouraged. I wasn't about to arrive without no flowers. Cars whizzed by but I was feelin planted on the bench. I started flippin through the phone book. The nearest flower shop was way over on Sprague.

Myrna said, Forget it, they won't have nothin this one don't.

I popped up. I got a idea, Myrn, come on. She was wipin on nail polish and didn't budge her butt. Come on, I said again, which you usually got to do with her, and I started walkin up Beeson Avenue to the shoppin plaza, where I got orange construction paper and a little plastic stapler and green pipe cleaners. You got to do everything yourself in this world. On the bus on the way over I made my flowers. I cut out little squares of construction paper with Myrna's nail scissors and rolled em into a cone and stapled em to my stems. Then I cut out big petals. Some tulips, Myrna said, leanin over the seat of the bus which we were ridin, it turned out, because once she found out we had three more miles to walk more money appeared like a miracle from the toe of her shoe. I buy em a little big for that, she said.

We didn't have any trouble findin it. I am not good at directions but Myrna knows this town like the back of her hand. It looked exactly the same. The grass was yellow like the stuff in Mrs. Leffer's front yard, and the black iron gate stood wide open, but no one was there. Except the dead people of course.

We had a little trouble findin my mom because one dead person looks pretty much like another. Myrna didn't say nothin while I went from stone to stone, readin. I knew she was over on the right side. I knew it wasn't very big, that it wouldn't grab my attention like some of them other stones did. None of the stones were much to write home about though, so crazy-lookin you have to see it to believe it, all different sizes and leanin over toward each other like girls at school that have some big secret to share. It aggravated me. I was tempted to walk over to em and give em a shove. Tell em to shut up. That would be disrespectful to em, since they weren't my relatives. So I didn't. But I wanted to.

We finally found her stone. It was one of the worst slouchers. Since I'm her relative I put my shoulder to it and tried to move it straighter and give it some dignity. It didn't budge. My feet sunk into the soft dirt. You'd think they'd have hard dirt in a graveyard. I don't know who runs the place, but I'd do a better job.

What're you doin? Myrna said. Always after me with the stupid question.

Nothin.

You're workin awful hard doin nothin, she said. I shot her a glare and she wandered off to look around.

I sat down on the grass next to where I figured she must be layin, because man it would be disrespectful to sit on top of her. I hit PLAY and Johnny started hauntin out I Walk the Line and I could practically feel her turnin over in her sleep down there, smilin, because it's her favorite song of all time. I poked my tulips into the soft dirt around her stone and they stood up straight and dignified.

ANGELICA RAE SKYLER it said. And there was her age in plain sight for anyone who could subtract 1961 from 1994.

After a while Myrna came back. She didn't ask but I could tell she wanted to go. My arms were all goose-pimply like the dead were breathin on us and she was shiverin. I picked up the tape recorder and was about to switch if off but she said leave it. That's OK, I said. She said leave it and took it out of my hand and put it down in the middle of the flowers. We walked back down the path and out the gate and then we stopped and looked back. The flowers looked real from that far away.

Walkin back to the bus stop we passed the little stone church with a bell in the steeple that I'd noticed earlier. I would of liked to go in but Myrna had already done about fifteen good deeds for the day by bein so patient and keepin her trap shut, so I didn't have no heart to make her do that too. Myrna is not the kind of girl you should take into a church anyway. She is too squirrelly. I like churches. They are quiet and they got the guy on the cross to remind you that your life is not the only one in the world that went off course.

~ ~ ~

HALLOWEEN WAS on its way. Roy brought home a pumpkin from school and he wanted to carve it on the table but Mrs. Leffer made him go outside in the backyard and she wouldn't even give him a decent knife. Probably thought he'd attack her or somethin.

My mom used to take me trick or treatin when I was

little. I always wanted to be a fairy. As if one in the family isn't enough, my mom would say under her breath while she worked on my costume. I'd say, Mom, will you for pete's sake try to get it right this time? I'll do my best, honey, she'd grin. She made it out of lace and satin for my first Halloween when I was five and every year after that she ripped it apart and sewed it back together again to make space for me. She liked to sew in those days. She hummed while she worked, and even though I knew it was either goin to be draggin on the ground or flyin above my knees, I liked to be around her in the kitchen while she worked. I appreciated her effort. I'd saw a wand out of a cardboard box with the steak knife and wrap foil around it and whack it against all the hedges as we walked up and down the street. I'd get a lot of candy.

I was exactly as tall as her when I turned nine, so she said this was goin to be my last year. My costume was clearly goin to be at my knees, so I called it a tutu, and I begged her so bad she finally caved and bought me real ballet slippers from the ballet school on the other side of Bean Park. The kind you can use to stand on your toes. So I got to be a ballerina for one night, my other goal in life besides learnin the harmonica. It's harder than it looks to stand on your toes. I had to use the kitchen counter and it hurt like hell. My mom said it was because I had a lot more height to support than your average ballerina. I told her she forgot to buy me lamb's wool for the ends. Before we went out the door I put on my regular high-tops. What about your ballet slippers? she said. You got to be kiddin. You think I'm wearin those on the street? I said. Then what'd I buy em for? she said. She said she was goin to take em back. But I hid em till I got em so dirty from wearin em around the house she couldn't return em.

I remember that last trick or treat night like I'm lookin at my hand. That's how clear I have it fixed in my head. We drove Lester's van to the good neighborhood we always went to, over on Jack Street by the water, where the houses have views that they pay through the nose for, my mom used to say, just for the privilege of watchin cars drive over the bridge. We parked at the end of a dark street and got out and she ducked back into the driver's side to light her match. We walked up the street together with the cozy smell of her cigarette between us. It was cold and I shivered, but mainly with excitement.

Some of the houses were taller than our apartment building. They had mile-high steps and I had to walk up em alone, past the lighted pumpkins with their big old grins to the front door, while she waited at the bottom. When you rang the doorbell at some houses witches' laughter would come out on the intercom. Trick or treat, I'd go, and the people would say, Oh, what a pretty fairy. Do you live around here? Whose child are you? Not the Greenlawn girl? No, the Greenlawn girl doesn't wear glasses, but she's about as tall as you. And I would just shrug my shoulders and take one candy bar off the plate even though I preferred clearin it. Especially since this was my last year, and I didn't have to worry about em rememberin me. But I didn't want to leave a bad taste in nobody's mouth on Halloween.

Then I'd go back down and over to where my mom's fresh cigarette gave her away. We walked up one side of the street and down the other in this fashion, then we went down one street closer to the water, and cleaned up one side, then the other. Each time I'd go up to the door I'd be so afraid they'd figure out I didn't belong to the neighborhood. It was worth riskin it for the candy though. Then when we got down to the very bottom and there weren't any more streets and we could smell the water and hear it against the shore and my pillowcase was cram full of candy, we quit. We hiked back up to the top of the hill and sat down on the curb by Lester's van. She said, Thumbelina, honey, you got anything for me? And I pulled out all the Milky Ways and Reese's and M&M's and set em in her lap because my mom *loved* chocolate. She said, You don't have to give me all these, and I said, I know, but I want to, and she poured coffee for herself from the thermos and lit a cig for her and one for me and told me not to breathe in. End of an era, eh, sweetheart? I couldn't answer because I had been tempted to imitate her and was coughin all over myself. She laughed but not meanly. And there we sat, takin a puff and then eatin some chocolate and takin a puff and eatin chocolate and watchin the lights from the bridge that curved over the night in a chain like all your dreams strung together, and I sat there tryin not to breathe to disturb the atmosphere because I didn't want the magic to end. It was up to her. I could of sat there all night with my head inchin closer and closer to her shoulder, but she made up her mind midway through some cigarette that it was goin to be the last one and she stubbed it out and crinkled up all the candy wrappers and said, Guess we better be goin. Do we got to, Mom? Thumbelina, she said. And that was it. You could never hold a moment with my mom. She had a personal schedule written on the back of her head that she wouldn't change for nobody.

~ ~ ~

WE RAN AWAY Halloween night although Myrna and me saw no need to move our butts past a walk. Mrs. Leffer was out leadin Roy around in the bedsheet with two eyeholes cut out in it from the kid who used it last year. He wanted to get one of them pirate kits at the Piggly Wiggly but Mrs. Leffer had wax in her ears when he asked her about it. Then he wanted to rip the sheet up and be a mummy, but I told him that would make her mad. So what? he said. I said, Roy, watch yourself. She gave him a plastic Safeway sack for his candy. I told him to use his pillowcase because I'm the voice of experience in partin people with candy.

The minute they were out the door we were packin. It took me about three seconds to get my drawer cleaned out, my horse off the windowsill, my guitar back in its case with my ballet slippers and comic books. But it took Myrna ages to stuff her clothes, makeup, shoes, tapes, rock and roll magazines, into two bulgin suitcases which we both had to sit on to shut, and which I carried because I've always had a tendency to carry other people's loads.

Our decision to clear out happened fast. We were walkin to school and Myrna put down her backpack to get out her cigarettes. I put down my backpack.

You're right, Thumby. It's humiliatin bein in eighth grade for the third year in a row.

Maybe you ought to crack a book once in a while, Myrn.

I got a sister, she said.

I eyed her. Who is currently hatin your guts. It sounds like.

Myrna lit her cigarette and didn't say anything, which pissed me off.

Right? So why'd you bring it up?

You don't have to be on good terms with someone to get em to feel sorry for you. And she heaved out smoke.

Myrn, this I got to see.

I thought we should bring Roy but Myrna said it would be bad enough with just us two showin up. Maybe you ought to call her, let her know we're comin, I said.

Naw, that isn't how old Agnes works.

I raised my eyebrows politely. Oh? How does she work?

Just don't be expectin her to be real happy to see us.

Oh, I've never had that problem.

I left Mrs. Leffer a note on the table: *Bye and please don't take this personal.*

Why didn't you tell her a reason? Myrna said.

Because I am not aware of any, I said.

How come you didn't tell her what a pain in the ass she's been to me all these months?

Shut up, Myrn.

Agnes Vanderwhacker lives on the south end of the city, out past the car lots. In the moonlight the house looked tall and lonely as we climbed up the stairs from Lumis Street. Somethin in the front yard caught my shoe and I stumbled and dropped Myrna's suitcases. She was up on the porch whackin the door. Nobody answered and I was formin apologies to Mrs. Leffer in my head.

Then a little kid with brown boingy curls opened up. Soon, thanks to her, I would discover that I am not a fan of kids.

Your mommy home, Dee Dee?

The girl put her whole fist in her mouth and looked at us. Myrna moved her gently out of the way and dropped my paper bag in the middle of the livin room floor and my stuff fell out. My guitar went *gongggg*. I left her suitcases on the porch.

You mind bringin those in, Thumby?

You mind not spreadin my stuff all over hell's half acre? I said, and started pickin up my raggedy white undies and my socks which are in slightly better shape and my catcher's mask and puttin it all back in the bag. Myrna got her own suitcases. I found the light switch. A little TV with rabbit ears out to there flickered in the corner. The couch was buried under piles of clothes and toys and the same with the floor. But here and there you could see polished wood.

Myrna started hollerin for Agnes and went up the stairs and came thumpin back down. She's not here.

Kind a get that feelin.

Where's your mommy, Dee Dee?

The little kid put her finger in her nose. She had a big head and big eyes and jelly bean stains spotted her Donald Duck T-shirt. Myrna whacked her arm down. Don't do that. Is Dwayne Junior with her?

Want some jelly beans? The little girl held up the bag. Myrna was on her way to the kitchen. Thumby! Get in here!

The kitchen walls were bright green. Dirty dishes spilled out of the sink, and the linoleum was torn up around the stove like somebody lost it and just started rippin.

We got to clean this up, get on her good side.

You got to be kiddin. I pulled out one of the chairs.

You want a roof over your head tonight?

We had a perfectly good one.

Myrna didn't bother arguin. She just got busy. She dragged dishes and bottles out of the sink and stacked them on the counter and put the stopper in and turned the tap on full blast. She yanked open the little white fridge at the end of the counter and it rocked back and forth like it had been punched.

You do the bathroom and the livin room, I'll do in here. She handed me a garbage bag.

What's this for?

She and Dwayne got a four-month-old baby, Thumby.

After I had picked up the clothes and high heels off the bathroom floor I saw that it was a pretty yellow tile pattern. It looked new and shiny and didn't match the walls, which were old white. I put the clothes in the hamper in the hall and sat on it to shut it. I dumped the diaper pail into the garbage bag and bumped it down the stairs. When I passed through the kitchen Myrna said, Mind takin that out too? and I said OK because I got a tendency to do everything that girl asks. I would of liked to stop and admire the moon but my teeth were bangin into each other by the time I'd made it ten feet to the can. I don't know what's with me these days, gettin cold so easy. Don't recall I minded paradin around town in my fairy costume at this time of year.

In the livin room I shoved the Barbie doll and little plastic cars under the couch, which in my opinion was a good place for em. I got the broom and the cig butts went under there too. I dumped the six ashtrays and found a pair of red lips in the bottom of each one and thought that was weird and stacked em neatly on the coffee table. I gave the black wire lamp a swipe with my sweatshirt sleeve.

We had just sat down on the couch with our feet up when she got home. We didn't even have time to run our fingers through our hair.

Hello, Sister, Myrna said cheerily.

She eyed Myrna and them eyes said: Don't even start, not after the night I've had. She wore black leggings and black clogs and a lot of black stuff around her eyes. She wasn't beautiful.

You've got five minutes to clear out before I call the cops, she said calmly, and headed for the kitchen.

What kind of pissy welcome is that? Myrna called after her, and rolled her eyes at me. But I could see her lower lip doin a little dance.

I followed Myrna at a safe distance. I didn't know how these two worked out conflict. If they did it like my mom and Lester, I wanted to lie low.

Four minutes, Agnes Vanderwhacker said, puttin down her bag of groceries on the counter and shovin the baby around to her other hip. She tried to light a cig, but the cig wouldn't light and she said, Hell with this, and put the baby in Myrna's arms, which was a good sign. Myrna bein useful. Then the baby started cryin. Well, that wasn't so hot. You could tell it was gettin on Agnes's nerves, not to mention mine. Wherever she'd been she looked tired.

She don't look nothin like Myrna. I used the word *not beautiful* already. To further that along, her hair is gold, and she doesn't have no freckles on her white skin, and is taller and a heckuva lot thinner than Myrna, like one of those long white dogs they race like horses.

Where's my two hundred bucks? the lady said, unloadin the bag. And my red skirt with the white polka dots? And my gold earrings?

Not to mention your fiancé, I thought.

Aw, Agnes. Can't we stay here tonight?

Those earrings are real gold, Agnes added, glancin at me, then back at Myrna. I guess you know that, that's why you took em. You could of stayed right where you were.

I miss you.

Her sister snorted.

Myrna moved her toe in a circle on the floor. I was hopin we could stay with you for a little while.

We? Her cool green eyes looked me over. The one thing they have in common.

That's Thumbelina.

That your name? Strange one, she said, gettin busy with the can opener on the pork and beans.

It was a strange lady that gave it to me, I said.

Thumby. Myrna shook her head at me. Shut up, will you?

I see that she is just as polite to you as she is to me. Agnes smiled a little starter smile at me, stickin her big toe in the water, if you know what I mean. I didn't know what to do. How'd I get in between em?

Myrna yanked my arm out of my body, nearly, and pushed me behind her, although my head stuck up high over hers. I didn't mind. I wanted out of the spotlight till I knew what to do.

Come on, Agnes, Myrna said quietly, changin her tone like a gearshift, gettin low and serious. We cleaned up your house for you.

Agnes Vanderwhacker stirred the beans around in the pot Myrna had recently cleaned and meanwhile didn't say anything. Just stood there and puffed on her cigarette and sipped from the wine she'd poured. She wore a yellow sleeveless blouse, which was weird, considerin we were occupyin the last hour of October. There was a big blue wallop under her arm.

He sure is gettin big, Myrna said. Jigglin the little kid. He's startin to look like you, Agnes.

Good old Myrna, workin it for us.

Me and Thumby's lookin for work. Does Sal need girls?

Not ones your age.

Aw, come on, Agnes. We cleaned up the place for you. That's worth somethin.

Agnes took her wine and Dwayne Junior the baby out

of Myrna's arms and went into the livin room and we followed. She opened her blouse and the baby ate. She lit a smoke and said, Shit, I'm not supposed to be smokin when I'm nursin him, and I was real impressed. Myrna took the cig, then passed it to me, and I took a mouthful and passed it back.

Thumby's pregnant too, Myrna said.

Turn off the TV, sweet pea, Agnes said. Dee Dee ignored her. Agnes closed her eyes very slowly and opened em. Dee Dee, do you hear me? Turn that shit off. She made a move to get up but I said, Allow me, and I went over and bonked the switch.

Mommy!

The baby started cryin and Agnes said he was wet and she got up and went upstairs. Dee Dee! she called tiredly down the stairs, You come up here and let me wash you up.

Dee Dee's dark little eyes were glued to a bunch of yellin cops on the TV which she had yanked back on.

You seem to have a hearin problem, kid, I said, and I went over and slammed the knob in. Her eyes got all squinty and her mouth sagged down. She plowed her hard little fists into my legs. I had a strong urge to return the favor.

The little girl fought in my arms as I carried her up the stairs to the bathroom, where Agnes was powderin her baby's crotch on the counter.

She got a nightgown or somethin?

Agnes looked up at me a second. Her eyes were the same fresh green as Myrna's. I know I mentioned that, but it's spooky, seein two people with the same eyes. She was not pretty but somethin about her seemed familiar, besides her eyes. I couldn't place it. She smiled, and it was bigger than it had been downstairs. You met my sister in foster care?

As a matter of fact, I did.

You don't seem like a troublemaker.

I puffed out my chest, grabbin this opportunity. I am pretty well behaved.

What's your story?

Long.

I got time, she said, rubbin powder all over her baby's body and holdin it still with one of her pretty hands while she grabbed a diaper from the big box behind her.

Your baby's kind of cute, I said. You know, now that I can get a good look at it.

Take one of my old T-shirts. Agnes nodded at her bedroom door.

It was that little bit of kindness that turned the tide if you ask me, helpin her with her kid, because Agnes came back from puttin the baby down and told us we could fold out the couch and that blankets were in the upstairs closet.

There was peace and quiet for about a half hour, and I started havin these wild thoughts, picturin us all sittin around the breakfast table in the mornin with mugs of coffee, bein friends. Maybe I could ask her for advice on how to get a boyfriend. Then Myrna dug through her humongous suitcase lookin for her extra nightgown for me. Out fell a red miniskirt with white polka dots and a gold earring. She tried to stuff it back but Agnes saw and hit the roof. I sat in the corner and tried to be invisible but it's hard because of my big head. I thought for sure we were headed for the Y to spend the night with the home-less men.

But they settled it finally. Don't ask me how. It involved

a lot of yellin and name-callin until one of em wore down. It's amazin to me, absolutely amazin, how Myrna can hold up her end of a argument when it's clear as day she's in the wrong. The girl's got to get onstage. She's missin her callin in life.

So long, orange month, I'll see you next year.

november

ME AND MYRNA OPENED OUR EYES IN THE MORNIN and looked at each other. (Well, first I had to find my glasses.) The TV was blarin and Dee Dee was sittin one inch from it.

No sign of Agnes.

She's at Clifford's, Myrna said, shakin cereal into bowls.

I thought his name was Dwayne?

No, Dwayne's in the navy, Thumby, don't you listen?

Who's Clifford?

Her boyfriend.

I thought that was Dwayne?

He's her ex-boyfriend now.

She was goin to marry him, you said.

Things change, Thumby, that's the world for you.

Did you screw it up for the two of em?

Here you go, Dee Dee. Myrna laid down a bowl of cereal on the table. Clifford's a bouncer.

What does he bounce?

People. If they get out of hand.

Dee Dee, don't throw your Froot Loops on the floor, OK? I said.

I want my mommeeee.

Your mommy's at work, sweetie. Open up, I said.

She's not goin to eat, Thumby, might as well give up.

Who asked you?

I used to live here, remember?

Yeah, before you went and slept with her fiancé. Swift move, Myrna.

Myrna shook more Froot Loops into her bowl and ignored me.

That's your second bowl, Myrna.

You didn't buy em.

So. You're piggin out big time.

You don't eat nothin. How's that baby goin to get big and healthy in your stomach if you don't feed it nothin?

I rested my chin on my hands. I didn't say nothin. I was feelin bummed. Everybody in life has a boyfriend but me.

I was plannin on askin Agnes for some advice about this subject. She got home from community college in the middle of *Get Smart*. She said in a loud voice, You guys have any smokes on you?

{73}

Kools on the table, Agnes.

Some real cigarettes, Myrna. Not your goddamn menthols.

If mine aren't good enough for you, that's too bad.

Myrna kept her eyes glued to Maxwell Smart who was dialin his shoe. Not me, I was gettin ready for trouble. Kissin my advice good-bye.

Will one of you get that?

Quiet, Agnes.

The damn phone, Myrna.

You, I'm watchin this.

Get the damn phone, Myrna.

I jumped up and ran for the kitchen. It was the Clifford guy askin for Aggie in a voice that seemed pretty normal. Couldn't imagine him thumpin people on the head. I'm assumin you mean Agnes, I said. That's right, he said. I told him to hold on.

If you don't go get me some cigarettes right this minute you can piss off out of here and not come back, Agnes said with her hand over the phone receiver.

So me and Myrna were walkin up Lumis Street to 7-Eleven with a list in our heads for Basic Lights, chocolate ice cream, chocolate bars, orange juice, and wine.

We turned onto South Pacific and they were workin on the sidewalk and if there are two of you, one of you has to walk down in the ditch if you don't want to get hit by the cars. I was wearin my high-tops and Myrna was travelin in green high heels so you don't have to wonder how that stacked up. There was a trickle of water in the bottom and my toes got wet, but I didn't care. You can find interestin stuff in ditches.

Hey, Myrna, look at this.

Myrna said, Look at what? and kept on walkin.

Course, it's a good thing I got four eyes, because the way she'd huddled up on the side of the ditch to keep out of the creek, her head burrowed into the dirt, she must of looked to normal eyes like a pile of hair under my mom's chair after she's just relieved you of what you've been growin all your life for a pixie style.

Is it alive? Myrna muttered.

I crouched down and my knees announced this fact to the world with a *kerack*. *Grr!* it muttered under its breath, and my hand, which had been about to land, swept up into the air again.

No offense, no offense.

You know anything about dogs, Thumby?

I think it's a poodle.

Maybe it's a puppy. Pick it up.

Can't hurry these things, Myrn.

I think it's a puppy.

Naw.

How can you tell under all that hair?

You go on and get the stuff. I'm stayin here.

It looks dead.

That's because she wants us to go away and leave her alone.

Then why don't we?

Because I'm goin to help her.

How do you know it's a girl?

I lifted the tail of my mom's brown corduroy coat and plopped my butt on the side of the ditch where the water wouldn't get me.

If a boy was out alone in the world like this, he wouldn't be so sad about it. How about you goin anytime, Myrn? Hi there, Black Bean. Nice day, isn't it?

Black Bean kept her head firmly in the dirt.

Black Bean?

Go get the stuff, Myrn.

You are fuckin weird, Thumby, if you don't mind me sayin so.

I did mind her sayin so but I ignored her. Hungry, Black Bean?

Nothin.

How'd you like some bread and milk? I said.

She's not a damn cat. A fat cut of steak, Black Bean? Myrna said, and *boy-oy-oing* went her dangly ears. A fat cut of steak? Myrna repeated, and that dog's head lifted.

Well, now aren't you a pretty dog. Myrna grinned and patted her and Black Bean's head dove into the dirt again.

Myrna, go get the stuff for your sister, I'm goin to sit here and talk to her.

Why do I have to?

Because I got a better personality.

Oh, fuck you.

Myrna went off. I told my dog not to take her personal. Appearances were deceivin. Bad taste in clothes but a good heart, Black Bean, I said. I'm Thumbelina. I'm an orphan also.

The dog's pink tongue cleared the dirt off her nose and whiskers. She was takin pride in her appearance already. Shows you what a little love can do.

I told her all about myself while I waited for Myrna to come back. I told her that my dad left this world before I was born, but don't worry, Black Bean, things were already bad between him and my mom before that happened. I told her about their band down in Oregon and California. They'd drive around with the curtains shut and get high and sing Simon and Garfunkel and Dylan at coffee shops.

This bein fifteen years ago. My mom had a voice worth hearin. People say I inherited it from her, along with this hair. The guitar that I have belonged to my dad. The Johnny Cash tapes are his too. I told the dog that sometimes I laid my fingers on the fretboard and thought how I was touchin exactly where his fingers had been. Did he have big fingers, like me? I don't know what he looked like except he was tall (obviously). They were gonna get married to give me a family name. But then he went over the guardrail on the highway that night in Oregon. So I'm an Oregon girl. But I lived all my life in Tacoma, thanks to Lester, because he was the drummer in that band and he brought my mom back up here.

When I got done tellin my dog all about me I said, And what about you? You from Tacoma originally? Or did you arrive here on the bus?

Black Bean looked at me and licked her chops. Personal information, eh? I can relate, I said. I didn't push it.

So I talked to her some more about steaks—round steaks, rib eyes, ham hocks, all the stuff I could remember seein in the meat case—till Myrna came traipsin back with her big old stomach pokin out from between the flaps of her cycle jacket. She set the bags down and bent over so her rear was showin to the whole planet.

You mind, Myrna? I said, goin around behind her and yankin down her skirt. Didn't help much because then her middle was showin. It was like squeezin a balloon.

Quit interferin with my attention, Thumby. She hiked her skirt back up.

It was so embarrassin with cars whizzin by and guys whistlin out the window. I mentioned I try to travel through life incognito. I picked up my dog. She stiffened and I could relate to that but I said tough beans and started walkin. Myrna didn't have no choice but to pick up the bags which any two-year-old could carry and follow me.

You're crazy, Thumby! she yelled. What do you want with a grubby old mutt! How you know it don't belong to someone? How you know it won't bite? Not to mention, fleas! No way is Agnes gonna let it stay!

It's her high heels pinchin her, Black Bean, I whispered. You can't hold her bad moods against her.

Myrna, her name is Black Bean, so please use it, I hollered over my shoulder. Myrna said somethin I better not repeat.

When we got home Agnes was watchin a movie with the sound turned down and her feet up on the table, her baby in her arms who was eatin on her.

The phone call had improved her mood. Hi, she smiled, and her face inched into pretty.

Hi, I said.

Sorry we took so long, Myrna said, shootin arrows at me from them amazin green eyes.

Myrna took the bottle out and twisted off the cap and went to get a cup. I headed straight for the cellar stairs. I had Black Bean buttoned down inside my coat and when I opened up she landed ten feet across the room and ran behind the water heater.

Be back for you soon, I told her.

Some guy was walkin up and down with the baby when I got back upstairs. Hadn't noticed him before. He had dark skin and he wore a black T-shirt and white jeans that could use a washin and one of them haircuts that is short on the sides and long in back that used to be in style quite a while ago. Myrna and her sister were arguin in the kitchen. I never know what to do in these situations. I

{78}

scooted between em—Agnes with her back to the stove, Myrna in the middle over the bad patch of linoleum, her little hands on her hips. Why didn't you tell me he called? Myrna was sayin. I got bread and slathered on peanut butter and pretended to be eatin it as I crossed back.

You tell her, Thumby.

I stopped in my tracks. I looked at Myrna, whose green eyes had a orange tint to em from the fire blazin inside em. Tell her what?

Stan's good qualities. He called for me last week and she's only just now tellin me.

That him in the livin room? I said.

That's *Clifford*, Agnes snorted.

Oh, I've never met your guy, Myrna. I smiled, spun in my socks, and headed for the cellar door. I exchanged smiles with Clifford as I zipped by, wonderin if I should give him advice about his haircut. Give him one of my mom's cards.

Oh, for cryin out loud, Black Bean, what do you expect?

She sniffed at the bread some more, then slipped back behind the water heater. I took my mom's coat off and reached around in the cobwebs, makin a bed for her.

After Agnes headed off to the place she went each night in that skimpy little dress and high heels (I was not askin yet), I went down to get Black Bean. I tried again to make good on my promise of steak, but all I could find in the fridge was a carton of sour cottage cheese Myrna bought to go on a diet. So I mixed the stinky cheese with bread and put it on the floor. She gobbled it down so fast I was afraid she'd get gas. Didn't lift her face up till Agnes's china bowl was empty. Then she sat there lookin at me with her big brown eyes, beggin me for more and cottage cheese hangin on her mustache.

Figured I had her right where I wanted her.

I took her up to the bathroom and rolled up my sleeves. She was not at *all* happy about gettin a bath. She didn't bite me but I could tell that thought was crossin her mind. But she didn't, that's the important thing. Not even when I splashed Tide in her eyes accidentally. That's a good dog for you. I was itchin to give her a haircut after that to see what kind of cut she had that had opened up like a envelope and poured about a gallon of blood into the water, but I didn't want to push my luck. I dried her off with one of my extra sweatshirts and wrapped a whole roll of toilet paper around and around her to keep her back from bleedin all over the floor, which would of sent old Agnes sky high. I cut the top half off a Pampers box and settled a blanket in it which I stole from Dwayne Junior's crib (he has got plenty). I took the box and my dog downstairs and set her house up by the water heater.

She wouldn't get in the box. She just sat there in the middle of the floor with her back to me.

Aw, Black Bean.

I went over and patted my hand on the bottom of the box. Won't you even come and test it out?

Nothin.

I stood up and went over to the cellar stairs. I said, Good night, Black Bean.

Like my mom she has got the ability to hold out. She did not say good night back.

~ ~ ~

I CUT MY dog's hair with Myrna's nail scissors. Took me *all* day through *all* the soaps. I am patient sometimes. I found bones underneath and I thought, don't we got a lot in common. I found the gash somebody'd cut in her back and when I dunked her in the tub it opened up and reddened the water and she started barkin and yelpin. What the hell are you doin to her, Thumby? Myrna yelled from downstairs. I pulled her out and wrapped her in my other sweatshirt. I am doin this for your own good, Black Bean, and I dumped alcohol into the cut and she shot up to the ceiling and whacked her head on the bare lightbulb. I said, Sorry, Black Bean, but she had already tore out of the bathroom and I went downstairs and put my head down on the floor and saw her huddlin back under the couch. Sorry, Black Bean, I said again. Fuck you, she said. She didn't come out till dinnertime when I put down a tasty meat loaf of Quaker Oats and baloney that was my mom's specialty. Meanwhile I cut my own hair. My mom showed me a trick once to cut my bangs. You twist the whole bunch of bangs up then you cut the ends right where you want em and they will be straight. I didn't cut nothin else of my hair. I like that it fits into my back pockets.

~ ~ ~

FINALLY met her guy. In the 7-Eleven parkin lot. Seemed like that's all we did for Agnes. Changed her baby's diapers and got her smokes. He was over at the air pump fillin up the front tire on his motorbike. *Steeeannnn!* Myrna screeched. I got a good look at his behind in tight black jeans before he jerked up like somebody'd kicked him. Myrna hoofed over. He didn't look too happy to see her, just bein honest. He tossed these herkin long braids over his shoulder, they whacked him in the back pockets. So right off we had somethin in common.

Stan, when did you get back to town?

Uh, the guy goes.

Then she's up on tiptoe grabbin his neck and kissin him. He held off for a few seconds but Myrna's pretty if you look at her from a certain angle.

They kissed for about two hours. I waited patiently.

I thought you were goin to do somethin about that, Myrna? he said, meanin her stomach.

Well, you give me the money. She glared at him.

I thought you had it figured out so the clinic would do it?

I—she drew up tall—changed my mind.

You what?

Myrna glared up at him. I got the right.

His teeth were white and tightly packed together. He had a nose like a big baked potato. I can't go through with this, Myrna sweetheart, I told you.

She looked like she was about to cry. He reached over and put his arms around her. You want to come listen to us practice? We're gettin back together.

I'm not officially talkin to you, Stan.

You're talkin to me now.

Only because you're pissin me off.

Aw, Myrna. I missed you. He was still huggin her and now he started into the serious kind of kissin, which involved their open mouths and tongues. Next thing you know she's on the bike behind him.

It's not fair, Stan, she said, you stayin out at the ocean so long. What you been up to?

What about your friend? Doesn't she talk?

Come on, Thumby. You can meet the guys.

I sing, Stan said, puffin out his chest.

So does Thumby.

You mean like in the shower? I said.

In my band, he scowled.

So you got three kids, I heard?

Thumby, stay out of it, Myrna warned.

Think I'll go back home, I said.

What are you afraid of?

I'm not afraid.

Could of fooled me.

Someday I'm goin to learn how to get out of that one. I went over and I swung on behind her. Only because I don't got nothin better to do, I told her, because I didn't want old Myrna thinkin, you know, that she could lead me around by the nose.

It was a tough squeeze what with her stomach and mine which is just beginning to bulge. Stan rides like how you'd expect. I felt like sayin, Hey, fool, would you mind slowin down? You got four passengers back here, but I didn't think he'd take it good.

They play in a old shed off Q Street on Alphabet Hill, about twenty blocks up from my old apartment building. The shed belongs to Stan's gramma who lives a couple streets up on E Street, because none of the houses on Alphabet Hill got their garage attached. There's no car in it because she got in a accident. It's pretty bare bones. A basic woodshed, no heat, in the ceiling one lightbulb without mother or father or sisters or brothers. The guys string extension cords across the floor from one plug by the door. Who knows where they go to the bathroom.

They got a warehouse space, Myrna claims, which they share with some group called Rain who once apparently opened for Fresh somethin-or-other, I have too much stuff in my head to remember details. What sharin means is they get it one day a week, Sunday.

Stan is thirty-four I've since learned from Myrn, and the other two are up there, but the kid is Todd, and he's takin a vacation from school. Todd plays guitar and Zonskey the Afro drums and fat small Mack plays bass when he isn't sittin there on his amplifier smokin little white cigs and turnin the page on some little paperback with a orange cover that says *The Failure of Our Education System.*

They all live in a house together way down at the bottom of the hill. They play at the Half Moon Tavern on Pacific Avenue Friday nights which is what they live on. That's why they're so skinny. Myrna must of asked Stan about five times to let her move in and cook for him but he said he don't want to die young.

Me and Myrna sat under the workbench on wood crates. I don't know if they're good or not because I didn't have no idea what they were playin, but they sure were loud. You can thank Todd for that. He has hair as black as Stan's but it's short and swept back and there isn't too much of it up there. He has Doc Martens and skinny legs and flat, wide eyes that are always half closed and he don't smile under no conditions. It isn't attitude he's got though, it's just concentration. He's always fiddlin. Even when he's blastin out your ears he's fiddlin. With the knobs on the front of his blue guitar or with the strings or with the metal bar or if he don't got nothin else available, his ear.

It was a wasted day though because he didn't ever play his harmonica. I saw it pokin out his flannel shirt pocket. He's got what you call a stretched-out body, which isn't no surprise. He probably eats three meals a day of guitar vibrations.

The only time me and Myrna budged was when we went down the hill to get em beer. She got two six-packs from the fridge and I followed her up to the counter and watched her slap down a ID like she owned it. I put down two Hershey's bars, figurin the guys could treat us.

Gainesville, Florida? I said when we were outside.

You want to get one? There's this shop on Agnes's street that sells em. Cheap.

Sounds like a great street to be . . . workin on, I said.

Ohhhhh, yeah. Agnes works on a real interestin street, Thumby.

I didn't say nothin. I wasn't in the mood for acquirin complicated information about Agnes, or nobody. She started eatin her chocolate bar but I put mine in my pocket.

My dad lives there, she said.

In Florida?

No, the moon, you dumb ass.

Stockin lightbulbs on the moon? Hmm.

Fixin *displays,* Thumby.

You're in big trouble if you get caught.

Fixin lightbulb displays?

I dug her in the ribs. Lyin, cheatin, and breakin the law, you moron, with that fake ID.

That's why I keep you in my life, Thumby, because you got one of them honest faces. As long as I'm with you, I'm touched by luck.

When we got back to the garage we gave em the paper bag and we got a beer each. Myrna gulped some and then she got up. It wasn't a surprise, I'd been feelin her restlessness for about a hour. She walked over to Stan. She said, Stan, I got to talk to you! and she roped her fingers through his belt and dragged him outside.

I took advantage of my opportunity. I said, Here, Todd, and I handed him my Hershey's bar. He gave me this look like, who are you? Mack snickered into his book. Todd put it in his shirt pocket next to his harmonica and went back to his fiddlin on his guitar. All my blood (I got quite a bit) jumped into my face. I got no clue why I did that. Probably made him think that I liked him.

I was out the door like that. Myrna was talkin to Stan and Stan was sittin on his motorbike smokin. I didn't even say bye to her. Myrna kept on yackin to Stan and lookin at him like the sun was settin on his head. I started walkin down the street. I walked slow. She caught up at full speed. She can run in them heels when she wants to. Will you wait up, goddamn you? she huffed and puffed.

So then we started walkin normal.

After about five seconds of walkin normal she got tired of not talkin. So where's your boyfriend again? she said, speakin real casual. Didn't fool me.

California.

Whereabouts?

California, I repeated.

How come you never call him up and say hi?

I don't phone boys, gives em the wrong idea.

What. That you just might like em?

Don't want to waste my money.

Where is he in California, exactly?

I don't know, I said, which is my usual policy when my lyin is about to get me dunked up to my neck in hot water.

Don't he know about your kid?

What kid.

She spit on the sidewalk. That's gross, I said.

You and Stan would make a great pair.

Then she added, for no reason whatsoever, For your information, Todd has a girlfriend.

Doesn't everybody.

But you can get him if you want him. She don't own him.

Who says I want him.

Myrna laughed. It's written all over your face in sky-high letters. You'd have to be blind to miss it. It's cool. So? Get him.

I shrugged and didn't say nothin.

Your kid could be a problem. Good thing you don't show. So the boyfriend in Cal's out of the picture for sure?

Oh yeah. I guarantee it.

What's his name?

Who's name? Stallin for time.

Your boyfriend.

I don't have a boyfriend, Myrna.

OK, the father of your kid. That guy.

Del.

Del what?

I pretended to be mad. It comes in handy. What. You goin to track him down?

Come on, I'm just bein nosy. Del what? What's his last name?

I wouldn't tell her. Because the fact is, I didn't have any idea myself. Haven't seen old Del since I was seven years old. He lived down the hall in Ravenhead Apartments, my first home after my mom's stomach.

Stan thinks I'm eighteen, you know, Myrna said.

Then he is dumber than I thought.

She gave me a look. Don't tell him I'm fourteen. He'd dump me.

For your own good.

Thumby.

He's got kids, Myrna. Three kids. He's thirty-four.

Old guys do it better.

It's not funny.

Oh, for crap's sake. This is not life and death, it's love, a happy thing, Thumby, if you've ever been knee deep in it, which I highly doubt. I love him.

You don't know the first thing about love, Myrna.

Even if you get mad at me, don't tell him the truth. Don't tell him my real age.

Since when do I get mad at you?

Thumby.

If you want to fuck up your life, fine. I won't say a word. But I doubt I'll be seein him again.

She elbowed me through my mom's coat. I'll help you snag Todd. We'll double-date.

With you and Stan?

No, me and the tooth fairy, you stupid ass.

Well, I haven't noticed Stan comin around to date you, Myrna, that's all.

She leaned back, exposin her whole, fat neck to the darkening sky. He misses me.

I let her have the last word.

~ ~ ~

A COUPLE days later we went to Safeway and put fifteen bucks down on a turkey. Then we had to buy the stuff to stuff it of course and cranberries and apple pie but Myrna was buyin so I didn't sweat it.

The house was empty when we got home. But plenty of boxes were scattered around.

Myrna? I said, followin her to the kitchen. What's Agnes doin?

Tryin to scare us into believin she's in love.

She movin in with him?

Agnes'll never leave this house, she's havin it remodeled.

I eyed the kitchen walls, lime as ever. I haven't seen nothin change since we got here.

Let's cook this turkey. She tossed the little bag of turkey parts into the trash. I fished em out and poked em down on the floor for Black Bean who got up off the mat and sniffed, then pulled back.

What are we goin to do, Myrna?

She's not a wild animal, Myrna said. You got to cook that stuff first.

I mean about payin rent if Agnes moves out.

Myrna curled her hair behind her ear and lifted the turkey into the sink. She splashed water inside it and stuck it on the oven rack and turned the oven on 550. I showed her the package which said 325.

You want to wait all day for some damn turkey? Myrna hollered.

Myrna found a candle and we turned off the lights and ate on the couch in the livin room. Myrna called Stan to ask him to come over but he was out accordin to the lady on the phone.

Liar! Myrna hollered, and slammed it down. I hate Claudia.

Myrna, like the guy said, have some mercy on him.

Myrna didn't say anything. Common sense didn't usually shut her up.

Have some more turkey. She forked me some on my full plate. We did a good job on it, didn't we?

She got up to get the apple pie out of the oven. I built a tower on my mashed potatoes with the lumps of gravy.

You ever hear from Lester?

I eyed her, a little surprised. She didn't ever ask me nothin personal, except all that crap about my boyfriend.

Why are you askin?

Where is he?

With Marcus probably.

Who?

His friend.

Why don't you ever go visit him? Is he cool to live with?

Why don't you ever go visit your mom?

Because she is more of a pain in the ass than my sister, even, I prefer keepin eight hundred miles between us. He's cute, you know.

I choked on my pie. How do you know?

You're haulin a picture of him around in your wallet.

You been snoopin in my wallet too?

So what's the story?

I stared at her. There is no story.

Why'd you come to Leffer's then, instead of stayin with him?

I didn't want to stay with him.

Is he a fag or somethin?

I blinked slowly. If you try really hard, Myrna, I bet you can find a more delicate way to speak about the guy my mom loved more than anything. Especially considerin the fact that she is dead and not here to defend her taste in men.

She was all eyes in the candlelight. You don't have to be ashamed about it. It's just that I've been alive for fourteen years and I've learned a few things. No guy that good-lookin lives with another guy unless he's queer.

She gave me a second to answer, but I was just tryin to get my breathin under control.

That's really cool, you know? Men that can go both ways. They're so free. They get the best of both worlds.

Caused my mom a lot of grief.

I'll bet. Whole world's your competition instead of just half of it.

My fork clattered down on my plate. She could tell I was near losin it. Probably her body remembered the last time she'd pushed me too far, back at Mrs. Leffer's on the first day I met her. She changed the subject.

I saw somethin else in your wallet, Thumby. She pricked the crust of her pie with her fork. Some number for an adoption agency.

You got a big fuckin nose, Myrna.

Yeah, I know. You got it off the bulletin board at the doctor's office, didn't you? The one where Mrs. Leffer took you.

Is this your business, Myrna? I don't think so.

You plannin on givin up your *baby*, Thumby?

My eyelids cut off those pushy green eyes. I thought about my mom in the ground in her wood box. I started to salt my pie.

I'm sorry, T. She squeezed my foot under the table. I mean, she said softly, if you're worried about bein a single mom, I'll help you.

Myrna. You don't want to help me raise my kid. You got your own kid to worry about.

Yeah. And I am worried about it.

How come?

Somethin don't feel right inside me, Thumby.

You goin to the doctor?

She forked up her pie and chewed and changed the subject, typical Myrna style.

Why don't you want your own baby, Thumby?

I didn't say I didn't want her.

Her? You'd give away a *her*? How can you do that? Man, I hope mine's a girl.

I picked up my pie plate and carried it into the kitchen. I took off my glasses and shoved my face under the tap. The water ran into my ears. I blotted my face with the dish towel. I went to the back door and pulled it shut behind me. My shoes squished in the soft, wet grass and then crunched on the gravel. I sat down on the garbage can in the alley and the sky was black and filled with silver lights and I thought about my mom and that damn ugly outfit we'd sent her off in and I hoped her feet were warm.

The kitchen door opened, spillin light into the backyard. Thumby? Myrna hissed. Thumbeliiiina?

What.

Where are you? She put her hand up over her eyes to squint into the night. Come here! We got company! she hissed.

I am busy, Myrna.

It's . . . a certain guitarist! she hissed. He's in the livin room!

I was over to her like a shot. No way! I grabbed her arm. What's he want?

Beats me. Are you in decent shape? She hauled me into the kitchen and took a look. You look like hell. Too bad, my makeup's in the livin room in my purse. He just knocked on the door and asked if he could come in. I said you were takin the trash out. She snagged a leaf out of my hair.

Make him go away, Myrna.

Comin, Todd! she hollered.

Grab a couple beers, Thumby, she whispered, and when

I didn't move she jerked open the fridge door, bangin the backs of my legs, and reached in.

I barely got my hair smoothed out of my face before she was pushin me through the kitchen door.

Hellooooo, Todd, she sang.

He was sittin on the couch with his knees near his cheeks. A cig burned the red lips in Agnes's ashtray. He straightened his legs and his head came up. He ran his hand through what's left of his hair. I just stood there, takin him in. Good thing Myrna was there. She pushed me over to the couch. Right by his knee.

You want a beer, Todd? Myrna said, plunkin two down. Thumbelina, you remember Todd, don't you?

Good old Myrna, keepin the ball rollin.

I eased my butt sideways, away from him. You look different without your blue guitar, I said. But your face is comin back to me.

Ann Marie.

I blinked. Scuse me?

I named my guitar for my mom.

Well, that's pretty weird.

B. B. King did it.

Nuh-uh, he named it for his girlfriends, Myrna said.

If B. B. King belly flopped off a bridge, would you? I said quickly, before he could bring his girlfriend into the conversation.

I grinned, to let him know I was teasin him. He didn't grin back. His mouth wasn't normal. His top lip was ruler straight from corner to corner. It didn't look very flexible.

He put his thumbnail in his mouth and chewed on it. The lightbulb went on in my big head, but before I could ask him if he was hungry, he was talkin again.

I brought you somethin. He reached into his leather

jacket pocket and plopped it down. There, between the red lips on the front of *Vogue* and the pair in Agnes's ashtray, sat a Mr. Goodbar. My eyeballs stared. I couldn't believe he was returnin the favor. I wanted to pinch my arm. You smoke? he said, and gave me another present. The cig sat in my big hand. He flicked his yellow lighter. I wanted to say, Nah, I'm keepin this forever, Todd, in my underwear drawer, except I don't have a underwear drawer no more. I put it to my lips and leaned over. I got a whiff of somethin nice. My heart whacked my ribs. I took a little puff and blew it out slow, tryin to look sophisticated. I tapped the ash on the ashtray. I kept tappin. He laid his cig down and put his hands behind his head. He seemed relaxed. Like he came over to say hi to strange girls every day.

You ever play that harmonica? I said, glarin at him because I was pretty sure my eyes were givin away everything.

What do you want to hear? He looked up at me through his eyelashes. My stomach flipped over like a pancake on the fry pan.

Are you goin to make him perform on a empty stomach? Myrna said, elbowin back into the conversation. Offer this man some turkey, Thumby.

Todd lifted his head. Turkey?

Myrna overcooked it, I muttered, glarin at her.

Turkey'd be great, man—

We got mashed potatoes and cranberries too, Myrna said, ignorin me.

And apple pie, I said, fadin and lettin her take over.

He put his hands on his knees and pushed himself up. I can't stay, I got to get over to Quik Stop for the graveyard shift.

On Thanksgivin? Myrna hollered.

He shrugged. I just came over—his eyes moved off Myrna and sat on me—to invite you guys down to the Half Moon this Saturday night. If you want to hear me playin harmonica, that is. We got some new songs we're tryin out.

Is that offer comin from the whole band? Myrna said, clutchin her waist with her little hands.

He held his left hand out like it was frettin a guitar and swept the air with his right hand. He didn't say nothin, which impressed me.

Myrna counted on her fingers. One, two nights' notice. I don't know, Todd, she said. We got busy social lives.

Come on, Myrna. Don't keep Thumbelina from appreciatin our talent just because you're pissed off at Stan.

We will think it over.

You promise I'll hear some harmonica playin? I said.

His top lip nearly hit his ears. I was surprised. Didn't think he had that kind of smile in him.

I guarantee it. Come down about nine. We'll give you free beer.

We walked him out. It irritated me that a guy could thump on our front door and turn us inside out in two seconds flat, but I couldn't help feelin happy. We watched his guitar player boots thump down the steps. He thumped up the brick walk. He ducked into the little Volkswagen Bug that waited for him and he waved, and we waved back. The car made a *bu bu bu* sound in the darkness. Then his taillights swung around the corner.

Man, Myrna said. Do you got the touch, Thumby. Her smirkin green eyes bugged me. I swiped my Mr. Goodbar off Agnes's table. I went over to the cellar door. I need some privacy, Myrna.

Don't stay down there all night, we got to make plans. What are you goin to wear?

I don't know. Somethin of yours.

Down in the darkness I ate my chocolate and held Black Bean's warm body in my lap. She snored like she didn't have no care in the world. I thought about Todd and my heart worked hard, pumpin, pumpin hope through me.

~ ~ ~

HE LIKES you, Thumby, Myrna said the next mornin, pullin on her thick tights. Trust me, he likes you. He wouldn't invite us down to watch em if he didn't like you.

What makes you so sure he don't like you?

Because that whole band would like to see me dropped off the Narrows Bridge with a couple bricks tied to my ankles.

Because you're complicatin their lead singer's life?

She smirked. She shoved her arms into her coat. Stan'll probably choke on his mike when I walk in.

She was gettin ready to go to the clinic, dressin warm because she was walkin. The bus never came reliably in Agnes's neighborhood.

What if Todd's girlfriend is there? I said.

You'll make short work of her. She heaved her green scarf over her neck. You got a lot to learn when it comes to guys, Thumby.

So you got to teach me, Myrn! I blurted. I don't got as much experience as you!

She cocked her eyebrow. You implyin that I've been around, Thumby?

This is one time I need you to be normal, so kindly don't read crap into everything I say, Myrna.

You comin with me?

Myrna, bein as you heard me on the phone with Agnes a minute ago, you know perfectly well that she's bringin her kids over for me to babysit.

You got to learn to say no to my sister, Thumbelina.

It's all my yessin that's keepin this roof over our heads, you dumb ass.

Well, then, call her back, tell her we got to be free this afternoon. Let's go to the mall and buy somethin sexy.

Usin what, Myrn? Our good looks?

Myrna winked. I know where my sister keeps her cash.

I was tryin to get lunch in them kids when Myrna called. Hold on, Myrna, I said.

I got bad news, Thumby.

I know, Myrna.

What do you mean, you know?

Why else would you be callin?

I cupped the phone under my chin and splashed a glass full of orange juice and then I hollered for Dee Dee to come in and drink it. I hitched Dwayne Junior higher on my hip and put the phone down and picked up the towel to get his bottle out of the hot water. I set it on the counter to cool.

It just sort of stopped growin, you know, Thumby? she said when I got the phone back under my ear.

What, Myrna?

It was missin most of its brain.

My heart slid out of its usual location and stopped in my shoes as I realized what she was tellin me.

They said it's been dead about a week.

I picked up the bottle and pushed it between Dwayne Junior's little hungry lips. Where are you?

The hospital. I had to come over for X-rays and stuff. It had everything, all its fingers and toes and a heart, it just didn't have the brain growin right.

The baby slurped at the rubber nipple and formula splattered all over my red sweatshirt.

I asked em if losin my mornin sickness was a sign, but they said it's normal to lose it in your seventh month. I'm warnin you, Thumby, you better be careful. You better start eatin better and takin it easy. You better go to the doctor.

I moved to the doorway. Dee Dee, last call to get in here and drink your juice, I called softly.

You hear me, Thumbelina?

Yeah, Myrna. I hear you.

They're holdin me overnight. They got to clean me out of the leftover bits. Maybe you could get the word to Stan for me.

OK.

Dwayne Junior started screamin. I jiggled the little guy, feelin his lonesomeness at missin his mom.

Don't you know how to shut up a baby by now, Thumby? She laughed softly, and all the sadness of her fourteen years was fillin that laugh. I don't know if I'll be out of here by tomorrow night. I don't know if I'll be up for seein em.

That's OK, Myrna.

You can go, I would go if I was you, Thumby.

I don't know, Myrna.

Go, man. This is your chance.

After she hung up I got her pack of cigarettes from the kitchen drawer and I sat in the rockin chair in front of the window, puttin away smoke after smoke, starin down into the puddly street. I hummed Johnny Cash songs and thoughts passed through my head like clouds.

•   •   •

I got this memory. My head keeps everything. I was in kindergarten and the teacher said, Fingerpaint your family doin somethin. I made me and her eatin dinner. I got all our favorite colors in: Our hair was yellow, the tablecloth was orange, and the mashed potatoes were knockout pink. I didn't put glasses on me because I wanted to be pretty like her. She said, What is it? It's beautiful, and she put it on the fridge with the apple magnets we got from the gas station after they stopped givin out free plates.

Lester came in lookin for a beer. What's this?

If you can't tell, don't worry about it. You're not in it, anyway, I said.

It's me and Thumbelina eatin . . . what, honey?

Mashed potatoes, Mom. I glared at him, wishin he'd go back in to the TV and leave us alone.

She stopped workin the crank on the can of pineapple. Thumbelina, don't be grouchy, sweetheart.

He was still eyein it. Why didn't you put me in it?

You're not my family.

He grabbed my ponytail like there was a sign on it sayin, HELP YOURSELF, and my cheek slammed into the counter. Pain shot over my face. I didn't see it comin. Then he went in the livin room and turned the TV louder. My mom got ice. She held me in her lap. She kept askin me if I was all right, but I felt it was the wrong question to be askin me. I was tired of my mom makin the rules, sayin who would be in our house and who wouldn't. Because I had to put up with him just as much as she did. Later she told me he only acted that way because it bothered him, not bein my daddy. He wants you to think of him as your daddy, she said. I don't recall replyin to her, but I had plenty of opinions in my head. That's about all that filled it in those days. Opinions on Lester. She taped my picture together and pinned it up at Betty's shop where she'd just got the job colorin hair.

In first grade we made candles for our moms for Christmas. I was still out to impress her. We were supposed to bring a pretty bottle from home to pour the wax into but I could only find empty beer and wine bottles, which would of been bad for my reputation. So I poured the ranch dressing down the sink and took that bottle. All these mothers drove us to Miss Kirkpatrick's apartment to use her stove. Then they drove off to leave us in privacy. Miss Kirkpatrick had stacks of Beatles records and wicker furniture and plants hangin from the ceiling like dead guys.

I didn't know anything about the Beatles and none of the other kids did either but we liked her and we sat down and listened to em on her record player. She showed us pictures of her mom and dad and little brother in a gold frame on this low little table, which was stacked with fashion magazines. She had all kinds of books in bookcases that went from the floor to the white ceiling. She gave us plastic glasses of grape pop. Everybody said thanks, bein on their best behavior. Then we went into the kitchen where the wax was mutterin under its breath in a big pot, complainin about life in general, and one by one we got up on the chair with our bottle and got it filled. Jess Beansley had a knockout pink vase like you'd put a rose in if you were askin a lady to marry you. I watched him fill it and held my breath till he'd got it full and done right because it was already mine. When it came my turn I held out my ranch bottle and some of the kids giggled into their shirtsleeves but Miss Kirkpatrick just poured in the wax like she didn't hear nothin, and some of it spilled on my hand and stung like a bee but I didn't say ow, it didn't hurt that bad.

We put our bottles on her kitchen table and she gave us labels. I stuck THUMBELINA on mine but I didn't press it down very hard. Then we went in her livin room to listen to more Beatles records and eat cookies. I got to go to the bathroom, I said. I went out in the kitchen cool as the bottom of the duck pond and worked Jess's name off his bottle and my name off my bottle and put my name right where I wanted it.

When Miss Kirkpatrick passed the candles out in class she plunked the salad dressing bottle down on Jess's desk.

Miss Kirkpatrick, this ain't my candle.

Don't feel bad, it's a very nice candle, Jess.

It ain't mine, and he started lookin around to see who had his.

Miss Kirkpatrick reached in her box and plunked down on my desk the vase that was as graceful as my mother's neck. Frosted clumps of wax ran down the sides of the pink glass. Jess's heart nearly failed him. He roared, That's my candle! Thumbelina's got my candle! He lurched out of his desk, comin down the row. Good thing I was in the far back, I had time to get my desk open and the candle inside and slam it down and get my elbows on it solid. Don't be bustin that vein in your forehead, Jess, I said.

Good thing Miss Kirkpatrick was dumb. Sit down, Jess.

Thumbelina's got my—

Jess, sit down.

He went up and dropped my ranch bottle in the waste basket. Miss Kirkpatrick said, Jess, step outside. Jess stepped outside. He didn't come back inside. After school I cut through the park to get home faster. I found stacks of wrappin paper in my mom's closet, a good sign, it meant she had plans. I wrapped her present in silver angels with long horns they were hootin on. Oh, isn't this gorgeous?

my mom said on Christmas mornin, takin it out of the paper.

It sure is, Lester said.

And she set it in the middle of the kitchen table. It lasted there till they got home from Betty's New Year's Eve party at three, four in the mornin. I was down the hall under my bed. I heard it bash the wall. All my hard work up in smoke. The next day she tried to blame it on Lester.

Nah. He wouldn't break nothin pretty, Mom, he likes pretty things too much, it's why he puts up with you.

She started to cry. She said she was sorry, it wasn't me she wanted to hurt. It was this guy from Seattle, some musician friend of Lester's from his army days called Marcus who'd been hittin on Lester and wouldn't leave him alone. I said, You sure you weren't drinkin too much, Mom? And she said, I'm afraid I'm goin to lose him, Thumby.

I told her she'd better leave her glasses at home the next party so she wouldn't have to see nothin that was goin on around her since it upset her so much and she surprised me by sayin, What a good idea, Thumby.

That was the only time she ever mentioned Marcus, in so many words. She just stopped seein the difficult things in life. She had an amazin ability to go blind.

And I didn't steal anything else for her. But a long time later, last summer, I stole somethin for myself. After Cynthia's slumber party it was time to get what I needed. I kept askin my mom but she said, Oh, you aren't old enough yet. I felt like sayin, oh Mom, you don't know the half of how old I am, but I wasn't ready to lay that on her, probably afraid she'd collapse. But where did keepin it to myself get me? I lost her anyway.

I was fed up with bein teased for not havin one. Fed up with changin for gym in the toilet. Fed up with the boys behind me feelin for it and hootin and hollerin as if I was lackin ears.

So I went to the mall and I went up to the underwear place and the lady said, Can I help you? And I said, No, thanks, I'm just lookin. I thumbed through the racks and I found one in a good color that I felt I could grow into. The lady cleared her throat behind me. Is that a gift? she said. Nope, I said, it's for me.

Why don't you let me help you? she said, takin it out of my hand before I could stop her. I got a good eye for this, she said, sort of grinnin. She whipped one out and handed it to me, in ugly old white and it didn't have no cups in sight. Jesuschrist, insult me a little more why don't you, I thought, and soon as some other people came over and took her attention I dug through everything till I found the purple one that I liked. I snuck out and stuffed it in my pocket and went down the escalator and out the door.

The buzzer didn't go off. They do it quieter than that. Two guys grabbed me by the arms the second I was out the door. Don't have no idea where they came from. Hand it over, they said. People stared. Oh man. I could of died.

Purple? one of em said.

Isn't it a little . . . large? the other one said.

I was plannin on growin into it.

You got the money to pay for this?

Of course I do, I said, because if you ask a stupid question you get a stupid answer. They let me go. I was pretty relieved. I blamed my mom. But I didn't say nothin to her about it. You kiddin? She would of busted the button on her jeans laughin. I just took a few bucks out of her purse next chance I got and went to Kmart and got one in a box that looked like the one the lady had recommended in the first place. I'm still wearin it.

~ ~ ~

Well, I had to break the news to Agnes about Myrna's baby. I hated havin this job to do. Nighttime came. I put Dwayne Junior and Dee Dee to bed and then I lay down on the couch without foldin it out since Myrna wasn't there. I must of fallen asleep because they woke me up, gigglin in the front door. Plastered. I got a ear for it. Agnes and her boyfriend with the out-of-style haircut who loves her and wants her and her kids to move in with him. She has a lot better taste than my mom.

She was tellin him, Shh! You'll wake my kids. Then it was daylight on the other side of my eyelids. Hey, come here, Aggie, he said, knockin into the end table. Come on, Cliff, it's been a long day, she sighed. I got the picture right off and I stuck to my plan of bein asleep, to give em privacy. Good old Black Bean who was under the blanket with me had no clue about the ins and outs of relationships. She popped out of the blanket and nipped Clifford, I wasn't sure where, I had to grab my glasses, but the guy yelled loud enough to raise the roof. This disappointed me. I had thought he was tougher than that. Sorry about that, I said. He was holdin his ankle. I got no idea why she don't like you.

What was that? Agnes said.

An orphan, I said, pullin on leggings and my sweatshirt. A charmin orphan that needs to learn some manners. I ran upstairs and found Black Bean huddled by the toilet, a position that I could relate to. I picked her up and whacked her on her behind. What'd you do that for? She grinned at me. Her warm little tongue touched my nose. I hugged her. What the heck. She was under the impression she was protectin me.

I snuck back out to the top of the stairs. They were arguin down there. Agnes was tellin him he had to go, he was sayin, Baby baby, I don't want to go, I want an answer, are you or aren't you? I've started packin, haven't I? she snapped. Then why can't I stay? Finally, she got him out the door. I crept back down. Light spilled into the livin room from the kitchen. I didn't quite make it back under the covers.

Come on in here and have somethin to drink, she called.

It's kind of late, Agnes.

You're goin to make me drink alone?

Then I remembered the job I had to do. So I went in there and she pointed the fingers holdin the cigarette at the red wine in the middle of the table. Her makeup had all pretty much disappeared into her skin. Her hair curled around her face like she'd been exercisin. Her long, skinny legs were crossed. On her feet were them stacked heels that have got popular since my mom has been dead.

Where did that come from Thumbelina? Referrin to the dog in my arms.

The basement.

Just appeared down there magically?

I poured some wine but I held off drinkin it. I looked into her dark green eyes that she shares with her sister.

No. I found her in the ditch.

She reached up and patted Black Bean's behind. Black Bean stiffened but held off on all other rude behavior.

I'm sorry Black Bean bit him.

She waved her hand. Oh. Cliff'll get over it. The kids sleepin?

Why wouldn't you let him stay the night, Agnes?

Because I'm exhausted, Thumbelina.

I pressed my lips together. You aren't that into him. At least my mom never got bored by her guys.

She let that sit there and didn't seem motivated to do nothin about it.

I pulled out a chair and sipped at the wine, to show her my heart was in it. I got bad news, Agnes.

I already know about your mother, Thumbelina. Myrna told me.

I blinked. My mother?

I asked her what was up with you and she said your mom had a accident.

Is that right.

Drove into some pond.

The one at Bean Park. Where all the ducks come every spring.

I didn't know that pond was deep.

It doesn't have to be when you bang your head in such a way that you are knocked unconscious.

Her long apricot eyelashes shielded her eyes. Pretty busted up over some guy, I heard.

Not some . . . *guy,* I muttered. Her boyfriend of fourteen years.

He must of been awful good-lookin.

I shrugged.

Rich?

No, just unavailable, which was sexier to my mom.

You mean married.

No, I mean he had a wanderin eye.

Had affairs, you mean.

Yep.

A womanizer.

Not exactly with women.

It took her a second to get my drift, her eyebrows marched straight into her hair. No kiddin.

It's not *that* strange, Agnes.

Your mother was into that stuff?

Be careful what you say of the dead, Agnes.

Her cig butt fell into what was left of her wine. I can never figure it out, when pretty ladies waste themselves.

How do you know she was pretty? You been snoopin through my wallet too?

She blinked at me. You ever look in the mirror?

Not too often.

Well, maybe you better start.

I turned this one over for a couple of minutes. Well, thanks, Agnes, for sayin that, but if I'm so pretty, how come I don't have no boyfriend?

She cocked her eyebrow. You had one, didn't you?

I ignored that. This guy came by last night. He asked me and Myrna to come down and watch his band play.

Which one's he after? You or her?

Hopin it's me.

You want to borrow somethin? I got a little black dress that would look great on you.

I eyed my feet. I got a lot workin against me, Agnes.

Don't we all.

I got more than the usual girl.

Her green eyes waited, patiently.

Agnes, it's not just my mom, my dad is also . . . you know, a ghost.

Thumbelina. You're fourteen, pregnant, wanderin around in the world with my sister. God help you. It's obvious you're a lone eagle. You're a six-foot-tall blonde, Thumbelina, that is obvious too. Don't forget that. She yawned. But I wouldn't worry too much about guys right now. You got a lot on your plate. You got the rest of your life to fool around. Wait till you get more experience, till you can spot one that won't go off and leave you . . . you know, alone with his kid.

Water gathered in the corners of my eyes and boiled over. She got up kind of delicately and went over to the sink.

I cleared sadness out of my throat with a great effort. Listen, Agnes, I shouldn't even be yackin about all this crap about guys because I have got some bad news to get out of the way.

Me too, Thumbelina. She was washin her hands. I hate to have to put you in this position, but I don't have a choice. I have to take care of my kids. I have to take the opportunities that come to me. Do you have any dancin experience?

I have watched a lot of ballet.

You want a job?

Doin what.

Sendin rockets to the moon, sweetheart, she said softly. I might as well tell you, Clifford asked me and the kids to move in with him.

That is not a news flash, Agnes. I nodded at the boxes on the kitchen floor. What are me and Myrna goin to do?

She blinked at me. Well, you're goin to have to get jobs.

It was startin to click into place. Bein dancers, you mean?

You're a little young . . . I got to admit that. But the money's good.

I better get my bad news out of the way, Agnes, while I'm still talkin to you.

Whatever you do, don't tell me my sister's in jail. I can't deal with that after the night I've had. She filled her glass with wine.

She's in the hospital.

Agnes swigged. Is she all right?

I don't know about mentally. But physically she's OK. She lost her baby.

I let the words settle in.

It was missin . . . important parts.

She sat back down and took out another Basic Light. What important parts? she said quietly.

Its brain.

It's for the best, I guess.

She won't see it that way.

My sister never sees things in any way that makes sense. You'd think she'd know what a drag it is, raisin kids on your own, from watchin me. But no. Same with you. She heaved smoke into the room, gathered up her hair, and tossed it over one skinny shoulder. A baby's goin to be a much different situation than haulin that dog around. You're goin to have to come down off your high horse, where, if you don't mind me sayin, you like to sit. You're goin to have to carry your weight, Thumbelina.

If you didn't have kids, you wouldn't be movin in with Clifford, would you?

I had a fiancé. A good-lookin fiancé. Good-lookin men are the worst kind, Agnes sighed, starin at the bad patch of linoleum. I feel sorry for your mom. She should have got rid of him.

You try tellin her.

You goin to stay up?

For a while.

She said, Night, and headed off to the sack, notice I say *headed*. The wine was showin. Couldn't call that walkin.

It was two in the mornin. I put on the kettle and sat there drinkin tea and lightin the rest of her Basic Lights and lettin em drift off in the ashtray and huggin Black Bean, who was awake also, and we admired the wallpaper for a long time.

I have a lot of fondness for kitchens. That's where my mom used to do all her serious talkin to me after she and Lester had a fight. Lester had this rule about himself. After beatin her up he had to go out and work off steam. He'd go out drivin like a maniac. My mom used to say, He's goin to hit someone and kill em. You have to admit that was pretty funny. Because he'd just got done hittin her. And her sittin there with a smoke goin and a mug of vodka and tellin me how she'd had it this time. She'd loop a wad of hair in her fingers and twist it round and round while she talked. Sometimes I'd wrap some ice cubes in a towel for her body parts but sometimes there wasn't none froze in the freezer. My mom didn't care too much about it as long as it wasn't her face got hit. Because my mom cared about her face. So did Lester, good thing.

Mostly I didn't have to say much, I just listened which was a good thing but once in a while she'd forget who she was talkin to and say, What do you think about that, Thumbelina? And I'd say, I'll tell you what I think. Why can't we leave, Mom? Huh? Why can't we move in with Betty?

That wasn't what she wanted to hear, of course. She'd get all huffy. She'd say, Thumby, you just don't understand. Life isn't that simple.

Seems pretty simple to me, I'd say. And she'd get all mad

and squash her cig in the saucer and she'd say, I'm goin over to Betty's.

Wait for me, Mom, I'd say, and of course I'd go after her. Because you always wanted to go after her. Because you never knew what kind of trouble she might get into on the way to Betty's.

Betty owns Betty's Beauties where my mom worked ever since the time I made that fingerpaintin. She didn't have no man in her life (still doesn't) to moan about so she liked to hear my mom's moanin. That made em tight.

Of course Betty was married once (wasn't everybody?) except hers was different. She didn't kick him out, he died. She sold the auto parts store and bought the beauty salon. She wasn't very good at colors and perms, but she had my mom and Chee Chee to do that stuff. She stuck to keepin the books and answerin the phones and once in a while if Chee Chee was out sick she'd trim someone's bangs. Course she wasn't good at that either. Mainly she was good at gossip. She had a problem gettin stuff even. She was always trimmin one side to get it even with the other side and vice versus so don't be surprised if you come out with nothin left on your forehead. She could do a decent manicure though if she embarked on it before she drank coffee which jittered her pretty bad.

One time Betty took me and my mom to the Betty Club of Tacoma meetin. You had to have the name Betty to join. We were guests. There was a whole bunch of people sittin around at tables in this gym eatin cake and talkin about famous Bettys like Betty Grable and Betty Crocker and Betty Ford. The Bettys were all old and me and my mom were young and we were bored as hell. We didn't let on, though. My mom was a polite lady and I inherited it from her.

Betty knew what to say to my mom. We'd come through the door and she'd sit her down in a kitchen chair and give her the cookie jar. My mom would be eatin them cookies whole she'd be so mad and Betty'd take the floor. Her favorite sayin in them days was, all in one sentence without stoppin: Drinkin don't make a good man bad but it makes a bad man worse you're a beautiful woman Angelica you can do better why don't you leave him he's goin to hurt you bad one day isn't it tough bein a woman?

Men, my mom would say, spittin out cookie crumbs, aren't they a pain? Why'd God invent em?

God's a man, Betty would point out. And my mom'd be off.

And meanwhile I'm goin tweedle-dum and tweedle-dee on the livin room floor playin with the goddamn cat and wishin. Don't know what I was wishin. For Lester to go away mainly. Course right in front of me I had the evidence on where she stood on that. I love you, Lester, she'd be sayin soon as he got back home. I love you, Angelica, he'd say back, pettin her head like she was Betty's cat.

Sometimes we'd bring our laundry basket over to Betty's because she had her own washer and dryer down in the basement. We'd pick up a layer cake on the way so we'd have somethin to eat over our coffee. (Accordin to my mom, but I knew better. She hated arrivin somewhere without somethin to give.) Them two would go at it in the kitchen, I'd be down in the basement swingin my legs off the table, readin about the famous people in *People* or *Us,* waitin for the spin cycle when you had to pull out the button because it was partly busted. I'd come up and tell my mom when the stuff was done and she'd go down and sort out what could be dried and what couldn't. Then we'd fold it all three of us and put it in our cardboard box and the night would always end with Betty sayin, You can't lead a horse to water, Thumbelina, while lookin past my head at my mom, who laughed.

~ ~ ~

WHEN I got to the shed the doors were wide open and nobody was there, but the blastin music from up above got me around to the back stairs and I went up. They were all sittin around this dusty little room drinkin beer. (So this is where they pee, I thought, seein the toilet in the corner.) It wasn't them makin the racket, it was this boom box. I went over and jammed it off.

Where's Stan? I said loudly.

Hey, Thumbelina, said Todd. What a surprise. He was sittin against the wall under the window with his blue guitar in his lap. It wasn't plugged in and he pinged at the strings.

Zonskey and Mack stared at me.

Why are you lookin for Stan? Zonskey said, eyein me up and down. This took some time.

I got a message to deliver.

He's not here, Todd said.

Kind a get that feelin, I said coolly, tuckin my hair behind my ear.

He's sick, Todd added, his eyes squintier than I remembered.

You talk a lot, man, said Zonskey.

Mind tellin me where I can find him, Todd?

He's sick, Mack frowned. Didn't you hear him?

At Claudia's apartment, Todd said.

I glared at him. Do I look like I got her address memorized?

Todd started to say somethin but the guys cut him off. He's got enough girl trouble as it is, the guy with the book smirked. You'd best leave him alone.

He's got a responsibility with orange hair to worry about, I informed them.

Does this little message involve her kid? Zonskey said.

Six-two-three Medford Street, Todd said, fiddlin with his strings and not lookin at me. Number seventeen.

I let off a couple curse words. Well, thanks. Thanks a lot.

He's sick, Zonskey hollered after me. Go easy on him!

Lay off, Zonsk, Todd muttered. Does she look like the kind of girl who's goin to cause trouble?

Todd caught up to me on the sidewalk. He grabbed my arm to slow me down. Hey, he said. Wait.

I stared at his hand on my arm till he let go. You got the charm of a chunk of concrete today, Todd.

I'm sorry, I just don't want to get on their bad side, stickin up for your friend. They're all older than me, and they're great musicians. They're pissed off at Stan. We all are. His women trouble is interferin with our music. You goin there now?

No, I asked for the address because I enjoy fillin my head with useless, stupid information, Todd.

He shifted his weight from one slick boot to the other. Is Myrna OK?

If she was, do you think I'd be here, humiliatin myself in front of the bunch of you?

He squinted at me. He lifted the collar of his jacket against the wind that gusted down the sidewalk. I shivered inside my mom's coat. You and Myrna are good friends, huh?

I figured it was decently obvious, so I didn't reply.

Well, don't be thinkin that I got somethin against her.

I'm just gettin frustrated with this whole damn situation, he said.

Seems like Stan's the one you should be pissed off at, I said coolly. If he can't figure out which girl he is in love with.

Man, definitely, he nodded. I take my music serious, Thumbelina. I got no patience for this crap.

I'm gettin that feelin, Todd.

I got a buddy down in Austin, Texas. The music scene is hot down there. But I got ties holdin me here. You know?

Well, aren't you a lucky guy.

My mom, for one thing.

I pushed my bangs out of my eyes. I had been expectin to hear about the girlfriend. Do you like your mom, Todd?

His straight mouth forked over another smile. Well, that's a weird question to ask a guy. Of course I do. Don't you?

His bony shins were available for viewin pleasure through the holes in his jeans. They were matted with interestin, black hair.

You and Myrna seem real different people. Maybe I don't know her too good, but you seem calmer. Like you got your head together, Thumbelina.

I smiled at him. I ran my fingers through my long hair and nearly fell over when his eyes left my face to follow my fingers, down through my hair.

The thump was a soft one. I blinked. Then it came harder. Thaaa*wump*. I stopped smilin. I took my hand out of my hair.

Maybe we could get together sometime, one of the guys said you sing, Thumbelina.

I pushed my hand through my mom's coat, against my sweatshirt, pressin hard on her to calm her down.

You ever been up to Seattle? I'm goin up there in a couple weeks to check it out.

You're one of those guys, I muttered.

Todd lifted his large eyebrows politely. One of what guys?

Them grass-is-greener kind of guys.

Sometimes the grass *is* greener, Thumbelina. I'm sure you don't exactly love Tacoma either.

I pushed my glasses up my nose. The wind was pullin tears out of the corners of my eyes. My fish thumped me with her tail again. I turned away, lookin out over the rooftops to the water out there which matched the sidewalk under my high-tops. Well, my fish was right. I had no right to be standin there, flirtin with him.

I got to go, Todd.

Hey! Thumbelina?

I turned around. Yeah?

Are you comin down to the Half Moon tonight?

I eyed my big, hairy toe which poked out the end of my high-top. Bare, because I was lackin in clean socks. My stupid toe, always tryin to struggle out and get a glimpse of the world.

Thumbelina? he said.

Myrna's in the hospital, Todd, I said, speakin to his left, leather shoulder. I won't be able to make it tonight, after all.

My big feet turned me around on the sidewalk and moved me away. It was my fault for startin it. Givin him that Hershey's bar. As if I was a normal girl. As if I could go around flirtin and leadin guys on. What would he say when he found out? Oh, bummer, you're carryin another guy's baby. Well, I like you anyway?

• • •

I waited for the bus on the corner of R Street and it took me down Alphabet Hill, around the far side of Bean Park on Washington Avenue, and out along the waterfront. I tried to just watch the scenery and not think about him. It wasn't easy, even for me, who is pretty good at shovin stuff out of my mind that I don't want in there. My mom would of gone down to the tavern, she would of tried to make him fall in love with her, got her heart busted when he dumped her.

But I am not my mom. I got a heart in good workin order. My mom had the dumbest heart around. God held it up on the day he made it and said, I goofed on this one, who wants it?

We hauled up the second-biggest hill we got in Tacoma and I got out at Medford Street. It's a big street of apartments that all got nine, ten floors to em. Number 623 was concrete with white drapes in all the windows. In the lobby area was a card table with a couple guys slappin em down and a bunch of mailboxes. I banged the elevator because I'm pregnant. Took forever to creak on down. Had no idea what floor 17 was on so I banged five buttons. Turned out I was two floors too high. The stairs were orange metal. The doors were orange with black letters. I applied my knuckles real gentle. The door opened and there was Stan in a white bathrobe, his hair loose and flowin down his back.

Well, you look comfy.

Thumbelina, isn't it?

Can't forget a name like mine. Can I come in?

Well, uh . . . actually—

This won't take long.

I guess it was obvious I wasn't takin no for a answer. He backed up and said, Careful, because of all the toys spread across the livin room. Two little boys with Stan's color hair were layin on their stomachs watchin cartoons on the TV. We stepped over their skinny pajama'd backs and into the kitchen where a dark blonde, thin lady in a white bathrobe identical to Stan's (noticed the Claudia wrote on the collar in blue) was feedin a baby who was also loud and clear Stan's. The nose, man.

Honey, this is Thumbelina. Could we have some privacy? Stan said.

The lady got up without sayin a word, picked up her pack of cigarettes, and disappeared down the hall. A door closed.

She's pretty, I said.

Thank you.

Well, Stan, I am not sayin it about you.

He pulled out a chair for me at the table, which was still holdin a box of cereal and a bunch of bowls. She's a good woman.

Myrna lost her baby, I said.

He wrinkled his forehead. She what?

Bam. I hit my palms together. It fell out of her.

His face all of a sudden looked younger. Even though he looked sad.

But I was on a mission. Her kid, I said. It was born dead.

He blinked at me. I . . . uh . . . thought she was goin to go to the clinic . . .

You guys. You're all the fuckin *same*. Men. She had a *mis*carriage. She wanted it, all right.

Do you have a cigarette?

I am not givin anything to you, Stan.

He shoved back his chair, went down the hall, came

{118}

back suckin on one. He eyed me from behind the smoke. Why are you tellin me this?

I believe you ought to know what Myrna is goin through.

I—

Saved by the bell. One of the little kids came in cryin, because the other little kid changed the cartoon. Stan swung the kid up over his shoulder and went into the livin room to settle it.

Well, you can't just change the show in the middle like that, I heard him sayin quietly.

He came back without the kid, pulled out his chair again, lit the other cig he'd brought with him.

Three kids already. You're what. Thirty-four? I said coolly.

I know what you're thinkin. I should of left her alone.

Nobody but God knows what I'm thinkin, Stan.

The problem with eyes that clear and blue, Thumbelina, is they give everything away that's goin on behind them.

Personally, I'm glad she lost it, I said, glarin at him. She would of just fucked it up, raisin it all by herself.

Well. I would of helped her.

Fuck it up?

You don't like me, do you.

Now, what gives you that impression?

He looked at the floor. My intentions toward her are good. I think of her like a sister.

God help your real sister, then, if you got one.

Now. I think of her like a sister *now.* I've got my head together. I'm stayin here with my family.

He knocked his cig in the sink. We did this free show in

the park last spring. A year ago. Claudia and I were takin a breather from each other at the time. Myrna came up to me after, she'd been dancin down front, I'd been watchin her. She was wearin this little outfit. This little yellow skirt and this top. It was sexual in the beginning but then it got emotional. She really digs me. Claudia is the only other white girl who ever dug me like that.

That why you went off to the reservation and left her with her crackpot sister, who in spite of everything loves her a heckuva lot more than you do?

I heard she was seein other guys while I was gone.

I wouldn't know.

Her sister's fiancé.

I waved my hand. You don't understand Myrna, Stan. That was just her little way of showin her sister what a jerk she was in love with. That he'd sleep with both of em.

So she did sleep with him?

You know, Stan, call me swift, but I get the feelin that this fact really matters to you, I said.

He eyed me. He looked about ready to cry. So where is she now?

Hospital. Gettin her guts sucked out, I said, lickin my lips meanly.

Poor, poor Myrnie, he muttered.

I didn't hear her comin but next thing I knew Claudia was pokin her uncombed head into the kitchen. Still holdin the baby. Am I interruptin? she said.

You got that right, I said.

Honey? Her eyes traveled right over my head to Stan. We have to be at the doctor's by two.

Stan walked me out. I could see he was turnin over a lot in his head, and I figured it was just as well I was leavin.

I am not sure if it was a good thing or bad thing, but

one thing I'll tell you, that part about me sayin Myrna was doin Agnes a favor by sleepin with her fiancé was a work of art.

Now I am warmin this bench, waitin for the bus. I have been warmin it for quite a while. Talkin helps pass the time. I can see the front door of 623 just fine. Wish I could tell you she was lyin about the doctor. But the front door opened and out they came. Her blonde hair was combed and in a ponytail. She wore purple ear muffs. She wore the baby on her stomach in a sling. They disappeared behind the juniper bushes. I heard his bike rumble. He drove it up to the red light. She was wrapped around him, the baby sandwiched between em.

What Myrna don't know won't hurt her.

So long, November.

december

I WOKE UP INTO THIS GREAT MONTH SLOW. NOT BECAUSE I was dreamin or nothin but because I was tired. She was thumpin me on the arm.

What do you want, Myrna?

She was sittin there in her pink robe the hospital gave her, doin the damage. Thumby, it's about time. Must be somethin awful special in your dreams.

Leave me alone.

You shouldn't sleep with your mouth open, Thumby. Somethin could fall in. Were you dreamin about your boyfriend comin back to you?

I put my glasses on my face and sat up. What's wrong, Myrna?

Nothin's wrong.

Then why are you pokin at me?

We got to be at Sal's in a hour.

I shoved Black Bean off my stomach but I didn't get up. I lay back down. Would you mind walkin my dog for me today, Myrn? I am not feelin my best.

Get out of town.

I coughed into my fist. Give me bus fare.

Then will you get up and get ready?

OK.

Myrna went off in her red miniskirt and green sweater which had a fancy-dance *M* stitched over her tough little heart and did not leave the state of her belly button a mystery (an inny). She was gone quite a while and it was Black Bean's wet little nose that busted up my sleep this time. She smelled like dirt and fresh air.

Myrna dragged me upstairs to the bathroom and took my glasses. Shut your eyes.

What are you doin to me?

I'm makin you beautiful.

How you plannin on workin that miracle?

Every bit of makeup I got to my name. Hold still.

She loaded up the wand with bright blue eye shadow. I dropped my eyelids. Why do I got to be beautiful, Myrna? She pulled the comb gently through my hair. You have got to ditch these jeans, honey buns. You got shorts on you?

It's wintertime, in case you didn't notice.

You got great legs, Thumby. I looked up, Agnes Vander-whacker was slouched in the doorway, dressed in a black skirt, black stockings, and a tight black turtleneck. Don't she, Myrna.

Yep. She does. Great, great legs.

Flatterin me is goin to get you no place.

Agnes shifted Dwayne Junior to her other hip. He was a lot bigger than when I'd last seen him. It don't really matter if she wears jeans, Myrna. Sal's got the eye to see through anything.

Agnes and Myrna passed a look between em which I didn't understand, lackin trainin in sister stuff.

We piled into Agnes's Impala and drove up South Pacific, past the restaurants and car lots and adult bookstore, and parked in back of a white concrete building with turquoise trim and a pair of big red lips on the sign over the door.

Inside was just a big empty room full of tables with chairs stacked upside down on em and on the far side was a plywood stage a couple feet off the floor and off to the left was a bar, dark and empty. We followed the path of light down this narrow hall between the stage and the bar, past TOILETS, and around the corner to this little cramped office where Sal was scratchin away in a little blue book. Sal's short for Salvadore. He was short and wrinkled and built like a beer can. His shirt was rolled up to his elbows. It looked expensive. So did the chains hangin around his thick neck.

While Agnes introduced us, I eyed the naked girl calendars hangin above the messy desk. (I mean, these girls were nay . . . *ked*. No swimsuits hidin their private parts like on other calendars I've seen.)

Great lookin December, isn't she? Salvadore said, pushin the junk off a corner of the desk and settin down the back pockets of his pants.

I just stared at him.

Girls? Please. He pointed at the orange couch on the opposite wall. Make yourselves comfortable.

So then we were sittin in a row with our legs crossed and he went, Ahhh. Just look at you. It's enough to give me a hard-on.

You got a hose nearby? I asked him.

Agnes dug my ribs. I gagged. Thumbelina and my sister here are lookin for work, Sal. They can do anything—

We want to be dancers, said Myrna.

Speak for yourself, I muttered.

Sal's shaggy black eyebrows crashed into each other above his surprisingly small nose. You've got one who doesn't seem to know what she wants, Agnes.

I'm shy. I smiled fakely at him.

Well, shy can work. If you work it into your tease. They love a shy girl. It's more mysterious. Girls are gettin so hard these days.

He passed a pack of Marlboros over to Agnes, who slipped one out and lit it and passed it to me. I passed. Myrna shook out two and put one down her shirt.

Sal watched her do it, and grinned. His teeth were nearly as yellow as my hair and one of em was missin in the bottom row. Well, who wants to go first?

I lifted my eyebrows with a great deal of effort and eyed him. Go first for what?

You got to audition, darlin.

Thumby, you go first. I'm goin to have a beer down front with my sister, Agnes said.

Scuse me. I don't—

But she had Myrna up and out the door before I could stop her. So it was just me sittin on the couch, lookin at him.

Well? he said.

Well, I said.

Sal grinned. I don't have all day, sweet thing.

What makes you think I do?

He scratched his nose. Well, why don't we start with some calisthenics. Stand up and touch your toes, sweet thing.

I figured whatever. Must be some kind of flexibility test like we used to do in gym to see if I got what it takes to be a dancer. So I bent over. Next thing you know my sweatshirt is over my head and I am standin there without it.

The bra too, he said.

No thanks.

He took a step toward me. I guess you want me to take it off for you, darlin.

So I reached up behind my back and unhooked it. I folded my arms over my boobs to give em shelter from his starin eyes.

Aw, come on, sweet thing, Sal said, give me a look. He took my wrists in his tough old hands and boom, there I hung as plain as yogurt in front of him.

Hmm. Well, I've seen better.

I squinted down at his crotch. Me too, I said.

He dropped my wrists and stepped back. Got a mouth on you.

Inherited it from my mom.

He nodded. OK. Let's see how the rest of you stacks up.

Can't you use your imagination?

My what?

So I unzipped my jeans and let em hit the floor. I pulled my undies down from my belly button. I slipped off my black socks.

He turned and rolled open the drawer in his desk. A pair of black high heels landed in front of me. Those should fit.

They're too small.

Darlin. You can't do a tease for me in your bare feet. He spoke patiently. Like he had all day.

So I shoved my feet in the shoes. I stood there, goose bumps pricked out all over me.

Well, come on, come on. He struck a match and smoke swirled around his black head. Move, sweet thing. Shake it.

Shake what?

Your ass.

I don't want to shake my ass.

Then what are you doin here?

They made me come.

He poked his finger into his ear, worked it around. You can make good money, darlin. A girl like you, with legs like that, you can make fifty bucks an hour. Easy.

Do I got to do anything besides dance?

His eyebrows knocked into each other again. What are you implyin about my establishment, darlin? That's why we got bouncers. To protect you ladies from the customers. You get em pretty riled up.

I am not sleepin with nobody.

Hmm. I like a girl who knows her own mind. He put his cigarette in his mouth and brought it to the end of its life. He pointed his butt at my stomach. Looks to me like you already been up to somethin. Looks to me like you got somethin in there.

I sucked in my stomach.

Now, don't do that. You look like you got a stick up your ass. They don't mind a girl with a little pot, especially when the rest of her looks like you do. But I'm hirin you on probation, and if you do got somethin in that stomach, we'll have to talk about it. It's against the rules.

I held out my hand. Mind passin me my shirt?

He passed over my red sweatshirt. So? Are you?

What.

Pregannint.

You're askin me?

These men that come in here, they're workin guys, darlin. They just want to come in here and drink a cold beer and watch some pretty girls take off their clothes. They don't want some complicated social commentary paradin up and down in front of them. They just want a nice piece of ass to look at.

I pulled on my black socks.

Can you see without those glasses?

Yeah. But I like to wear em so that no guy asks me out on a date.

He chuckled. Oh, you'll be gettin plenty of attention, darlin. I'll be happy to take those glasses off your hands before you go out there for the first time. It takes some gettin used to, takin off your clothes for a pack of guys.

I lifted a high-top. You think I could dance in these?

We don't pay you for the sense of humor, darlin.

When we got home Clifford's orange pickup was double-parked next to a white Chevrolet. In the back was Dee Dee's bed and Dwayne Junior's crib and boxes of their clothes and Agnes's dresser.

Clifford was rollin up the livin room carpet when we hiked through the door. His eyes shot to Agnes's face. He knew where we'd been. He didn't say nothin. He just went back to rollin the carpet.

Agnes said she'd leave us two plates, two cups, the kettle, the sofa bed in the livin room, and the TV.

We said, Thanks, Agnes.

I needed peace and quiet. I went down and got my dog out of the cellar. Now that me and Myrna were footin rent she could live in the light of day. I went upstairs and slammed and locked the bathroom door.

I told her I was strippin for a livin and I asked her if she was goin to disown me. Her warm pink tongue swiped my nose. Then she hopped off my lap and curled up in the bathtub. I didn't take it personal. My dog just needs a lot of elbow room. I paged through the *Rollin Stoner* magazine that was sittin on the back of the toilet. I decided to shave my legs. I got my pink shaver out from the drawer and then her little knuckles came, curious, on the door.

I'm busy, Myrna.

Open up.

I'm busy.

Thumby. Come on, man.

So I leaned over and twisted the knob. She busted in, startlin Black Bean's head up.

What are you doin?

I pulled the shaver up my leg. Gettin ready for my big performance, Myrn.

For Christ's sake. Don't that hurt?

A little.

Then why don't you use some cream? She opened the cupboard under the sink and shoved a can at me. You ever heard of shavin lotion?

No.

Who taught you to shave, Thumby?

Nobody.

She shook her head. I shot a wad of shavin lotion into my hand and spread it up my stingin leg.

He liked you. Myrna settled down on the tub. You want him?

For what?

Real funny.

My heart beat faster. How do you know he liked me?

I got eyes, Thumby.

He's a creep.

He's rich.

So what.

I don't see you up to your ears in choices, Thumby. With Agnes downstairs, clearin shit out, Myrna said.

You can't blame her for wantin to move in with Clifford. He's a nice guy.

You've said all of two words to him before runnin up here to—she chuckled—shave your legs.

I'm shy around men. In case you didn't notice.

I'll say.

~ ~ ~

So I was a dancer after all.

We didn't like the bus, we took a taxi like we were rich kids. He let us off across the street in front of our competition: Girls, Girls, Girls. Then we clopped over in our high heels and coats, tryin to hide our short little dresses from the guys slouched in the doorways. We went around back of the building and said hi to Tony, who guarded the door marked EMPLOYEES. He opened it for us. We headed for the dressin room to bend over and touch our toes and fix our lipstick. That first night I convinced myself my mom had a blindfold on in heaven, but after that, when I realized that guys were likin the naked me, linin the stage with money, then I wanted her to watch me. I wanted her to be jealous of me. I wanted her to turn to the guy next to her and say, That's my daughter down there, what a dancer, man.

At first it was a little weird to take off my clothes with my friend Myrna watchin me and Agnes who isn't exactly my friend but was close enough that I was goin to buy her a Christmas present. It was also pretty weird watchin them do likewise, especially Agnes. She is in pretty good shape for nineteen. She has big, high boobs, which make up for her fat stomach. Her butt also sits high on her, not like the saggin behinds of the older ladies who are into their thirties and forties. The guys like Agnes. I learned a lot by watchin her. She really enjoys teasin guys and makin em hard in their pants. She's got it down. She goes out there in her little bitty gold bikini with tassels shakin from the titties and she has this rhythm. She holds on to the pole and moves her hips around so bad it makes you seasick to watch. Then she rolls around on the floor and arches her back and what not.

Sal gave me a whole supply of black and red lace underwear. It was not normal underwear. There were all kinds of straps and hooks and this underwired bra that shoved my little boobs into my chin, makin em look almost as big as Agnes's. Amazin. I lost my own bra the first night. Dropped it on the floor and never found it. It was a bra for a kid. If Geena could of seen me. I had bras she never dreamed of. Plus a garter belt and black lace stockings and high heels. I wore this little string up my rear.

First time out, the men down there seemed to think I looked pretty good. They whistled and clapped and cheered over the music as I took off my clothes. I had trouble with the fancy-dance bra. It wouldn't come unhooked. So I yanked it down my body the long way. To make up for bein so clumsy I gave em a treat I had seen the other ladies doin. I ran my hand down my stomach and pushed my middle finger into my hole. At first the door was closed. I pushed pretty hard. Pulled it out, pushed it in. He did it to me like that when he was kissin me down there. He was pretty good when it came to stuff like that. When I uncrossed my eyes and looked, there was money all along the stage.

After we came out alone we came out in groups of three, because one of you naked isn't enough. We'd be wearin short little silver skirts and tops which showed our belly buttons. The skirts unzipped down the sides and we had these little strings over our privates which tie at the sides. We untied em. All the girls have different-colored hair between their legs. Jessica has black because that is her skin and hair color, and Myrna has orange, and Agnes is dark brown even though her head is gold. I am yellow in both places.

They played music for us while we danced. You could tell when it was good stuff to take off your clothes to. It didn't have no harmonica.

~ ~ ~

STAN SHOWED up when December was about a week old. I knew he'd be comin. He was wearin his usual: black jeans and a motorcycle jacket. He wore a cowboy hat. His hair was out of the braids and it was beautiful, wavy and black. Myrna was layin on the couch watchin *The Price Is Alright*.

Hey, babe, he said, settin the potted violets down on the table. Myrna said, Oh, what pretty flowers. They were beautiful purple. He bent to kiss her but she turned her cheek. I thought, Come on, Myrna, forgive the guy, but course I didn't say it. She's my friend.

I just came by to make sure you're OK. Can I sit down? You sure can, I said.

Well? Are you OK?

I am not, she said.

He looked a little guilty. Well, he said. You want to come down to Rafters to watch us play tomorrow night? It's a new gig.

I'm workin, she said.

You got a job?

Money don't fall from the sky, Stanley.

He lit a cigarette. I'm sorry, babe, that you had a . . . you know. Did it hurt or anything?

What if it did? What do you care?

I care.

You would of been there if you cared.

He sighed and stood up and went over to the window. His shoulders were all hunched over in his jacket. He looked old.

Maybe I ought to go.

She changed in the blink of an eye. You aren't goin already?

He looked at her. You want me to stay?

You want a beer?

OK.

She looked at me. Thumby?

No, thanks, I said.

Thumby, will you get Stan a beer?

I only did it because she's still recoverin from a tragedy. I handed it to him. She had got herself snuggled into his lap in the two seconds I was gone in the kitchen. He let her sit there. It's his fault far as I'm concerned. Stan likes Myrna a heck of a lot more than he lets on.

Soon as I was back down Myrna's fist comes flyin out of nowhere and whacks me in the knee. I looked at her like, huh? what's your problem? She raised one of her picked-clean little eyebrows and I got the message. But where else could I go in that house? I took the quilt and went upstairs. It was lonely in Dee Dee's empty room. I fell asleep.

Her little knuckles worked on the door. Thumby?

What.

You know what time it is?

I yawned. I could see the yellow moon through the alder branches out Dee Dee's window.

You in there, Thumby?

Where in the hell else would I be?

You in a bad mood?

I'm in a perfectly good mood. Can't you tell?

We got to go to work. Thumby?

I didn't say nothin.

She opened the door and flipped on the light. I slammed my eyes closed.

She was dressed in a short green skirt and black tights and her green plastic high heels.

I sighed. Will you iron my skirt for me?

I already did. Now come on.

The girls at Lips were OK. They tried to help each other look beautiful. They borrowed each other's lipsticks. They said, You got some extra eyelashes I can use? My kid glued mine to the fridge. They gave each other fashion advice and said, Don't lose sleep over that guy, he ain't worth it, and blah blah blah. And Jessica the black lady was always tryin to shove her purple bra on me because she said it flattered my yellow hair.

But I knew it was not our pretty dresses the guys were comin to Lips to see. They were not goin to lean over into the next table and whisper, Do you suppose them underpants are silk? Beats me, but what a great shade of lavender, eh? Yeah, and those high heels on the blonde, where do you think she got em? It was not our Coquette lipstick or our turquoise eyes they were admirin. Or the stuff we hung from our ears. When I first started I'd watch the ladies get all dolled up backstage and feel lonelier than I got words for. They were so nice to me. They wanted me to be beautiful and get lots of money. But this didn't make me no happier than I'd been with the softball girls. I felt like I had dropped in from outer space. I speaka no English. But I was speakin it and so were they.

~ ~ ~

YOU ARE due on April the twenty-seventh, miss.

That's not what I asked you.

He was eyein the photographs they had snapped of my stomach. Is your mother outside?

You aren't supposed to be nosy at this clinic. That's why my mom liked to come here.

Forgive me. I am merely making conversation.

I was layin in a room of the J Street Clinic, the place my mom used to come for her birth control pills and Atarin to calm down her anxiety and once in a while to get her head stitched up when she didn't duck in time. The doctor was dark skinned and with a funny accent. A new guy. I'd never seen him before.

Dr. Miligiwamny?

Hmm?

How come I feel so crappy?

You're pregnant, miss.

You're sure the fish is OK?

Yes, yes, I said all is well. You are due in seventeen weeks.

Dr. Miligiwamny?

{135}

Yes, he said without lookin up from his chart.

You know the queer disease?

He flipped through his chart. He didn't answer me. I slipped down and reached for my black socks.

If a person had the queer disease . . . because they slept with a queer. Dr. Miligiwamny?

He lifted his eyes. Pardon?

How would they know?

Know what?

If they had the queer disease, Dr. Miligiwamny.

The queer disease, miss? He blinked. You mean—

Ohhh ohhhh say can you seeeeee, I sang loudly. By the dawn's eeeeearly lieeight.

He put down his chart and eyed me with a puzzled expression above his mustache. Is there something you would like to ask me, miss?

If a girl sleeps with a guy who has the di*zeeez,* is it automatic that she's goin to get it?

Miss. Have you had sexual relations with an infected man? His eyes were so honey brown you could scoop em out and spread em on toast.

Like for example, I said, reachin for my T-shirt, if she happened to be pregnant at the same time as bein afraid she might be sick. How would she tell what was comin from pregnancy and what was comin from the queer disease? In other words, is she just coughin all the time and feelin rotten because she's growin a life inside her, or is she actually growin this disease thing?

Dr. Miligiwamny folded his arms. Perhaps you want to be tested for—

Naw. Not if it involves a needle.

He opened a drawer and pulled out a card and pressed it into my hand. INFECTIOUS DISEASE CLINIC the card said in black letters. It is just down the hill, across from the hospital on Y Street, miss. They won't ask you any nosy questions there either. Miss. He smiled his white teeth at me. It is better to be safe than sorry, no?

I headed down the hill from the J Street Clinic. Rain sprinkled in a irritatin way from the sky that was the color of the sidewalk. I couldn't see the water out there for fog. In my pocket I had a Christmas card for Delores Vitrielli. The old lady who lived downstairs of us, if you remember, who picked out the clothes my mom is buried in.

I wanted to get her this card with Jesus in the manger on the front and his mom and dad standin over him lookin proud. Because Delores is a Bible thumper and would appreciate it. I was all the way up to the front of the line at the cash register when it occurred to me that I was bein a little bit of a hypocrite because of what I'd been doin onstage the last couple weeks. So I said sorry to the lady and went and put it back and got one with Santa Claus on a reindeer with his fat little legs stickin out and MERRY CHRISTMAS spelled out in candy canes over his head. Had to wait in line all over again but that's life.

When I passed the ballet building I saw the girls up in the windows and I stopped. Could of sworn the one over on the end was Cynthia Kazlowski, with her long-ass blonde hair up in a bun and her arms wavin over her head like grass in the wind. I used to lay under my bed and draw ballerinas. I don't care about all that anymore, but I gave it another run for my money last summer.

You're too tall, Thumby, my mom replied. Not to mention clumsy. What's the point? Where can it take you?

I don't want it to take me nowhere, Mom. I just want to take lessons.

You won't fit in. You want it to be like softball?

What are you sayin, Mom?

Those girls were mean to you.

It was a accident, Mom.

A accident, my foot.

One tooth, Mom. It could of happened to anybody.

But it happened to you.

It was a accident, Mom.

Accidents always happen to the weak one, Thumby.

I'm not weak, Mom.

You're not rich, dear. Ballerinas are rich little girls. You'll just feel left out.

I want to learn to dance, Mom. That's all I care about.

They don't want tall girls for dancers, Thumbelina. Their partners aren't weight lifters.

And we'd start all over again. She wouldn't ever just say it. Sorry, Thumby, I don't have the money. She just took me on the runaround instead.

I'd come down on Saturdays and sit on the curb by 7-Eleven and watch em come in and out. The first class was at nine o'clock. Them were the real little girls, steppin out of the car doors with their short little legs pokin out from the bottom of their coats and wearin cloppy shoes and their hair in buns on the back of their heads. I love hair in buns. It's so romantic and graceful lookin. I used to put mine up in one and practice my dance steps to my Johnny Cash tapes but my mom used to say, Your neck is too long as it is, no sense in emphasizin the fact, Thumby, and she'd sit me down and pull out the bobby pins. I respected my mom's opinion. She knew what looked good on you.

Them little girls were boring because they were too short to see in the windows. After a while they'd come cloppin down the stairs with their shoes untied and get

{138}

in cars that were waitin in a line by the curb and doors would slam. Then a whole new bunch of cars would come with more girls that were a little older and wearin different-colored leotards. They'd go runnin up the stairs light and quick with their coats open over their pink tights. You'd see em a couple seconds later upstairs at the window, warmin up, arms all graceful and wavin. Then they'd disappear because they were dancin on the floor. Then after a long time they'd come back to the bars to warm down and you'd see em, still lookin fresh and clean but not movin so quick. When they'd come down the stairs they'd go slow, walkin with their heads down. Once I sat on the curb all day drinkin a Coke and watchin till the teacher with the nose like a tomato but with beautiful legs came out in a yellow skirt and got in her car and drove away.

After I was done rememberin all that stuff (how long can you stare at a building?), I walked around to the other side of the park. ViewCrest Apartments looked about the same as ever, the place where I spent the second seven years of my life. Same old muddy stucco two-story with the same curtains in the window, includin Delores's yellow butterflies on the bottom left, behind the Dumpster. I went around to the back and saw that our curtains had changed. I thought of our yellow kitchen and the table by the window and the coffee rings on it from all the times me and her'd forget coasters, which pissed Lester off who was a fanatic for order. The avocado fridge with the little magnet that said DAD'S MOOD IS ... and you could turn it so it said GOOD or BAD. It irritated me, her buyin that. Always tryin to shove him on me as my dad, not takin no for an answer.

I went over to the mailboxes. The A. SKYLER was gone (the lease was in her name) and it said FREEMAN. I knew in my heart that he'd moved out, but still.

I opened the big door that leads into the lower hallway. It was quiet inside and smelled like pine needles. It's the air freshener that Delores kindly donates for the whole building. Soon as I smelled it all these memories came rushin at me, throwin their little arms around my neck like little kids when their mom comes home. I had to pull em off and say leave me alone man.

It was weird goin down to the end of the hall to her blue door that I'd knocked on a hundred times before: Can I borrow a cup of sugar, Delores? My mom needs some coffee, Delores. You got any smokes, Delores? At first I wasn't goin to knock. Who knows what she'd do. Chain me down with them great macaroons of hers and call the cops. She had to know I ran off from Mrs. Leffer's. She'd want to know what I was up to. Strippin, Delores. She'd grab her heart and keel over.

But my knuckles hit the door of their own free will and I heard the chain scrape back and there was her long powdered nose holdin the gold glasses, starin at me. Thumbelina? Good heavens. The chain dropped. Come in!

It was good to feel her arms around me again, to feel her saggy shoulders against my chest. She took my arm and tugged me through the livin room where I'd slept that night on the floor and into the kitchen which smelled like bakin bread.

I can't stay long, Delores, I said right off the bat, because there was all this hope shinin in her old eyes.

How are you, dearie?

I'm pregnant, Delores, I said, because I am not the kind of girl to beat around the bush.

Oh! And her old wrinkled hands that as far as I know never did hold a wedding ring went up to her cheeks.

I unbuttoned my mom's brown corduroy coat and lifted up my sweatshirt.

She pushed her glasses up her nose and bent close. Then she pulled back. She didn't say nothin, just got busy gettin strawberry jam out of the cupboard and cuttin off a piece of hot bread sittin on the wire rack. She plunked down a glass of milk.

If Delores would of been my mother how would I of turned out?

That thought zipped through my brain and flew south for the winter.

Aren't you goin to say congratulations or nothin, Delores? I said, chewin bread.

Congratulations, dear.

And aren't you goin to ask me who the dad is?

She fixed her old blue eyes on me. Do you want to tell me about it?

Nothin to tell. Thanks for the congratulations. How's your arthritis treatin you these days?

Oh, Thumbelina, what's happened to you? Why did you leave that woman's house?

Aw. Mrs. Leffer's cool, but she's got a lot of rules.

You're only fourteen! Where are you stayin?

With my friend Myrna.

Who?

She's fourteen too.

Oh, Lord.

I concentrated on eatin while all this sank into her brain under that cottonball.

You know he no longer lives here, I suppose?

Guessed as much, Delores. I reached for another slice of her sunflower and pumpkin bread.

He stopped by last month. He was gettin some things out of storage and came by for a cup of tea. He looks . . . thin, dear.

You don't say?

Is he ill?

Well, Delores, I don't like to gossip about people, and I think you should ask him that question, not me.

I didn't have the heart. I think he misses your mother terribly.

Like the rest of us.

She lifted her teacup. Her eyes disappeared for a second. You're angry at him. You blame him for your mother's—

What gives you that impression, Delores? I ripped off another chunk of bread.

I know their relationship was troubled, dear, but try to understand.

Delores! I rolled my eyes at her.

Well, I think you should go to him, let him know you forgive him. It will lift your heart. You need your heart to be light for what you've got comin. She eyed my stomach in a meaningful way and pushed back her chair. He left the address for you, he thought you'd drop by sooner or later. I've got it written down here. She fumbled around in a drawer. Oh, where is it. It's on one of those streets over by the bridge.

Jack Street, Delores.

You know?

I know he's livin with Marcus.

Who's Marcus?

You don't want to know, Delores.

• • •

It was gettin dark as I ducked under the wet tree branches and slid down the hill into Bean Park. I passed the glass conservatory with all the plants from around the world and the little book where you sign your name sayin, I was here, and the basketball court where a ball slapped between the hands of a couple guys and the whirligig and the locked-up brick building of toilets and showers and the empty wadin pool and the swings and then, right before you come out on the other side, the duck pond.

Nothin like the algae smell of a duck pond to kill you with memories.

We used to come over here all the time in the summer to feed them ducks. Used to stand on this bridge and throw the bread down to em. This is goin back a few years. She had more bones in her face back then. Cheekbones that were sharp and strong. She'd wear her pink bikini and I'd wear shorts and we'd wear thongs we got at Kmart so our red toenails would show. Her legs were always brown from layin in the sun but mine wouldn't ever get off white because of bein under my bed too much. People looked at her a lot. She didn't seem to notice. We'd toss the bread at the ducks and I'd say, Mom, that guy's lookin at you, and she'd say, Which one? Thinkin I meant the ducks.

Every day we brought over a bag of bread that we got for fifteen cents at the grocery store on Beeson Avenue because it was old. (The bread not the store.) My mom figured if she could keep them ducks fed all summer she could convince em to stick around during the winter too. She used to get so mad when they'd fly off. It wasn't just Lester that she thought she could change.

After stuffin the ducks we'd go over to the wadin pool

to dip our feet. She'd put on her horn-rimmed glasses and open her romance book and say, Don't be hangin on me, Thumby, can't you go make some friends?

I don't need no friends, Mom, I got you.

Well, don't be hangin on me, do you mind?

There isn't no law against sittin beside you, is there.

She'd put up with me for a while, then she'd give me money to go get us dinner at 7-Eleven.

I'd walk slow because I knew she wanted time alone. Time to sit there in the sun and pretend she was single, maybe. No Lester, no me.

I'd get us potato salad and burritos. We'd eat in the kitchen on our orange plastic plates we got free from the gas station for fillin up on regular. When Lester got home she'd have a couple beers with him while he ate and I'd go out and watch the guys throwin the baseball in the street. Sometimes they'd keep on drinkin all night. That was all right because in ViewCrest I had my own room. My own walls where I could put up my posters of harmonicas in metal stands that rested on famous guys' shoulders.

It was almost dark and I was cold. The yellow moon had appeared loyally in its corner of the sky. I tightened up the piece of rope in my jeans because I hate havin cold air down my back. My waist isn't supposed to be shrinkin. My high-tops slipped as I hiked up the slobbery wet hill to Washington Avenue. Division comes down Alphabet Hill and splits at the bottom and becomes Jefferson on the ViewCrest side of the park and Washington on the side with the ballet building. When my high-tops smacked Washington I turned to look back. The duck pond looked shiny in the park lights. The bridge where we dropped bread looked delicate and lonely. I was lookin down the hill that my mom blasted down last August in Donny's

Corvette. He wasn't my friend. She was datin him to make Lester jealous. He wasn't in the car with her. You kiddin? You should of seen his face at the funeral. He loved that car. But my mom didn't care about Lester's van and she didn't care about Donny's Corvette. She smashed that car into lily pads and shoved the crickets' song down their throats. She woke the frogs and ducks that had tucked away for the night. A clump of yellow hair delicately broke the black water. The trees along the bank sighed—I got to believe this—and lowered their branches over her.

~ ~ ~

BY CHRISTMAS EVE my fish was really showin her face. I stood on the tub so I could see in the mirror. Myrna came in and caught me.

You're gettin big, all right. She tapped my bare belly. But the rest of you is so skinny.

I grabbed on my jeans. I'm all right.

What'd the doctor say about that cough?

He was very happy about it and he said congratulations.

Fuck you.

I reached for my socks. Fuck you.

She sat down on the tub and crossed her little bare legs, which were available for viewin pleasure because of her yellow stretch skirt.

Stan called.

Yeah?

I don't want to talk about it.

Don't even try gettin my hopes up by sayin that.

He's goin back to the reservation.

Excellent. I pulled on my shoes.

He says his uncle can put him to work in his junkyard. He's leavin Claudia and the kids. He said I can come with him.

I tied my shoes and waited.

She didn't say nothin. She was goin to make me ask. Damn her.

Are you? Goin with him?

I got to take care of you.

I'm doin all right. (I didn't put my heart into it.)

I am not sure I want to head off with a guy who leaves his kids behind. What kind of a father is that?

Maybe he'll send em money.

And you make loads of it, Thumby, pullin hubcaps off cars. She sighed, spreadin her little hands out on her fat little thighs. I don't know what to do. Why'd I have to lose that baby?

Myrna?

She looked at me.

I'm not goin to work.

You got to go to work.

No. I'm not. Me and my little fish are tired of bein paraded up and down the stage in front of men.

Your little fish. Myrna smirked, but I could see hurt brimmin in them green eyes. You speak about it like you know it personally. Don't get your hopes up, I'm tellin you, Thumby, it might be missin . . . it might not turn out like you want it.

Fuck off, Myrna, I said, which was mean, but she left me no choice. That's my final answer.

How're you goin to swing rent?

You are goin to loan me the money.

Right then Agnes came knockin on the door with

Dwayne Junior in her arms and Dee Dee by the hand, beggin us to babysit.

No can do, Agnes.

Come on, Myrna, please? I got to have a hour of peace and quiet to sort somethin out with Clifford.

Oh, cheatin on him already? And let me guess, he found out.

Agnes turned her eyes my way. I am a sucker for such facial expressions. Come on, Myrna, I said.

No, you come on, Thumby, and she hucked my coat at me. We went Christmas shoppin. I had to give Myrna some of my money to buy me a present. It better be a good one, Myrna.

It's not my fault I fell in love with a guy who has three kids who need Christmas presents and I got a soft heart, Myrna said.

We split up and met at the marble fountain two hours later. I got Myrna a gold watch. It was a combination birthday present because she was goin to hit fifteen on December 26. It's one of our most sophisticated watches, the lady said. Great, I said. It is apparently real tacky to give the price of somethin but I'll tell you it's a good thing I only had one other person to buy for. And it wasn't Agnes. I got her a package of hamburger.

I didn't forget my mom. They had a flower shop in the mall but they only sold dried flowers. It seemed kind of a bad idea to put dead flowers on somebody's grave. I went to the candy counter and I got her five pounds of chocolate instead.

I woke up early the next mornin and went to give my mom her present. The gates of the graveyard were locked. Nobody was around but me and Black Bean. That was OK.

I said, Wait here for me, and I climbed over the fence. It was just iron railings painted black, there was plenty of footholds.

Black Bean poked her face through lookin lonely so I reached through and said, Come on, man. But she wouldn't jump through. I had to grab her by the front legs and haul her through the bars myself. She got stuck. Couldn't believe it. That's a good sign. Means she's puttin on weight. She didn't like gettin tugged. She didn't like the graveyard either. She kept trippin me up so bad I got the message and picked her up.

The orange tulips were gone off my mom's grave and so was Myrna's tape player. I leaned the box of chocolates against her stone. Merry Christmas, Mom. I kissed her. The cold gravestone kept the outside of my lips. I wiped the blood off with the back of my hand. Then I sat down on it because I needed to think. I looked at the rows and rows of stones spread out in every direction like rows of little children. It didn't bug me no more about em bein crooked and whatnot. Lookin at em just made me feel lonely. Why do we got to die. Huh? Why do we got to die. I lowered my head and watered her dirt. Black Bean's nose snuffled into my bare ankle where my jeans end. Sayin, Come on, Thumby, we got to leave, because for now you and me are still livin girls.

When I got home Myrna was still in the sack. Somethin about the way her bright orange curls lay on the white pillow made me run over and yank off the covers. Merry Christmas, Myrna, I hollered to make that feelin go away.

She said somethin I better not repeat and rolled over.

I went into the kitchen with Black Bean and got busy makin us breakfast. I got out flour and eggs and bakin soda. The pancakes bubbled and hissed on the fry pan that looked like it came with the house (missin bits of its finish). If I closed my eyes I could of been back at ViewCrest with my mom on a Sunday mornin, but I didn't close my eyes. Myrna opened her watch and she said, Oh, man, Thumby, and water fell onto the sleeve of her robe. She gave me a little box and when I pulled off the lid two silver guitars were layin on the white cotton. Hooks in the ends. Oh, wow, Myrn, I said, now I'll get my ears pierced.

Stan came by late with a song for her which he performed in the livin room. He is short of cash so he had to show his feelins for her in that way. Notice I say feelins. I am not sure it's love. I am not sure a guy with three kids and his stomach over the top of his jeans can really love a girl who hasn't even started ninth grade.

We went to Blockbuster and got some movies. She picked out some horror thing with the lady's mouth open and her eyes bugged out on the front. I said, Not on Christmas Day, you don't, and put it back, and I got *Arsenic and Old Lace,* which is a Cary Grant me and my mom were always meanin to see together, but never did because we always picked the romantic ones, in the end.

~ ~ ~

IT IS NOT that I forgot what Dr. Miligiblah blah blah said. I just take a while sometimes. All the rain that was fallin down from the sky landed in my high-tops as I walked up Y Street and up the front steps of the little white house that said INFECTIOUS DISEASE CLINIC over the door. Christmas lights blinked in that window. People sat in plastic chairs havin smokes on that big porch. I tracked mud across the blue carpet and went up to the faded-lookin lady behind the desk. I got to talk to a doctor, I said, and showed the slip of paper from Dr. Miligiwamny.

You aren't the only one, honey, the lady said, noddin at the chairs along the window filled with wet people with their heads down from tiredness. Sign in—she passed me a clipboard—and take a seat.

I took up three lines with my great big name, and I went over and sat on the floor because there were no empty seats and leaned my head into the window and closed my eyes so I wouldn't have to look at the posters on the walls sayin HYPERTENSION, THE SILENT KILLER. I drifted off on a fat white cloud. Then some lady in a white coat woke me up and said she was Sandra somethin or other, a medical student, and she took me into a room and wrapped the blood pressure thing on my arm and stuck the thermometer under my tongue and asked me what they could do for me. I told her they could do plenty for me. Dr. Miligiwamny gave me the impression I needed a certain test. I don't want some test. I just want you to give me some pills. I am not feelin too great these days.

How are you feeling?

I hacked into my fist. Tired.

What else?

Grouchy.

Has your lifestyle changed recently? Any major upheavals?

Naw. Naw.

You're pregnant. That's a major change.

I got a pillow in my pants.

Her face bunched up a little like a dirty sock. Who are you living with?

You aren't supposed to be nosy at this clinic. Dr. Miligiwamny said so.

The doctor will want to know.

Then let him ask.

She sighed. She said I had to go back out to the waitin room and wait. I said, Jeezlouise. How many doctors do you got workin?

Two.

Jeezlouise.

Finally this lady in a baby blue outfit came out and took me into another little room with a table and a paper gown folded on it, and she told me to take off all my clothes includin my undies and put that gown on, and so I did and then I sat there goin hum de dum at the ceiling for about fifteen years. Then the door opened and the doctor came in, the top of his out-of-control gray hair scrapin the doorway, and he shut it and I nearly said howdy to the floor from surprise.

It was Dr. Kazlowski.

He looked thinner but he was dressed in the same old hikin boots and baggy pants and a yellow and purple tie-dye T-shirt, and all of his cement-colored hair was still bein held down by a red bandanna. He had his white coat in a ball in his fist and he shot it into the sink. Two, he chuckled, bangin his clipboard down on the counter. He rolled his stool over to my feet and sat down. And what, sweetheart, can I do for you today?

I blinked at him. Thinkin, don't he recognize me? and, please, God, don't let him recognize me, all at the same time. He grinned, and I saw that his teeth were just as crooked as I remembered em, like the stones in my mom's graveyard. Next thing I know he's shinin a light in my ear and in my eyes and then he's unwrappin a Popsicle stick and sayin, May I? and pokin it into my mouth and scrapin at my tongue.

Hmm.

Meanin what? I said, because I was gettin worried.

He straightened up and pressed his thumb into the

bridge of his glasses and pushed them against his face. I remembered that habit too.

Have you noticed anything unusual about your mouth, sweetheart?

People say it's big.

His thin lips went sideways in a smile. He scraped the stick off in this little plastic cup and put the lid on it. Then he put his heart thing on my heart.

It's workin.

It certainly is, he said quietly. He slung his heart thing over his neck and crossed his arms full of strawberry red hair over the bull's-eye on his T-shirt. Tell me about yourself.

I raised my eyebrows at him. What do you want to know?

Let's start with your boyfriends.

My what?

A pretty girl like you probably has a lot of boyfriends.

Excuse me, Doctor. But you can probably tell by lookin at me that I never was in love.

Never? Well, then, you've had sex with someone you weren't in love with. You didn't grow what you've got in your stomach all by your lonesome.

The mother of Jesus sure did.

He gave me a one-second view of his graveyard teeth. Well, you aren't the mother of Jesus.

Now you tell me.

We shared a smile. Then he got right back to business. Have you had a lot of boyfriends?

I put my thumb and my first finger together to make the zero sign.

Let me rephrase that. Sexual partners, he sighed.

I eyed him. Are you tryin to insult me?

He stroked his chin. Well, if you want to play hardball,

we can do that, sweetheart. I have scraped something peculiar off your tongue.

What?

I don't know for sure yet.

What do you mean you don't know?

He shrugged. I'm only a doctor, sweetheart. Not God. He smiled. At least, not today.

You never were much of a softball coach either.

His eyebrows ambled into his bandanna. (Nothin about Dr. K. moves fast.) What's that?

Don't you recognize me, Coach K.?

He just looked at me with his eyebrows still in his bandanna.

I shrugged. I wasn't a star or nothin. I think I was a pain in your butt. Nearly drownin on the bottom of your pool . . .

The lightbulb blinked on in his big, crowded head. At my daughter's birthday party?

During the relays. I was on your team.

And your name—

Is Thumbelina.

Thumbelina, he sighed.

That's me.

Well, I'll be damned. He squeezed my knee. How've you been?

Not too well, obviously, or I wouldn't be sittin here now, would I?

With an abnormality on your tongue, he nodded, which I suspect is candida, commonly known as thrush. Often found in the mouths of people infected with—

Hack! I went loudly into my hands.

He blinked.

Hack, hack, hack! I coughed, pourin it on.

I hopped off the table and picked up my lonely black socks off my jeans.

He grabbed my arm in his big hand. Would you be so kind as to get back up here on the table?

No, I'm all out of kindness for today.

That was a mistake. Next thing you know I'm sittin on the end of the table, still holdin my socks. He wasn't even breathin heavy.

That's quite a cough you have.

I'm all right.

I am afraid I cannot agree.

Fine. We didn't agree about a lot of things, you and me. Like how come you benched me? How come you didn't let me stay on third base?

Thumbelina. Please—

All season I sat on that bench.

Half the season.

Till Cynthia's barbecue.

Then you disappeared.

Well, obviously. I wasn't needed.

Our eyes met. He looked down first. And now you may have the AIDS virus. That's why Dr. Miligiwamny has sent you to me, isn't it? And you are pregnant. His eyes were calm. How did it happen?

Oh, man, Dr. K., I sighed, it's bad luck to say that word out loud. Why'd you have to say it out loud?

I'm going to have to test you.

With a needle?

He eyed my arms, bare in the gown. Yes, with a needle.

I hate em.

You must have had a sore throat lately?

I haven't really noticed.

He pulled his hands out of his pockets and bent down

{154}

and opened a cupboard. He tore the plastic off a cup and handed it to me. Cough into that for me, please.

I don't feel like coughin now.

Well, my dear, at some point in our lives we all have to do things we don't feel like doing.

I went hack! into the cup.

Harder.

I scowled at him.

I went *hack!* Hackety hack *hack!* into the cup. Then I couldn't stop hackin for about five minutes. He wrote in the chart and pretended he didn't notice but I could feel him watchin me from underneath his eyelashes.

Somebody's knuckles hit the door. Yes? he called. The nurse in the baby blue outfit said, Doctor? I've gowned two more, they're waiting for you.

In a minute, Carmen.

His watch hung off his wrist and clacked against the chart as he wrote. I assume that Dr. Miligiwamny at the J Street Clinic is your obstetrician?

Somethin wrong with him? I slid off the table.

Other than the fact that he beats me at squash, nothing. He's a resident at TC. A guy that sleep deprived shouldn't be such a holy terror on the squash court. And I'm it for your ID doc?

I don't really need you for nothin.

Au contraire, sweetheart. He was smilin but there was nothin warm about his voice. Would you mind getting back up on that table?

Yes, I highly would.

Now, Thumbelina. Up on that table, *now.*

After he got done emptyin me of blood he picked his coat out of the sink and shoved in his arms. He said he was at the clinic on Monday, Wednesday, and Friday afternoons, and that Monday at three would be our special time. He said to make an appointment with the lady at the front desk for Monday at three.

I thought this was a first-come, first-served kind of operation, Dr. K.

I make exceptions for attractive young ladies, he replied.

Our eyes met for a couple thumps of my heart then went their own separate ways. The door moaned shut and I got down and picked up my clothes. Since I felt pretty sure I wasn't goin to be comin back because Dr. K.'s personality has gone to hell since last April, I fished out the Popsicle stick from the wastebasket. I wrapped it in a paper towel. I took his plastic gloves which he'd also chucked in there. I looked around for other stuff of his. He travels pretty light. He'd left nothin. Not even a lousy gray hair.

Might as well finish tellin the story. I got three teeth knocked out. I told her it was only one. I got em knocked out because I was good at softball. That was a mistake. When you got my kind of reputation at school you shouldn't lift your head and be good at nothin. It makes people mad. I didn't start out benchwarmin. Heck, no. I started out as catcher. Because I have always been good at catchin things. But lookin at some of those girls in action, I figured early on that my skills at duckin would also come in handy. Because they were wild with their bats, throwin em every which way when they were through with em.

As I mentioned, Geena Delaney had it in for me. Because she did not like Cynthia bein my so-called friend. But she waited about three practices. I was catchin and she was pitchin. The reason she got the place of honor was because she was Cynthia's best friend, when the season started, anyway, although in my opinion I think that changed. Cynthia could of been pitcher, since she was the coach's kid, but she preferred manning first base. Geena was real smart. She waited till Dr. K. had wandered out into the outfield to look at the hole in the fence. Then she started throwin wild. Susan was supposed to be battin but she was stayin politely out of the way. Standin there holdin her bat under her arm and filin her nails with the file from her purse that was leanin up against the cage. Surprised she didn't carry it with her when she ran the bases.

The outfield was supposed to be goin, Hey, batter batter, at Susan, tryin to imitate real field conditions so we'd be ready when we faced our opponents. Today they were hecklin. Not the batter, the catcher. Because Geena had it in for me. Because I was startin and because Cynthia liked me. And if you were unpopular you shouldn't be occupyin a startin position and neither should a girl like Cynthia K. who is pretty and rich be likin you. Them were laws of the universe. So they were yellin names at me, nothin original, goin 2, 4, 6, 8, Thumbelina is a ape, stuff like that. You can only take it so long. I stood up and ripped off my mask and said, Hey. Would you all mind shuttin up?

Touchy, touchy, Susan said, filin her nails.

Then it was Geena's turn to bat. She came in from the mound and took the bat from Susan who was the relief pitcher. Susan hucked right over the plate. One, two, I hollered. I lifted my catcher's mask. Strike thr—*Wham!* went Geena's bat. Right in the kisser. They must of had it worked out between em. I landed in the dirt and all of a sudden I was chewin on some Chiclets. Geena said, Thumbelina, are you all right? in the sweetest voice. Batter up! Susan shouted. Cynthia ran in from first base. You OK? she hollered. Somebody get my dad! Someone got Coach

K. from the stupid hole in the fence. He came runnin up. You all right? he said, and *kerackkkk* went his knees as he bent down. Of course I wasn't all right. My mouth was bleedin. I am not a fan of blood. Especially if it's mine.

He scooped me up, which is amazin because I weigh a ton, and took me over to his car. At the emergency room they gave me stuff to kill the pain. That got me in a better mood. Then he drove me home. I stopped him on the corner and got out.

Don't you want me to come up and explain to your mom? he said.

Naw, I said. I took all the gauze out of my mouth and stuffed it in my pocket.

The next day he showed up after math class to take me to his dentist. Unless you have one of your own that you'd prefer? he said. You can have him send me the bill. Naw, yours'll do, I said, thinkin, how long was it since I've been to the dentist? The guy made me three fake teeth. Plus he filled up seven cavities. I guess I got a pretty good deal out of it.

So after all that I didn't feel too good about catchin no more and we hadn't even played a single game. Which position do you want to play? Coach K. said. Take your pick.

I would like to be pitcher.

Except for that, Thumbelina.

Why can't I be the pitcher?

Geena's the pitcher.

So I didn't know what to choose. What do you want me to play, Coach K.?

We could use your strong arm at third.

OK, I said.

I was a changed kid. All of a sudden I was out to win. For him, why else. It's like that when you're in love. But I'm tellin you it was frustratin as hell workin with what I had. Them girls were pathetic. They'd drop the balls or, worse, watch em pass right through their legs. I'd be yellin at em to shape up. Dr. K. would say, Calm down, Thumbelina, it's only a game. Only a game? Like hell! It was his reputation on the line! Didn't he care nothin about bein a loser?

One game I had to leave third base in the middle of the second inning to personally yell in Geena's face because she walked four in a row. I caught Cynthia starin at me queerly with her pale blue eyes from way over on first base. I thought, You don't know the story, Cynthia. Nobody was teasin me no more, you'll notice. Nobody was callin me names. I was hittin them balls out of the park and helpin us win. Then one game it was the bottom of the seventh, we were tied, bases loaded, and Geena hit a girl in the shoulder, givin em the game on a silver platter. I walked up to her and—to hell with my mom's rule—socked her with my glove.

There. How's it feel?

She went down without a sound, holdin her face. It was satisfyin.

Dr. K. was waitin for me when I got back to third base. Why don't you sit down and rest for a little while? he said. Jeanie? He turned and called to a bitty little sixth grader with brown hair flowin like a river down both sides of her bitty white face.

I'm not tired, Dr. K., and number two, we're in the middle of a inning.

We don't want you to wear yourself out.

Don't worry, Coach, I got lots of energy.

Sit on the bench, Thumbelina. He didn't seem so friendly no more.

Dr. K., do I have to?

{159}

Sit, Thumbelina!

So I sat. I'm tellin you I felt lower than the bottoms of my shoes. I sat there on my rear for six games of the season because I am a glutton for punishment, then I went to Cynthia's birthday party and then I figured I would take the month of May off and when June came I figured why quit now I'm on a roll.

If I have a regret, and I got a ton of em, I should of spent the extra time on my mom. I didn't have nothin to do all day, I should of been appreciatin her. How come I didn't appreciate my mom? I should of been goin to see her at work to say hi, talkin to her while she was streakin ladies' hair. Goin out and gettin her a Diet Coke and a Hershey's bar. Sittin on them red plastic chairs and readin her interestin articles out of magazines. Instead of layin under my bed just gettin older.

I should of gone to watch more of the old movies with her at that theater. They show em every Monday and Tuesday afternoon. Course, it wasn't my fault we only got there once a month. We were on the Lester Plan. Because she was afraid. She'd have to come rushin home about a hour before they were startin because Lester wouldn't be home yet and say, Come on, Thumby, and pull me out from under the bed. I'd say, Mom, are you sure it's worth it? She'd say, You aren't goin to make me go myself, are you?

We'd sit in the dark theater and eat M&M's and popcorn and watch Cary Grant who was my mom's favorite. She cried at everything and I'd get up and trip over the seats to go get her toilet paper. She'd say, Man, that Cary is one classy guy. I'd say, How do you know, Mom? You never met him. My mom was a romantic. *An Affair to Remember* was her favorite of all time because of the crippled red-haired lady who made Cary cry. And plus *North by North-*

west because it was so suspenseful comin down them pres-
idents' faces at the end, and pretty darn romantic. She liked
Gary Pecker too.

We'd get home late because we'd be goin by her watch
which was slow because it was in her head. Lester would
already be home. We'd go round the back and check for
the lights. She'd say, Oh, no! pretendin to be surprised.
She'd say, I'll let you off here and I better go to McDonald's and get us some dinner. I'd say, Mom, we got stuff for
dinner in the fridge.

I'm in the mood for a burger, hon. And you know how
he loves burgers.

He's pretty much a vegetarian these days, Mom.

Oh, Thumby, don't be like that.

(You couldn't argue with her.) OK, Mom.

He'd be sittin in the livin room with the sports page on
his knee and a beer. Where've you been? he'd say.

Out.

Where's your mother?

Isn't she here?

You know damn well she isn't.

Must be at work then.

She's not at work.

Now don't be thinkin I fell for that. Because I knew
Betty and Chee Chee better than that. They were always
coverin for my mom. Lester'd call up all the time sayin, Let
me talk to her, and they had ways of puttin him off. Sorry,
Lester, she's permin hair.

So all I'd say was, She must be on her way home, Lester.

My ass, Lester'd say.

Whatever, I'd say. I'd go down to my room and he'd
come after me and stand there in the doorway. Is it another
man? His voice would be unexpectedly quiet.

I'd lift my eyes off my comic. A movie, Lester. A simple stupid black-and-white Cary Grant, who you can't stand anyway because they never do nothin but kiss at the very end.

His butt would touch my leg, the springs would squeak. So why'd you lie?

To keep in shape.

His big hand would gently stroke my ankle. You never do anything with me.

Sometimes the front door would open then, sometimes it wouldn't.

Honey? she'd call sweetly, and slam the door.

He'd get up, tighten the belt on his bathrobe, his eyes still on me. Down here, he'd say. In Thumbelina's room.

Sometimes she'd get away with it. She would pull out a TV dinner and get his stomach full and he'd let it go. Sometimes he'd be too drunk. If she was drunk too then she would fight back. One time he hit her in the head with a can of peaches. Because she didn't have no sports trainin to teach her how to duck. They didn't have PE in her generation. Mostly he was pretty careful not to hurt her face, except one time he broke a beer bottle over her head and she had to go to the emergency room for stitches because the J Street Clinic had closed. I drove while she held the towel on her head. Tears were floodin down her cheeks. I thought now was the time to put in the plug.

You want to stay at Betty's tonight?

Don't start with me, Thumby.

Oh, for crap's sake, Mom.

I'm warnin you, Thumby. I'm gettin just as sick of you as I am of him. You're a real pair.

They shaved off around the gash so they could see to

sew it up and all my mom's cryin was nothin compared to how she cried then, seein two-foot-long strands of hair drop onto the floor. I held her hand. I said, Mom, don't cry. It'll grow back. I almost passed out watchin em dig the needle into her head.

The nurse sat down with her afterwards. Angelica, she said, we have places you can go, places where you'll be safe.

My mom leveled that nurse with her blue wide innocent eyes. Safe from what?

The nurse just looked at her. I looked at my shoes. I sure have spent a lot of time lookin at em.

Where'd you go, December? I got to say bye already?

january

I SAT IN THE DARK DRINKIN COLD RED WINE FROM THE bottle and smokin Myrna's menthols and knockin my hand against the strings of my guitar. Thumby, keep it down in there, Myrna hollered from the livin room where she was watchin Oprah. I sang louder. *I shot a man in Renoooo just to watch him die.*

Thumby!

I winked at Black Bean who did not wink back from the back-door mat.

Myrna stood in the doorway. Thumby, why in friggin

hell are you gettin drunk? We got to go to work soon. It's car wash night tonight.

Guess I'll have to call in sick.

You'll get fired.

Oh, well.

How are we goin to pay rent?

We got a place we can go and live for free.

She narrowed her green beautiful eyes. What in the hell are you talkin about?

I want to go back there and live where livin was easy, I sang.

Thumby, Jesuschrist, what's with you. She dragged out a chair and grabbed the bottle from me. She swallowed some.

I would be careful about doin things like that in the future, Myrn.

She set it down on the table and eyed me. Can't share your wine?

I got somethin in me that I could pass to you that could kill you.

Yeah, your bad breath. Don't take it personal but it's gettin bad.

She wore a new white bathrobe and white bunny slippers and her hair was wet from the shower. Her freckles stood out like pimples.

The queer disease, Myrna. The disease that queers get from other queers and pass on to girls when they are tryin to pretend that they are not queer.

God she has pretty hands, I thought, watchin her light a cigarette. She got up and ran the tap over them hands and wiped em off on the old towel that came with the house and came over and sat down heavily in the chair. She smoked it all the way down and still did not say a word and I didn't either because me and silence have always understood each other well.

For fuck's sake, Thumby. She covered her eyes. You got a way of droppin bombs on me.

All this tenderness for her gathered in my eyes and spilled down my cheeks. She tugged my sweatshirt sleeve. Her Rose Body Bath filled my nose. Don't cry, Thumbelina, she ordered in a whisper. If I can hold it off, you can.

It took me a while to stop. I'd been savin up.

Am I right in assumin I know who the father of your kid is?

(I didn't say nothin.)

You want to talk about it?

(I didn't say nothin.)

It would probably help to talk about it.

I sopped up my eyes. The doctor did a test on me. Took my blood I happen to need. What I got is, I got somethin growin in my mouth. It's been there a while. Makes my breath bad. It grows in the mouths of people who got this disease, Myrna.

She squashed her cigarette on the sole of her slipper. You die from that disease.

Don't treat your shoes like that, Myrna. You got to take care of your things so they last.

You die from this, Thumby.

Well, Myrna, that is a news flash. Thank you.

What are you goin to do?

I swallowed some more wine which had got warm, it soured the roof of my mouth. Did you ever see *Gone with the Wind*, Myrna? I'm goin to worry about it tomorrow.

What are you goin to do tomorrow, then?

I am not goin to nude car wash tonight.

OK.

I am not goin tomorrow night or the next night.

OK.

I got better things to do with the time I got left.

How much time is that, exactly?

I got to talk to the doctor about that.

What are you goin to do about your baby?

I put my hands under my shirt and stroked where I felt that her head was.

What kind of choices do I have, Myrna.

Are you goin to have her?

Of course I'm havin her.

Then what?

I took off my glasses so I could work out a lash that was scourin my eyeball. You see anything in my eye, Myrna? She came over and stared. Nothin but blue green.

It's known as turquoise to intelligent people.

You waste them eyes behind those glasses. Then what? she repeated.

I blinked, feelin the lash like a two-by-four. I can't see in front of me. I can't even see your face clearly. You are goin to have to respect that, Myrna.

~ ~ ~

I TOOK the rope out of my jeans and tied it around my dog's neck and we went out the door early the next mornin with Myrna snorin on the pillow. The bus driver didn't put up no stink about Black Bean in my arms. Mrs. Leffer however did when I knocked on the door and she opened it and she wore a yellow sweater stretched to the breakin point over her fat old arms. I had to sweet talk her quite a bit to get her to take me back, but after I told her

{167}

that Myrna had lost her little baby all her anger dropped off her face like clothes before you get in the bathtub and she told me I could stay.

These are the conditions. Her ringlets shook. The dog goes. You go to the doctor once a week for checkups. You return to school. You avoid boys.

Avoid what?

You heard me.

I tried not to laugh at the idea of me avoidin boys.

Black Bean is a orphan and has nowhere else to go, Mrs. Leffer. Even Agnes put up with her.

She whacked her cigarette in the ashtray so hard that the orange end fell off and she had to relight it.

Don't remember you smokin, Mrs. Leffer.

Probably don't remember me drinkin, either. She lifted her mug. Why didn't she come with you?

She'll be comin one of these days. She can't do without me. So if you let me stay, she'll be back.

Is she awful upset about the baby?

She's gettin over it.

She's not still hangin around him?

Who? I said, to buy time.

That Indian fellow.

How do you know about him?

They tell us about you kids before we agree to take you on, Thumbelina.

They're goin to make life hell for me at school, Mrs. Leffer. Them girls.

You have made your bed, dearie, and now you are goin to have to lie in it.

The tears farted out of me, rollin down my cheeks, my long neck, into my sweatshirt.

Mrs. Leffer's soft arms came around me and I shut my

eyes and smelled her light body odor and sweet baby powder. She was puttin out heat like a fire.

You're goin to be all right, Thumbelina. I know you are. Good girl for comin back to me.

She went over to the big yellow bowl on the counter and pretty soon the smell of fryin pancakes filled the kitchen. I pressed my forehead to the slidin glass door. I fogged up an area as big as my head. Sadness filled me. Rain plonked into the backyard. Does Black Bean have to sit out in that all day?

You can put her in the garage.

It bein Sunday the next step was church. You want to come? she said, and I felt that a yes would be a good move. There was nothin on the cross but a shine. Roy sat beside me. He's the same old little kid, all hair and them eyes. I mentioned church shoes. Peein in em. Well, my mom used to drive me to this stone church on the Ravenhead Apartments side of town where I used to live one floor above my friend Del who was goin to marry me. She said this church was Catholic and my dad was Catholic and if I had to go to church, there you go. I liked the statue of Mary out front with her head bent with the weight of everybody's sins. I liked the stain-glass windows and the guy in the robes who talked as loud as a bus on the altar. I liked how everybody got down and kneeled after they went up and got the little bread in their hands. I got it too sometimes. I liked lookin around at people and smilin at em and all of us speakin together in one voice. About an hour after everybody'd left my mom would finally show up. Psst! she'd whisper loudly, one inch inside the back door. Thumby?

Excuse me, God, I'd say. I'd turn around. I'm busy, Mom.

Doin what? Settin her big white purse on the holy-water stand.

Prayin.

Can't you do that at home?

You have got to be kiddin.

Well, you're goin to have to walk then, and the door would be shuttin on her tight-butt jeans.

I'd finish up quick: SotomakealongstoryshortGod-makeherleavehimamen.

When we got home from church Mrs. Leffer made us ham sandwiches, then she took me out to the garage, a place I had only thought of as the home of her silver Ford Escort. Black Bean had moved from the old towel in the corner to the wheelbarrow.

She handed me a pair of stiff cold garden gloves.

What do I need these for?

She took me into the front yard and pointed at the weeds along the walk.

Are you punishin me?

I am givin you a reason not to run away again, she said, and smiled and shook her ringlets out of her eyes.

Those weeds are nearly dead, I told her. We are occu-pyin wintertime.

She said when I got done weedin to pick the beauty bark out of the grass and put it back in her rhododendron beds. Then I had to sweep out the garage. I got a big nose and I sniffed around, lookin for clues under the shelf. But all I found that might have belonged to the Mister was a hammer and a paper bag with a couple of nails inside that was so old it fell apart in my hands.

~ ~ ~

MRS. LEFFER had softened. Took me about a week to understand this, but she was lettin me off the hook about school. She'd knock on Roy's door at seven in the mornin, but not mine. I'd hear water in the bathroom. I'd hear the mornin TV show in the kitchen. The garage door would rattle open like somebody bangin a hammer on the garbage can. Roy would bang out the front door a while later. And nobody came to tell me to get up. I'd drift in the bottom bunk till about nine. I'd force myself to shower, even though it took a lot of energy. I'd drink some orange juice. I'd even use her hair dryer, puttin it back where I found it. I'd rinse off their breakfast dishes. I'd haul out the vacuum cleaner and cover every inch of carpet. I'd gather up the newspaper in the livin room from where I'd spread it around the night before. I'd go out into the garage and check out the situation and if Black Bean had pooped I'd pick it up with toilet paper and sprinkle the spot with Ajax. Mrs. Leffer saved me. I couldn't of faced those girls at school.

One night she was stirrin stuff in the pot and keepin her eye on *Wheel of Fortune*. I was eyein the funnies. Roy was down in his room. He kept to himself, same as before.

Hungry, Thumbelina? Mrs. Leffer asked like she always did about this time.

Yeah.

You're lyin, dear.

I raised my eyes from Beetle Bailey. Then why'd you ask?

You're never hungry.

My throat hurts.

She wiped her sweaty hands on her lace-trimmed apron. What's wrong, Thumbelina.

I got a sore throat.

You mean an ulcer?

No, I mean a sore throat.

Your mother had an ulcer.

How in the heck do you know that?

She came over nearer to me, a worried look pullin her eyebrows together. They tell us these things, dear, what to look out for in our kids when we take em on.

I folded the newspaper. I am not my mother.

I am takin you to an ulcer doctor.

Aw, for cryin out loud. You want me to cut some carrots or somethin?

They're in the crisper. I've also found this OB for you. The social worker recommended him. Since you didn't like the other one.

That other guy wanted me to have an abortion. I ran my finger across my throat.

She sighed. He was concerned about you havin a child at your age.

I am already goin to the doctor.

I made you an appointment for next Tuesday.

You got ears? I got my own appointment for next Thursday with Dr. Miligiwamny down on Alphabet Hill. I can take care of myself and I have been, Mrs. Leffer.

She fixed her little eyes on me. Thumbelina, I don't have the energy to argue with you.

You think I got the energy to argue with you? I'm the one that's pregnant.

He's an OB?

No, a garbageman.

I started slicin the carrots with her biggest knife.

How did you hear about him? she said.

He works at the J Street Clinic. My mom used to go there.

Isn't that a homeless clinic?

It's a keep-your-nose-in-your-own-business clinic. They don't ask you personal questions, it's the rule.

She whacked the spoon on the pot. Your kind of place.

I eyed her. She wore yellow slacks and a long black sweater. Her feet were bare in slippers. You lost any weight, Mrs. Leffer?

Why, yes, I have.

You on a diet?

Why, yes. Nice of you to notice.

We both held off speakin for a while, while we got busy finishin dinner. I don't mind cuttin vegetables when they are raw, because they don't got much of a smell to em. Somethin very smelly was comin from her pot though. I went over to the door to smoke a cigarette and get the smell out of my nose.

That isn't good for your baby.

She's fine.

How do you know it's a she?

I know.

They say that mothers do. I didn't have a clue about mine.

I waited for her to go on, but she had got stuck. So I helped her out.

You got kids?

Three.

Where are they?

Spread around. She shrugged. They didn't come home for Christmas. They have families of their own now. Two boys and a girl. We don't get along that good, especially me and Annie.

Are you nice to her?

To Annie? Of course I'm nice to her.

I blew smoke through the crack in the door, into the night air outside. If you're nice to her, she'd come home.

Mrs. Leffer sighed. We've had our problems, that's for

{173}

sure. She blames me for losin her daddy. She was just a little girl, she doesn't understand the kind of hassle he was bringin into our home. The boys were older, they remember. They were glad to see him go.

Did you invite her here for Christmas?

Mrs. Leffer lifted the pot lid off. Steam shot out into her face.

Scuse me? Are my ears not workin?

I was waitin for her to invite me to her place.

Ahhh.

What does that mean, exactly?

What kind of a attitude is that? You got to call up your daughter and invite her home.

Well. It crossed my mind that she could invite me to her place in Spokane.

Did you ask her directly?

That would be rude.

I sighed. I went over and stirred the carrots around in the pot, admirin the yellow centers, which were nearly the color of somebody's hair.

~ ~ ~

I WALKED through the waitin room and up the stairs that were as flimsy as the eleven in Agnes's house, went down the gloomy hall to the last door on the left, across from TOILETS. I opened without knockin because I am that kind of girl. The nurse said I was supposed to see you, I said loudly. Dr. K. was jumpin on a trampoline in the corner. He wore those same dark green corduroy pants with the baggy butt and a white T-shirt with a hole near his belly button and a necklace of beads that whacked him in the chin as he jumped. He hopped down and used his bandanna to sop up all the water rollin down his face, then he tied it back down on his seriously out-of-control hair. He dragged his hikin boots out from under his desk.

Sit down, Thumbelina, make yourself comfortable.

On the purple couch, he meant. So I did. Why don't you just go joggin like normal people, Dr. K.?

What have I done, sweetheart, to give you the impression that I'm normal?

I smiled but Dr. K. didn't.

He reached for the other boot. Normal people don't go into medicine, Thumbelina. The few that do certainly don't choose infectious diseases.

Behind his desk was a big window, round like a hula hoop, with the curtains tied back. On the windowsill sat four ladies. All of em pretty. The one on the end I recognized from the day of the birthday party and knew as Mrs. K.

Them other three your sisters?

My wives.

Four of em.

Well, he shrugged, don't forget the *e* and the *x*.

What about that one on the end?

Lauren?

Cynthia's mom.

Lauren left me last summer, he said, meanwhile listenin to my heart under my shirt. His hands were warm. She lives in Ann Arbor now. Going to graduate school.

She left you?

They all left me.

You're that hard to live with?

I am intolerable to live with. Dr. K. moved the heart thing around to my back.

Cynthia go with her?

She did.

He straightened back up, saw me lookin at number two, who had slanty eyes and straight black hair and a red dress that went down kind of low but not in the range of none of the girls I've been hangin out with lately.

That's Beatrice. She was born in Taiwan.

How'd you meet her?

My, you are curious.

From the look in your eye you are plannin on pickin up where you left off, askin me questions. It's only fair.

He smiled. It touched his eyes this time. At an ear, nose, and throat conference.

Married to number one at the time, probably.

He looked at his watch, then he leaned his butt into his crowded desk. Which do you want first, the good news or the bad news?

I thought it over. I was still thinkin when he started talkin.

Given enough time we will develop a vaccine for the HIV virus, and it will become benign. It will live symbiotically with its host. That would be you. But not this year, and not next year.

What are you sayin?

We'll clear up the thrush soon. You'll find it easier to swallow. But you are profoundly immunocompromised, Thumbelina. You are vulnerable to infection. I mean, you are wide open. You've got to take care of yourself, kiddo. You can't laugh this off. No more missed appointments.

I thought you said there was good news, Dr. K.?

I just gave you the good news. I have some questions to ask you. Personal questions, I'm sorry.

Yeah. No kiddin. That's all you do is talk, talk, talk.

Well, I would be glad to turn the floor over to you. How long have you been sexually active?

Lookin straight at me and not even embarrassed. He didn't have no right askin me that.

How long have you been sexually active?

I dropped my eyes to his red boot laces. I felt like we were tuggin opposite ends of a rope. Both of us tuggin hard.

Not too long, I said.

Could you be a bit more cooperative with me?

Yeah, if you ask me decent questions.

He nudged his wire frames up his long nose. You asked me about the women in my life, I'm asking you about the men in yours. Did any of them engage in high-risk behaviors?

What makes you think there was more than one?

He started pacin back and forth between me and his big messy desk. Them were the good old days when I had energy to burn like that.

Where is your mother in all of this?

I sort of live my own life.

You don't live with her?

No.

What kind of a relationship do you have with her?

I don't want to keep you here all day.

He smiled. Could you bring her in with you next time?

She don't go out much.

It would be helpful to see her.

Naw, I highly doubt it.

Does your mother have a husband?

Nope.

A boyfriend?

Doesn't everybody?

Except for you, apparently.

I lowered my eyes.

Tell me about him.

{177}

What do you want to know?

Anything you think is important.

He was in the army once. He drove a truck. All-right lookin. He wasn't my dad.

You speak about him in the past.

Yeah. I kind of do, don't I.

He took a pen out of his shirt pocket and started clickin the ink in and out. May I ask why?

No.

He crouched down in front of me. I could smell the soap he had used to wash his long body that mornin. Did this boyfriend . . . what's his name?

Lester, Dr. K.

. . . ever hurt you?

Not for a long time.

But he used to?

A long time ago. We're talkin way back when. Then I got smart. He likes it when you're smart. My mom, on the other hand, never got smart.

So he used to hit you?

Your ears, Dr. K., are workin.

Did he hurt you in other ways? Did he ever touch you?

I leaned back to get some breathin room, settin my hands protectively over my fish. Dr. K. was gettin too close for comfort.

It's pretty hard to hit someone without touchin em, I said.

That isn't what I mean.

Well, you better say what you mean.

Did he ever touch you in . . . certain places?

He touched me in all kinds of places. The livin room, the bathroom, the kitchen—

Private places.

The bathroom was pretty private.

Private places on *you,* Thumbelina.

I don't got all day, Dr. K., will you cut to the chase?

He went over and pulled out the bottom drawer of his desk and unscrewed a mason jar filled with orange stuff and emptied half of it down his throat.

Lester is the father, isn't he.

No question mark on the end, so I didn't feel the need to answer. I just looked at the ladies lined up on his windowsill.

Are you still in love with em?

It's carrot juice. Would you like some?

Too healthy for me by a mile, Dr. K.

He pulled a brown leather wallet out of his rear pocket that looked like it had gone through the wash a couple times and set it on the desk. I stared at it, thinkin, is it full of cash? He saw me starin and reached over and opened it. All these cards and bits of paper spilled out. Book reviews, he said. Of all the interesting books I am never going to get the time to read.

I pointed at the Mrs. K. that I knew. She's the prettiest.

Thank you. I've got approximately two minutes before Carmen's going to be banging that door, sweetheart—

Don't thank me, it's a fact that has nothin to do with you.

—telling me she has five patients gowned and waiting. Tell me this and tell me honestly. Did you ever speak to your mother about Lester?

You would ask me that.

Is that a yes?

I put my big toe into the subject, Yeah.

The flat, low sky knocked against the window.

And now she is dead, Dr. K. I guess I should have told you that sooner.

Why didn't you? His voice was calm.

Because you are divin into my life makin a big mess, and I'm not your swimmin pool. You are screwin everything up that I've worked hard to set in order. I don't really like you, Dr. K. That's the main problem here.

He poured carrot juice down his throat. If I had hurt his feelins he was as good at hidin that as I was. He set the jar down by the fourth wife. A man was yellin downstairs but I couldn't make out the words. Then I heard a lady's voice, mellow and calm, then things got quiet.

All right, he said. Perhaps we've talked enough for today.

Aw, Dr. K., I like some things about you. I just don't like you pryin all this personal information out of me.

We have talked enough for today, Thumbelina.

We? *I* had talked enough for fifteen years.

~ ~ ~

HAD A dream.

I was in the graveyard lookin for her grave, but I couldn't find it because it was so little and it was unmarked because remember she was embarrassed about her age. I got tired of walkin around in circles and I started hollerin, Mom! Mom! You here? I brought you some flowers! This hand poked up out of the ground a long way off and waved. I heard this thin wail goin, Thumby! Thumby! I ran over to the hand. Right before I could grab it the ground caved in. When I opened my eyes I was in her coffin. I didn't have dirt on me. She was sittin cross-legged, a big old grin. She wasn't a skeleton. She might of put on a couple pounds.

Took you long enough, Thumbelina. I've been so

lonely. You got any idea how boring it is down here? Don't have no romance books and no TV.

It sure is nice to hear your voice again, Mom. Water trickled out my eyes.

She was holdin the orange tulips I'd brought her, crushed by my fall. This was sweet of you, she said, but I would of preferred chocolate.

I was plannin on leavin em on your grave, Mom. It's what people do.

I rubbed my head. A bump the size of that softball I used to huck around was growin above my right ear.

Did you bring any cards?

Before I could say a word she reached into the pocket of her coat which I was wearin and pulled em out. Oh goodie! What do you want to play? Go Fish? Gin rummy? And by the way, why are you wearin my coat?

Meanwhile, I got down to business. Mom, I got a problem.

Thumby, I'm dead. I don't have to worry about your problems no more.

It's a big problem, Mom.

You were born with big problems, honey. You were my kid. Alls I can say is I'm sorry. Now let's leave all that behind us and have some fun. She started to deal the cards. How about five-card gin?

I got the disease, Mom.

She dealt the cards and ignored me.

You know which one I am referrin to. Don't tell me you got that short a memory. Your hair is still wet and I can smell the algae on you.

Oh, sweetheart, it was a accident.

Were you afraid you had it, Mom? Come on, tell me, I got to know.

Pester pester pester, it's all you've ever done to me my whole life, Thumby. I'm dead, can't you respect that and give me some peace?

Her blue eyes were clear and empty. I started to cry.

Oh, Thumby, poor old Thumby. She pulled me into her arms. I could smell the duck pond in her hair.

I am goin to have a baby up there on earth, Mom, I whispered into her neck. But I'm not goin to be there to raise it, and you know what happens to a kid when it don't have its mother no more. Just look at me.

It's pretty hard to avoid it, sweetheart. She pushed me away from her, smilin. You're fillin up the landscape.

You made me this big, feedin me all that food.

I just wanted you to be healthy.

Givin me that name.

Thumbelina's a pretty name.

She was the size of a *thumb*, Mom!

Thumby. It's a silly fairy tale. It doesn't mean anythin.

You did it to be mean.

You always did think the worst of me.

My other problem, Mom, is this doctor.

She had let me go and her head was down, her face hidden by all her yellow-white hair. But at the word *doctor* I had her full attention. I always did want to meet one of those. Can you introduce us?

No.

Keepin him for yourself? Smart cookie. But it's no good. Doctors don't date girls like us.

I looked down at my hands.

Damn it, Thumby, don't look so sad. Not now. I'm so lonely and you are goin to play cards with me.

Good thing me and Delores bought you a big coffin. I

am goin to stay here with you, Mom. And I lay down and shut my eyes.

Thumby.

Good night, Mom.

Thumby! Wake your big butt up! You're playin cards with me. She punched me in the arm.

I woke up all right. I lay there a couple minutes starin at the boards of the bunk bed above me. Then I rolled over and got down on my hands and knees and felt around in the darkness. But there was only the cold floor. I put down my head, I screamed into my hands without makin a sound.

One time last summer we were fryin burgers in the kitchen. Well, I was doin the fryin and she was sittin there drinkin vodka from her coffee cup and knockin ashes in the plant. The sun came through the window and sat on her head, makin all the other heads in the city wait. Under her breath she was singin, *Hey porter hey porter please open up the door,* with Johnny Cash on the tape player. I was so happy my heart ached like it had run ten miles.

What do you think it's like bein dead, Thumby?

I gave her a look but her head was down. She was hidin behind her hair. Depends if you go up or down.

Where am I goin, do you think?

Let's just put it this way. You're probably goin to want to pack water.

She didn't say nothin. I kept my eye on her but she stayed hidden behind her hair. I was jokin, but I thought, oh man she took me seriously now she's goin to hold it against me.

I salted the meat. Mom, you have to have an interview, see. But you got to wait your turn because with all the stuff goin on in the world, he's busy. While you're waitin you turn into a ghost and you come out after dark and sit around on your gravestone and get to know other ghosts and have a party. You better not get drunk, Mom, and miss your name. He only calls once.

Ghosts can't drink, Thumby.

I feel sorry for you then.

She shook her hair back from her face. I got a confession to make.

I jammed the pancake turner under her burger. I'm not your real daughter.

I'm seein a man.

You aren't the only one.

He came in wantin a haircut, but I told him I am not experienced with Mexican hair. I didn't say it meanly, just matter of fact because of its texture. He said, I can help you with that muffler. Because the place was busy and he'd been waitin in line and heard me tellin Chee Chee that it's draggin, see. I said, Yeah? He said, Yeah. That he works for Al's Muffler on Beeson Avenue. He was cute and I'd seen him get out of his white Corvette. That, honey, is one of the advantages of havin the window chair.

I squirted on a blob of yellow and a blob of red and dropped her plate on the table. Lester's goin to find out.

She wiped the back of her little hand across her chin. Are you goin to tell him?

I might.

Then maybe I'll just move in with Donny and leave you behind.

You wouldn't last a day without me.

I wouldn't mind tryin.

I slapped my burger between the bun. I dare you, Mom, I whispered. I just dare you.

Where are you goin? There was somethin in her voice
that needed me.

Outside to get some fresh air because the air in here has
got all hot, Mom.

I got up off the floor and went to the window and let in
the cold air. The stars were crowdin each other in the night
sky, seein which one could pour the most light down on
me. I regret treatin her that bad. It is somethin I got in my
heart and that I am goin to take with me even though they
say you can't take nothin with you not even your toothbrush.

~ ~ ~

Myrna came back a week ago. We were eatin mashed
potatoes and peas and hot dogs. Thumby? My suitcases are
sittin on the front porch.

I pushed back my chair.

Thumby's pregnant, Mrs. Leffer said. Sit down, dear.

Myrna looked at small little Roy who was scoopin in
peas. Want to earn a buck?

So Roy went out and hauled in her seriously big-ass
suitcases and dragged em down the hall.

It's about time you showed up, Mrs. Leffer said.

Don't start, please.

Are you hungry? There's food on the stove.

Not really. Think I'll just go have a shower.

Miss. Sit down, Mrs. Leffer said firmly.

Myrna's green eyes filled with a rare quality: surprise.
Then those eyeballs rolled in her head and she plunked her
behind down in the chair, her body language sayin loud
and clear, I don't believe her, is she for real?

She is decidin at this very minute whether or not she's goin to let you stay, Myrna, I said, so it would be a good idea to zip your big lip.

I could feel Mrs. Leffer smilin at my lowered head as she clanked a plate of food down in front of my orange-haired friend.

I stole looks at her as she picked at the potatoes and peas. She looked tired.

Are you back here permanently? Mrs. Leffer said.

I have come to talk to Thumby.

She is stayin, I said quietly to Mrs. Leffer.

Later we watched TV and drank Cokes and it was like old times. She sat in the bathroom for a hour and made me wait to wash my face. I finally just went to bed.

Why'd you sneak out on me, Thumby? she said when we were lyin in the dark.

I snored loudly.

So what's the doctor say?

About what?

So you're not asleep.

I was tired of takin off my clothes, Myrna, I already told you. I have always had the feelin that Mrs. Leffer likes us.

She was quiet awhile. I had no idea what she was thinkin. But do I ever?

How's your AIDS comin along?

I rolled over in the darkness and faced the wall. It's not my AIDS, you dumb ass.

You goin to the doctor?

I'm goin.

Are you takin all the pills he gave you? For your AIDS?

How many times are you goin to say that word, Myrna? AIDS AIDS AIDS AIDS AIDS. I kicked her through the bed board.

Would you mind gettin me a smoke out of my back-pack?

Yes, I highly would.

Please?

I rustled around in the darkness. I handed up the stuff. Her cigarette was orange and beautiful in the dark. I got back in bed. Soon there was a thump and I felt her butt take a seat beside my legs.

I heard about this place in California, Thumby, this mail-order place, one of the girls at work told me about it—

I suppose you're tellin the whole world about my AIDS, I said sarcastically.

Nope, only a few people. You can order all these Chinese herbs and stuff. It's supposed to be a cure.

There is no cure.

Who says?

Dr. K.

Who's he?

My doctor.

So who made him God?

He's pretty darn close.

You in love with him?

I didn't even honor that with an answer.

You can order anti-HIV herbs and pills and alfalfa and tea. It's called TCM and they use it in China for curin disease. It works. I ordered you some stuff.

If you want to waste your money, Myrna, would you buy me *Patsy Cline's Greatest Hits,* please.

What's your CD4 count?

I elbowed her in the darkness. How do you know about that?

I got friends who tell me stuff. What is it?

Dr. K. says it's closin in on two hundred.

She swooshed out smoke, it was a soft comforting sound. That isn't too good.

I know, I whispered.

You got the best chances of livin when you start takin this stuff early on. Well, you'll have to make up for it with a positive attitude.

I am plenty positive.

Your attitude sucks, Thumby.

Will you quit knockin ashes on the floor? I'm tryin to stay on her good side.

No kiddin. What for?

I told you, I like her.

Jesus lovin savior.

Shut up, Myrna.

You tell her?

No, and if you do you are goin to suffer.

Oh, I am so scared.

I'm crossin over to the other side, Myrna, and I'll come back and make your life hell if you tell her I got AIDS.

Quit talkin that way. It's irritatin.

I am gettin skinny just like Lester. (I thought about this a minute.) Course, I have always been skinny. But I am coughin just like he was coughin. He was takin all kinds of pills, me and my mom didn't know why. We thought he was just gettin healthy on us.

I'm goin to take care of you, Thumby.

Silence for a couple minutes while we both just breathed. What am I smellin, Myrna?

Poeme by Lancôme.

Classy.

I got class.

You sure keep it in your ass.

Look. I didn't come back here to argue with you. I can't stay long, Thumby. She drives me bananas. But I will stay as long as I can. Till this Chinese stuff comes.

She stood up. I didn't want her to move away from me, I didn't want her to go to sleep and leave me alone.

Don't let em bury me, Myrna.

Oh, for fuck's sake. She sat back down. Don't speak like that.

I don't want to be down there in the dark and cold all by myself.

I heard the click of her lighter, a long sigh as she breathed out smoke. It could be peaceful.

I saw my mom last night. She didn't look peaceful. She looked lonely.

She came into the room? (There wasn't a joke in her voice.)

You got to be kiddin. Come to see me? Here? I went to see her. I always got to go to her.

What'd she say?

She wanted to play cards.

Well, that makes sense if she's bored.

You believe in the afterlife, Myrna?

I am willin to entertain the notion, yeah, she huffed, tuggin herself back up into her bunk.

I turned it over in my mind a few minutes before I said it.

You could come with me.

She didn't say nothin dumb like, where? She just took her time thinkin it over. Yeah. I guess I could. But I doubt we're goin to the same place.

Aw, Myrna, we are so.

You are a better person than me, Thumbelina.

I only wish at this point in my life that I was. I have fucked up too much.

{189}

I don't believe it.

I wasn't very good to my mom.

Your mom, it sounds like she had a lot of problems, Myrna said gently.

So tender I got hard-edged. Careful how you speak of the dead, Myrna.

So then Myrna got hard-edged back. She sounds pretty fucked up.

No, she could be very nice, actually. She could make good pancakes. She could sing. Those are basically the things I inherited from her.

You mind spinnin somethin out now?

What?

Somethin lonesome.

You'll dream sad dreams.

I'm already goin to, nothin you sing is goin to make it worse.

So I sang Walkin After Midnight and then I did Hey, Good Lookin What-cha Got Cookin. For her. My orange-haired friend. Even after her breathin was deep and regular I kept on singin softly all the songs I knew.

~ ~ ~

I SAT in the paper gown in the little room for about one hour.

Thumbelina, sweetheart. Dr. K. breezed in.

Oh, you decided to come today? I glared.

He looked me over, puttin his heart thing here and there and his hands. Miligiwamny sent over another chart. He nodded at the counter. You've been visiting him regularly.

Yep.

So why do you stiff me?

{190}

The pills you give me don't work.

Yes. We have to talk about that. Your blood smears indicate that you haven't been taking your AZT.

Hum de dum, I went at the ceiling.

Why is that, Thumbelina.

That stuff makes me feel funny.

I understand—

You don't understand nothin. Myrna is orderin me other stuff.

What stuff? he said sharply.

Oh, I don't know, anti-HIV herbs. Chinese tea made of oyster shells.

I swung my legs off the table, admirin my toenails which I had just painted black. It's supposed to clear the heat out of my lungs.

He wasn't smilin. How long have you been following this regime?

I haven't started yet. It's comin from California.

His eyebrows disappeared into his hair. He started to say somethin but I interrupted him. I'm livin in foster care again. Did I mention that?

He told me I could put on my clothes now. Does your foster mother know you're ill? he said.

I'd appreciate it if you don't use that *m* word, Dr. K. OK? I smiled. Of course not. Nobody but Myrna would stick by me if they knew.

Give people a chance.

I pulled on my black socks.

We have to talk, Thumbelina.

What are we doin now, fartin?

You have to think of your baby's welfare.

Oh, Dr. K. I only smoke one or two cigarettes a week now.

That's one or two too many. That is not what I'm talking about.

Well, cut to the chase.

He folded his arms. There is no cure for this disease.

You told me that already.

Because you are so profoundly immunocompromised you are vulnerable, exceptionally vulnerable, to infection. I'm worried about pneumonia, lymphoma—many things. How is your swallowing?

Fine.

You've got to take the Diflucan regularly.

OK.

And the AZT.

Yeah yeah.

Which you haven't been doing.

I told you it makes me feel funny. I feel tingly in my hands and feet. It bugs me.

Peripheral neuropathy, he nodded.

It won't go away.

No, I'm afraid it won't.

Well, then I don't want it.

I don't care what you want. You must take it—

Dr. K., I said. You missed the war, didn't you?

What war?

Oh, you know. *The* war, with the hippies. But that's OK. There is probably other girls that wouldn't mind you pokin your nose in their lives. Why don't you find one.

He shuffled over to the sink and washed his hands. Then he did somethin stranger than fiction. He put his hand on my arm and squeezed. I'm sorry, he said, pullin out a big checkered hanky. He dropped it in my lap. I thought he was givin me a present. If you feel like crying, I understand.

When I didn't cry he took his hanky and stuffed it back in his pocket. I can't force you to take medication against your will, Thumbelina, but I want you to understand that it's not just to help you. It's to protect your child. You can possibly infect your child, you see.

I thought it over. I'll take the crap. Now tell me somethin useful. How long do I got to live?

A lot of that depends on you. Whether or not you take care of yourself!

Are you shoutin at me? I have to get goin.

You had better sit down, young lady!

Then don't be goin around shoutin at me.

I've got a person you should contact. Who can find a home for your child.

A *what?*

Now, Thumbelina—

You mean give her away?

We call it adoption.

I don't care what you call it.

Even if you were fourteen healthy years old, sweetheart, and you came to me, I would give you this same advice. So take it. Make your life easier, and for God's sake think of your child. You're in no shape to be a mother. If you do it now you can at least choose the parents.

I'm the parent.

His lips flattened into a line thinner than a single hair on his head.

Maybe I'm plannin on givin her to somebody I know.

Are you?

I'm kickin around Myrna. She is my best friend.

Wonderful.

Hey. I'm the only one around here who gets to insult her.

Do you want your best friend to be the mother of your

child? The duality of roles is not always a good idea. I moved in with my best friend during medical school and we almost killed each other.

That wouldn't be your first wife you're talkin about?

His beeper went off then. He looked at his watch. He pushed back his chair and said, Follow me, and rushed out of that door and down the hall and up the two flights of rickety stairs to his office on the third floor. I was sloggin up the last few steps when he came back down the hall holdin a little white card with gold letters on it. He pressed it into my hand. Candace Conn runs a private adoption agency.

I started cleanin under my thumbnail with the card.

He stared down at me from the top step. We have a pack of social workers associated with this clinic, Thumbelina, and I've been keeping them off your back. Telling them I have a personal relationship with you. I don't know how much longer I can do that. Don't make me turn manipulative now. Normally, like most members of my profession, I don't think much of lawyers but they come in handy once in a while. At least with Candace you can choose the parents. If you wait too long the state will handle it. I'm sorry to be so blunt—

He shoved his fingers under his glasses and rubbed his eyes.

—it's just that I hate to see our wacky, screwed-up government choose a mother and father for you. When I know you can read people excellently and make a fine choice.

Thank you, I said. I bent the card and fit it between my front teeth.

He grabbed my arm, his eyes firin sparks. It's important, young lady, that you be absolutely up front with her about your disease because there's a certain percent chance that your child will be born infected. There are things that we can do medically, however, to greatly reduce this possibility. If you deceive Mrs. Conn, you could be willfully endangering your child. Are you listening to me?

That thing is cryin for you. I nodded at his beeper.

He bonked it quiet. He shook his head at me, he looked pretty irritated all right. Excuse me, he said between clenched teeth, and he went back down the hall. I wasn't sure if I was supposed to follow him. I wanted to see his wives again. It was a comfort to look at their four faces. I had the feelin his glasses belonged to one of em, they were too delicate for his big face. She must of left em behind on the table when she stormed out with her suitcases. Now he wore em to remember her.

~ ~ ~

I DIDN'T expect to get such a busy lady on my first try. She sounded nice. You're one of whose patients?

Dr. K.

Dr. . . . ?

From the—you know—clinic. He gave me your card. Big, sloppy-lookin guy, I muttered. With a real big nose about everything.

James Kazlowski, she chuckled.

Do you know him?

Only philanthropically.

I turned that one over in my head but I couldn't get a handle on it so I moved on.

I'm pregnant.

Of course you are, dear. How old are you?

Fourteen.

And how far along?

I am due on April twenty-seventh.

We don't have much time, then.

Don't rush me, Mrs. Conn, I'm not in a very good mood.

But you are considering adoption?

With a capital *C*.

What does that mean, dear?

What I just said.

I was bein rude, all right, but it didn't seem to bother the lady. She wanted to come over that afternoon and talk, but I said, Hold your horses, I got to think this over. I told her we would have to meet in Bean Park by the duck pond. She said, Oh, come on, now, I've got to see where you live, meet the people you live with.

Later, ma'am.

All right. When? Your call.

Let me check my social calendar. I counted to twenty-five under my breath. She waited patiently in my ear.

Saturday afternoon good?

At, say, three o'clock?

OK.

How will I recognize you?

I got yellow hair. I will be the only one sittin on the swings at this time of year, Mrs. Conn.

Call me Candace.

No, thanks, Mrs. Conn. I think we should stay strictly professional. Mrs. Conn?

Yes?

I am real, real healthy.

~ ~ ~

IT WAS rainin, which it figures, and I forgot a umbrella which it figures (well, actually, I don't have one), and I was late, which it figures, because my name is Thumbelina. I got off the bus and slapped up the sidewalk and ducked under the wet trees and past the statue of Mr. J. Bean himself who started the factory down on the water, which makes this town smell like everybody in it lit a fart at the same time.

I spent about five minutes gettin my butt wet before I saw a lady runnin down the hill. She was medium height, medium weight, I could tell through her flappin red raincoat, and she was swingin a big red umbrella. She looked and smelled expensive. She shook my hand like a man and said, Come along, dear, you must be frozen, and we slogged up the grassy hill to her big white Lexus, which was as comfortable as a livin room inside, and we small talked for a while. She tried to make me feel relaxed by tellin me a little about herself. You know how they do that. She has two kids, eight and ten, named Merry and Matthew, and she said she loves em dear so she knows how it must feel to be in my position. I felt like sayin, Mrs. Conn dear, you don't have the foggiest notion what my position is, but I didn't want to piss her off until I knew where I stood.

Her hair fell down her head in big curls—hot rollers that mornin, by a mile—and was the color of wet beauty bark. She asked me who I lived with. I said, People.

What kind of people?

You aren't goin to be nosy, are you?

I just want to make sure you're being taken care of.

Foster care.

And your mom and dad? Where are they?

(Knew it was comin.)

My dad is down in Sacramento, California. He's a folk singer. (Not exactly a lie. He's buried down there.)

Oh? she said, gettin all interested. So I coughed up the information that my mom and dad were both from Sacramento and they had played in a folk band called Be Air.

Be Air? Never heard of them. I love folk music. Perhaps I've heard of your father. What's his name?

Charles Volkner.

Charles Volkner. Volkner. You didn't take his last name then?

Nope. Then I added, because her eyes were askin, that my mom and dad never got married. My mom liked her independence. Anything else you need to know about me? I had my hand on the door.

Oh, dear, I thought we might go and get some coffee and a bite to eat? Do you like McDonald's?

I put my nose in the air. The food is bad for you, ma'am. I'm carryin a life inside me, or didn't you notice?

This earned me points, loud and clear.

I know a great bagel shop. How does that sound? Are you hungry, Thumbelina?

No.

Oh, of course you are. No need to be polite, dear.

She started the car and the wipers swiped off the windshield and we weren't in our own little world no more.

So a couple minutes later me and her were sittin at a round high funky table with our feet hooked in the rungs of our high chairs, starin out long windows at the water lappin the dock.

I was freezin cold but she obviously wasn't, takin off her raincoat and settin it down on the stool beside us. So I didn't let on. She might get suspicious. I was feelin crummy in my wet jeans and muddy shoes next to her lookin like a fluffy cat in her white sweater and white slacks which magically appeared from under the red raincoat.

My Herbie Turkey on a sesame bagel came and sat in front of me. I wrapped my hands around my glass of decaf coffee and stared at it. She dug in, like as if to say, don't be shy. I'm not shy, I passed to her with my eyes, I'm just not hungry.

You want to see a picture of my mom? I said.

Love to.

So I hauled out the one of me and her on the teeter-totter and passed it over. We don't look alike, I said real quick, to keep her from sayin, Oh! She looks just like you! but she said it anyway. Oh! She looks just like you!

Probably thought it would earn her points. It didn't.

So then I took my picture and put it back into my wallet.

Mrs. Conn said, What have you been up to today? I said, Not much. She said, Isn't the rain depressing? I said, Yeah, but it's kind of mournful and nice in its own way. She said, It is? Well, I'm from California, I must be missing something. I said, You are? My friend Myrna wants to move there.

People do, don't they? I can't understand it. I couldn't wait to get out. So much more wholesome up here.

Yeah, I said.

Yeah, she said. Well, it sure is raining.

She had nice holes in her cheeks when she smiled. So you spend a lot of time in Bean Park?

You should see it in the summer when it's full of kids—I stopped, I was about to drop water everywhere.

She changed the subject. What are the qualities you want in parents?

My friend Myrna says that everybody wants a pretty baby.

Well, that's probably true for natural parents as well. At any rate, you have nothing to worry about.

She took a mouthful of her Curry Chicken. She's one of those people that seems comfortable eatin around strangers. I've just spent a week in China arranging adoptions for American couples.

China? I'm buyin medicine from them.

Medicine? Her eyes were suddenly alert.

I thought quick. I mean, I'm orderin all this health food from this company in California, to make me healthy for my . . . you know. Baby.

Are you seeing a doctor?

I'm in foster care, ma'am. Of course I'm seein a doctor.

We'll need to discuss all that. I'd like you to use my doctor.

I opened my mouth to tell her about the clinics I was already goin to, but she lifted her hand and put it on my head. Any couples you meet will fall in love with you, dear, you'll be an easy one for me. Her hand slipped down my hair and gripped my shoulder lightly. I didn't know what to do. I sat there. One day, and there will be a one day, when you are happily married to a man who loves you, you will have another little child. Many more. As many as you want.

I pressed my lips together. I didn't let that comment get near my heart. I just shoved it out my ear. I said, Mrs. Conn, can we get back to the subject?

Did we leave it?

How long will it take to find em?

Parents?

Do you have to use that word?

Mrs. Conn's mouth sagged. I know this is painful for

you. I'm sorry. It depends on how many couples you want to meet. I've got a list as long as my leg. Many of them have been waiting years.

That's a lot of pressure to put on a little baby.

She patted my hand. Don't worry, dear. Everything will be fine.

When people say that, that's usually when I get worried.

Back in her car she dug out a white card and gave it to me, it had a bunch of phone numbers written on it. My work, my fax, my beeper, my home number. Call me if you need anything, she said. I'll drive you home now.

Back to the park is fine.

Thumbelina, let me take you home.

The park is fine.

Is there something you are trying to hide?

I opened my eyes wide and innocent. Why, no, Mrs. Conn.

I am going to have to inspect your home situation sooner or later.

I looked out her expensive window.

So she took me back to the park. When I got out she idled her car for a few seconds, waitin for me to get started walkin so she could see which way I lived. I stood there with my hands in my pockets till she finally drove off. I went to the phone booth and called Mrs. Leffer.

How'd it go, dear?

All right.

Will she find you some good parents?

I looked across the street at the girls' pretty arms movin in the windows of the ballet building. I'm cold, Mrs. Leffer, just come and get me, will you?

Myrna flipped out when she heard the news at dinner. We were all of us shovelin in SpaghettiOs. Some of us more than others.

What did they say about payin you?

Payin me? I eyeballed her long and hard. You got a screw loose in your head and it's causin you brain damage, Myrna.

Jesuschrist, you're a dumb ass. Your baby is goin to be blonde and gorgeous. Don't give her away for free.

Thank you, Myrna, for that roundabout compliment, but I am only half the equation. There is another person involved who is passin on hair color and things.

Mrs. Leffer cleared her throat. Her cheeks were red. But it had nothin to do with what we were talkin about. She had a full glass of vodka goin. I think it's a very good idea that Thumbelina is goin to put her child up for adoption.

Nobody asked you, Myrna said.

Don't talk that way to the roof over your head, Myrna.

You shut up too, Thumby. Listen to some sense. Why should they get your baby for free?

Because they will love her.

She isn't theirs.

Once they adopt her, she'll, she will be.

But they didn't give birth to her.

I didn't give birth to Black Bean. I love her plenty.

That's because she doesn't love you back!

I squinted at her. Run that by me again?

It's the truth, Thumby, I'm your friend, I only tell you what I see. You got a habit of lovin things that don't love you back. Now, if you're goin to be dumb enough to go through this adoption thing, at least get some money for it.

She put down her fork. It's no different than goin on a car lot and pointin at a car and sayin, That one, please.

It is totally different, Myrna.

She poured milk down her throat. The women can't have babies of their own so they buy em off kids like you.

Then she started goin on about this TV show she saw once. Normally, she said, she wouldn't mention it but since I had obviously gone over the deep end in stupidity she had to. There was a bunch of couples on who'd adopted kids and then after a while these kids started fightin at school and shopliftin, and they didn't have the best IQs or whatever, and they weren't much to look at which was too bad because that can help, so they gave em back to the government.

Myrna, you are makin it up.

I am not.

Are too.

Girls! Mrs. Leffer's head was in her hands. Girls, please. Do your fightin somewhere else. I've had a long day.

Just like any time Mrs. Leffer gets that tone in her voice, Roy pushed back his chair and carried his plate to the sink and toddled solemnly out of the kitchen.

I couldn't let it go. It's against the law, Myrna, I hissed, followin her down the hall. You can't give birth to a kid and then shove it back where it came from.

Adoption is a different ball game, dumb ass.

Just what in hell am I supposed to do then?

Oh, she said, lookin at the ceiling.

Then it clicked. You think I'm leavin her with *you*? Is that it? Hah! It'll be a cold day in hell when I leave her with you! You would bring up a kid worse than me and that takes talent!

Yeah? Myrna snapped. Well, you can just fuck off and thanks a lot if that's what you think of me as a mother since I am going to be one in eight months and twenty-seven days!

We were havin this argument in the bathroom. She was puttin on lipstick. I was yellin at her. Soon as she said that I walked out on her. I went into our bedroom and dropped all these inches of me down and slammed my pillow over my head.

She ripped my protection off and hollered into my ear that she was three days late.

I eyed her calmly. Three days is not late, Myrna, it's just your blood stoppin along the way to smell the roses.

I am so pregnant. I am so pregnant! she hollered. Fuck *you*. I am *so* pregnant. My leg is still sore where she jammed me with her high heel.

I don't have the energy to deck you, Myrna. Is that stuff from California comin when hell freezes over?

She was heavin too hard to answer.

Because the doctor said I can pass this crap to my fish. He says I have to take his pills. They make me feel like shit. Is your stuff comin?

I am so pregnant, Thumbelina.

The case is closed, Myrna.

You're bein mean.

It's about time.

Her big red purse banged her butt. She was out of there. The front door closin nearly knocked my teeth loose.

I waited till my heart slowed into its normal thump. Then I walked calmly into Roy's room.

You're supposed to knock, Thumby, Roy said, without lookin up from the model airplane he was workin on.

Lookin good, I said, floppin down on the bed.

He didn't reply.

Thank you, Thumby, for that compliment, I said loudly.

He didn't even look up.

You're a mouthy kid for eight years old, Roy.

Are you really havin a baby, Thumbelina?

I ran my finger over the antlers on one of the moose in his bedspread. They were the first words he'd said directly to me since I'd come back.

I sure am, Roy.

You were mean to her.

His black hair curtained off his eyes as he sorted carefully through a pile of plastic plane parts.

What was it like, Roy, livin here with just Myrna before I came?

She was nicer to me then.

Nicer how?

We'd watch TV. She talked about her boyfriend and goin to California.

Were you sad when I showed up?

Won't you miss your baby? Roy said, without lookin up from his model airplane.

I held my chin in my hands. I was havin trouble breathin.

Do you miss your mom, Roy?

I saw her at Christmas.

What'd you do?

He rubbed glue along a piece of plane with his wide thumb. We opened presents.

Why'd she bring you back here?

Because I live here, Thumby.

~ ~ ~

I TOOK some money from my sock. I went to church and I lit a candle. My bony knees sunk into the kneeler. I cleared everything out of my throat. I had the place to myself and I filled it up with my talkin. I told em I was sorry for bein mean to her. It was her fault for rubbin my face in it. Once I got that out of the way I got down to business. I asked em all up there for help in locatin a decent mom and dad. Anybody who's free, I told em, and wants to pitch in. Except you, Mom. Why except me? she hollered in my head. Because all your taste is up your ass, I said. I thought she'd fire somethin back, but there was only huge, heavy church silence in my ears.

January, it was nice knowin you.

february

FEBRUARY TRICKED ME, STARTIN OUT DECENT. FOUR days in goin to hell in a hen basket.

That little dingbat was goin to make me come crawlin to apologize. I don't got any pride. On the fifth day I said, All right. I knew where to find her. I could hear em arguin from the front porch. I looked down at Black Bean in my arms and there was a scared look in her eyes. It's OK, I whispered. Their bark is worse than their bite. I pushed open the door. She and Stan were standin in the middle of the livin room, which has got a lot more furniture in it these days, arguin over the screechin boom box. Her eyes flicked over me and went back to his face. Her hands were in fists and them fists were lookin dangerous. I said, Come on, Black Bean, and I went upstairs to Dee Dee's old room. I stood at the window and stared at the puddles in the alley, clothes on the line that were too heavy with rain to move in the wind that stirred around in the branches. Reminded me of my mom for no reason. She didn't ever hang up clothes.

I sat down cross-legged on the floor and got my stomach comfortable and pulled out a Veronica and Betty comic from my coat. Black Bean sat in the opposite corner with her nose on her wet paws. I kept whackin the floor beside me sayin, Black Bean, won't you come over here? But she was in one of her depressed moods. She wouldn't even look at me.

Stan and Myrna were really goin at it downstairs. I figured she must of told him about her blood takin time to smell the roses. Nothin else would get his voice raised like that. Plus they were downin beers while they were at it. That never helps. Take it from a expert on the situation. I didn't hear nothin breakin so I figured whatever man. Fightin people don't want your big nose in their faces. That is one thing I know about life.

I love my Veronica and Betty comics because they are always havin adventures. I love their clothes and all the fun they get to have and the way they talk and did you ever notice how many friends they got? I used to say, Mom, me and you are pals like Veronica and Betty, don't you think? and my mom would say, Is that supposed to be a compliment?

In the back are ads to win stuff like radios and clocks. When I was little I sent away from the back of my Casper comic to sell Christmas cards, because you could earn enough to get a watch. What they did was send you a book of samples and you went around and knocked on doors and said, Scuse me, ma'am, would you like to buy some Christmas cards? And then you showed em the different types they could choose from.

I didn't sell any cards because I didn't have a knack for partin people with their money, but the thing was you got to keep the book of samples. They were beautiful samples with gold pop-out Christmas trees and sleighs stuffed with brightly wrapped presents and reindeer with nice eyes. I stuck em on the inside of my door and looked at em. One day Lester tore em down. He wanted to hit me, but he had made a promise to himself that he wouldn't hit me, so he had to do somethin else with his energy. Lester didn't like no signs of Christmas spirit. He didn't even want no Christmas tree in our livin room but every year my mom would say, Lester, we're havin one, in that voice of hers that meant no arguin, of course Lester didn't argue, he'd just hit you, he wasn't the kind of guy to debate it. But on Christmas mornin the tree was always there.

I was readin Veronica and Betty and not payin any attention to my dog, which was dumb of me. I got up to go pee and left the door open a crack. Next thing I heard was Stan yellin downstairs and Myrna screamin, Thum-*byyyyyyy*. I yanked up my jeans and tore down there, nearly flyin down on my stomach but catchin the railin just in time. He was chasin my little dog around the room with the broom. Then Stan's boot snagged in one of the guitar cords he had layin around there and he went flyin. Myrna went flyin on top of him. I ran over and opened the door, I was givin Black Bean a way out of the situation. She was thinkin the same thing. I didn't even have to say, Come on Black Bean, she flew out. Couple seconds later I heard the tires screech like fingernails down a chalk-board. A white Cadillac shot up Agnes's street. Why in heck didn't she stop in the front yard and wait for me?

I ran down Lumis Street. She was halfway down with her neck on the pavement and her bottom up on the side-walk. I called out to her, practically shoutin in her ear. But she didn't move her tail or her head, but since when does she do that? I carried her back to the front yard and sat down in the dirt with her. Her sides were movin. I checked her over for blood. I wiped her spit off on my sleeve and lifted my sweatshirt and pressed her head and neck against my swimmin fish. Her body was puttin out heat, but her nose was wet and chilly. I sat there waitin.

It took a while. Her breathin got lighter. I kept sittin there, lookin out over the rooftops below me, green and gray shingles. I thought of this TV show I'd seen where the fireman pulled a baby out of a swimmin pool and pushed its chest to get it breathin again. I didn't do that with Black Bean. I told her, It's up to you if you want to stay. After a while she was gone.

I felt pretty normal. I lifted her and I was glad that her body was still warm. I appreciated that. I carried her around back and laid her in the dirt and went in the kitchen for the mixin spoon and started scrapin out a hole under the kitchen window.

Myrna stuck her head out Dee Dee's bedroom win-dow. She saw me buryin my dog and she came down cryin and with this T-shirt to bury her in, sayin, Sorry sorry Stan is so sorry. The T-shirt landed on my spoon, and she was in the dirt cryin and sayin, This is like an omen, Thumby, isn't it? I covered Black Bean with TOO HOT TO HANDLE.

I kept on diggin.

You can't dig a deep enough hole with that, she said. I

started usin my fingers. I was down farther than you think. I wanted to get my dog in the ground and forget that I ever had cared about her.

You can't dig a decent hole like that, Thumby.

Shut up.

She planted her feet in my way. I shoved her. She landed on her ass on my pile of dirt. Fuck you, Thumbelina! Dirt came flyin at me. I ducked. Fuck you, Myrna.

She came at me hard. I shoved her back, her head thunked the side of the house. Then we went at each other with everything we had. She grabbed my sweatshirt, I sank my hand into her hair, she dragged her nails down my face, I smashed shoe marks into her bare legs. We screamed terrible things into each other's faces. We dragged each other down into the mud. She pulled my hair that I'd been growin all my life right out of my head. I let go of her. She fell on top of me. We weren't screamin for Black Bean.

Stan came and cleared his throat quietly and we saw that he had a shovel and that our legs were in the way of the hole and we dragged ourselves sideways. He gave Myrna his pack of Winstons and his Budweiser lighter and we rested our backs against the house and smoked cigarettes in the rain while he dug out a good deep private hole. I picked up the T-shirt bundle and her body was still warm and I couldn't go any farther. Here, honey. Stan took my dog from me and he laid her carefully in the hole and dropped the dirt in gently. Then he said he had to take the shovel back and I stood there in the rain feelin confused.

Maybe you ought to marry him, Myrna. We were standin in the kitchen waitin for the kettle to boil for tea.

Now she tells me.

Dishes were everywhere, but she'd had the floor replaced. The linoleum was bright and new for this minute anyway.

He says he don't want to be a daddy a fourth time. He don't have it in him.

My face felt numb. I touched my lips with my fingers. Myrna, go easy on him. I felt my lips move.

It's his fault what just happened to your dog, Thumby.

Myrna. You've been after me all this time to like him, now I got my toe in the ballpark of that feelin, please appreciate it.

I went into the livin room. She was right on my tail. What's takin him so long to return a shovel?

My long finger hit the buttons of her telephone. I didn't expect to get her this time either, but the secretary said, Can you hold? Then the lady came on, Thumbelina? What a surprise, I wasn't expecting to hear from you again.

I spoke quietly. They don't got to be rich, Mrs. Conn, but they got to be nice.

Good attitude, but money never hurts.

She needs a room of her own and a horse would be a bonus. And for Christmas, nice things under the tree like stuffed animals and perfume and the good kind of chocolates. The dad has to work every day. And I'm not talkin drivin a truck. The mom better have her head screwed on tight.

You drive a hard bargain, Thumbelina, Candace Conn said.

I do?

She sounded pretty when she laughed. It was a nice sound to hear right then. I think we can manage it all.

The chocolate doesn't have to be that good.

How about a college education instead of the horse?

Don't find me a lady who cuts hair.

You can trust me, Thumbelina.

I kicked it around. Mrs. Conn, I will do a first and trust you.

She said the Christofolettis were right up my alley. That he was an investment banker and she was a pediatrician. No kids. I said, What's a pediatrician. A doctor for babies, she said. I said, Oh, man, not another doctor in my life. She said, She makes pottery in her spare time. She has a pottery wheel. She sells her teapots. She makes amazing teapots, dear, Candace Conn said. You can meet them in a couple of days and see for yourself.

I said, Are they nice? Mrs. Conn said, That's in the eye of the beholder, but I think so. Then a long silence came between us. I didn't touch it because she had put it there.

Thumbelina?

Yeah, Mrs. Conn.

Another silence, just as long.

Thumbelina?

What, Mrs. Conn.

Presentation is very important, Thumbelina.

I got her drift right off. I asked her what she wanted me to wear. She said she just wanted me to take extra-special care with myself on the day that I met them. She said, Could I wear a dress? I said, OK. Actin like I had one. Just like I used to act like I had a father who was away on business. She said, Would I comb my lovely hair and put a ribbon in it? That pink would be a lovely color for me because of the pink in my cheeks.

You are very pretty, Thumbelina.

Aw, you're just sayin that because you feel sorry for me.

I think your life has been sad.

I waited.

The way you look at me. And you don't speak of your mother.

More sad than most people's?

Yes.

So what am I supposed to do about it?

Let me help you.

You shouldn't drop things like that on me, Mrs. Conn, when you don't know anything about my life. That's a pretty heavy thing, to tell somebody they've had a sad life.

I want to help you, Thumbelina. Will you let me help you?

I'll think about it. Yeah. You're helpin me already.

I can help you find parents . . . *people* that you like and that you trust.

Tears rolled down my cheeks. You think there's people out there that could love a baby that's not their own?

I don't think it, I know it. It's my business. I see it happen every day. Her voice was firm, like her handshake the day I met her. When a woman can't have her own baby she has a special love for the one she adopts, because she knows she doesn't have any right to it but by the grace of God and the generosity of the girl—*woman*—who gave it up.

Thanks for sayin that, Mrs. Conn.

The lady asked me if I was all right. I said, Yeah. She said, You're sure? I can come over for a while, we can talk some more.

I looked at Myrna who was starin out the window.

I'm all right, Mrs. Conn.

After I hung up the phone I kept sittin there in Myrna's livin room lookin at my bare, white toe in my shoe. My body felt weighted down by what I'd just done. That was my sadness. I knew I was doin the right thing and my heart felt bigger, knockin in my body. My baby was goin to arrive in this world free of me and my mom and our past of yellin and fightin and hurtin each other. I grew her, but I didn't have no right to her. I had to lay her in somebody else's arms. It broke my heart thinkin, what if they hurt her, but I thought, I'll just have to find her people that are perfect and won't. Dr. K.'s lectures nagged at me. But I shoved his voice out my ear. If I told that lawyer I was dyin my baby's chances would be shot. Mrs. Conn's jaw would hit the table, she'd ditch me. Nobody was savin up to go to heaven these days. Nobody would touch my girl with a ten-foot pole. I didn't want people usin my daughter to get a place in heaven anyway. I didn't want nobody usin her for nothin.

Nobody could tell by lookin at me that I was dyin. You die so slow. Lots of girls in the world are thin. Lots of em cough once in a while. Now they were tellin me I was pretty, man that was in the nick of time.

My mom always did things half-assed. I am not my mom. I was goin to find her parents with money in the bank and a driveway and a garbage can at the end of it. They would own a lawn mower and good clothes. She was goin to have a room of her own with lots of little bottles of perfume on the dresser and she was not goin to have to drag that dresser over to the door every night. She was goin to buy presents from the mall that people were goin to go ooh and aah over, not be dumpin 7-Eleven candy bars out of no paper sack.

I knew this like I knew my feet that I was starin at.

~ ~ ~

THE CHRISTOFOLETTIS live on a lake near Seattle. We left the highway and winded down a road into the woods, but not the kind that you shoot animals in. These were private. (I saw the sign.)

We went through this gate (luckily Mrs. Conn knew the password to say into the little black box) and over the little hill. There were six houses on the lake. Mrs. Conn headed for the biggest one. The lawn rolled from the front porch down to the water and it was green as a golf course (amazin for February) and short as Lester's hair in the picture from his army days. And all the windows shinin down like mirrors on us, and the wood and stone in all its glory.

Mrs. Conn wanted to come up with me but I said, No, thanks, ma'am. Because I wanted to see em on my own first, even though my heart was knockin all over my chest.

You're sure you don't want some moral support? she said. It's not that I don't want it, I said. Well, you look lovely, Thumbelina, really lovely, they are going to love you.

With that pep talk in my ears I crossed the driveway, which could pass for that highway out there, and walked up the wooden steps lined with planters. I whacked the doorbell with my fist. Did it again in case they were deaf. You got to act like you mean it with rich types man.

Mrs. Christofoletti is pretty. She is almost as pretty as my mother. That's what I noticed when I stood on the welcome mat waitin for her to finish lookin me up and down and let me in. She wore a turquoise dress like my mom's ring and my two bad eyes and it hung like quality and I took that as a good omen. On her feet were tiny little black slippers with tiny little heels and her hair was striped light and dark blonde, and didn't move when she moved her head. I washed my hair last night because even though it was pretty far down on my list of important things to do with my energy supply, I wanted to make a good impression like Mrs. Conn said. Of course then I went and fell asleep on it when it was soakin wet and there was no repairin it.

So she noticed that. And she noticed how thick my glasses were and the fact that I was about a foot taller than her, and most of all in that first minute of meetin each other, she noticed my classy dress I bought from the mall. Forgot to mention that. I went shoppin alone, without Myrna, because I needed somethin classy, and I didn't want her distractin me. The mall doesn't have too many classy shops and normally I don't mind, because I like sweatshirts and regular old jeans. But I needed somethin special and I had a hundred bucks in my shoe which Mrs. Conn had folded into my hand for spendin money. I went in the shop by the china store where my mom's plates were stacked in the window. Can I help you? the lady said, and I said, Yeah, I need a classy dress for an important occasion. What occasion is that? My eyes shot past her to the merchandise. I didn't want to get too chummy. I pawed around, her tailin me. I found it on a rack behind some other dresses that weren't half as classy. It was navy blue with a wide collar and sleeves that stopped halfway to my wrists when I tried it on, but it was the style. It skimmed straight over my stomach and stopped below my knees. I sure looked classy.

Nice to meet you, Thumbelina, I'm Fran Christofoletti, won't you come in?

I didn't hike up all your steps for the exercise, I said.

Below me, Mrs. Conn's car backed up slowly. Then the door closed. The smell of cookin meat knocked me over. Man. That's a smell I would of appreciated a year ago. Now it just gagged me.

She shoved my coat in the closet that was stuffed with

long important lookin coats and took me down the hall. Got a glimpse of a fireplace in the livin room, then the kitchen opened up all clean and shiny, the lake right there through the windows.

She pulled out a stool for me at the counter and said, Anything to drink?

Coke.

I'm afraid I don't have caffeine free.

Regular's fine.

Thumbelina? You aren't supposed to drink caffeine when you are pregnant.

I'm not?

She licked her lips. No, honey. Didn't your doctor tell you that? You are seeing a doctor?

Oh yeah. A real good one.

One of her eyebrows cocked as if to say, What kind of doctor is he that he didn't tell you to avoid caffeine? How about herbal tea? she said.

You got Sprite?

Diet all right?

Fran Christofoletti had a quick way of smilin like a eye blinkin. She poured the pop and said, Thumbelina is a beautiful name (what a salesman), then she asked me if I'd like a cookie and hauled down a plate of chocolate chip from the cupboard. They were still warm.

She eyed me as I chewed. I didn't like the way she was lookin at me, or maybe I was just mad at her for ownin a house my mom would of killed for. The countertops were white and black tile, the floors gleamed, there was a microwave and dishwasher and electric can opener and a bunch of other appliances that did who knows what.

So how far along are you? she asked.

I'm due in eight weeks and some change.

You don't look it. Who *is* your doctor, sweetheart? You should put on at least twenty-five pounds.

I've put on ten, ma'am.

I don't believe it, dear. Where is it hiding?

This is a slimming dress, Mrs. Christofoletti, I smiled.

Well, dear. All the toes and fingers will be formed by now, the heart and lungs, your baby is just sleeping off its last little bit of peace and quiet. Have you found out the sex?

Her eyes were bluish gray.

She is a girl, Mrs. Christofoletti.

The lady smiled. So many of the mothers I see tell me they had similar premonitions. Invariably they are right.

No boy would have the nerve to live inside me. I reached for another cookie.

Please call me Fran.

The kettle whistled and she poured it over a teabag. Somethin beeped on her. She took it off and eyed it. I told them not to page me. She went to the phone. She said she was busy, not to page her, into the mouthpiece. She said, No I'm sorry, call Dr.—She hung up. She pulled up a stool opposite me. She picked up a cookie which was a good sign, a lady that eats sweets. But then she put it down.

This must be a scary time for you, Thumbelina.

I eyed her suspiciously.

You're so young, and this is such a stressor for your body and mind. Having a baby without a support structure around you.

I got a good friend.

One thing I am worried about, being a pediatrician myself, is the kind of OB care you are getting. I can arrange for a colleague to see you in her practice. Free, of course.

You make these cookies? I reached for another one.

Irvina did. Our help. Now, I know you have a doctor at your own clinic—

You mean like a maid?

She sipped her tea, watchin me a second. Well, with the schedules that Victor and I keep, we need somebody to keep the place in order.

I moved right in for the kill. So you work a lot?

Well, to be honest, right now I do. I have a pretty heavy patient load. The new mothers get so anxious. But if we adopt, my partners will cover for me for three months. After that I'm going back only part-time. I'm forty-three years old, and I've given a lot of my life to medicine. Precisely because I couldn't have children. Now I'm ready to be a mother. I think I have a lot to give a child.

Out the window waves rolled on the green lake. Where's your husband?

He'll be here any minute. I thought it would be nice if we had a little time alone, to get to know one another.

Candace Conn said he's an investment banker.

Yes, that's right—

Mrs. Leffer works in a bank. That's the foster lady I live with.

She lifted her tea. Her fingernails were oval and covered with clear pale polish. And what about your father?

He's a folk singer down in California. That was his coat I was wearin that you hung up, my mom stole it from him. She sewed the fur collar on it to make it more feminine. I play guitar and one day I'll learn harmonica. How long have you been waitin to adopt a baby, Mrs. Christofoletti?

Over two years now.

That's a long time.

Yes. Yes, it is.

If I waited two years for somethin I would be expectin it to be the coolest thing around. I would have real high expectations of it. No matter how great it was, I would still be disappointed. I have wanted a horse for fourteen years, for example. No way could any horse live up to what my idea of ownin it has become.

Mrs. Christofoletti was starin down into her tea as if the meanin of life floated in it. Yes, I know what you are saying, Thumbelina. But by the same token, perhaps after waiting so long for something, you know how to appreciate it. You don't and never will take it for granted. When I was a medical student I did six weeks in OB. I saw so many girls come into the clinic to have their babies. Girls your age, girls that had dropped out of school, run off from home, girls that were abandoned by their boyfriends. It was so easy for them. They didn't realize how lucky they were. They took it for granted. I was so jealous. It's why I didn't go into OB. It was too painful to deliver babies. I settled on just taking care of them once they were born. Would you like more Sprite?

Her shoulders were very narrow. I watched her pour. She's goin to be a lot taller than you, Fran. I'm just under six feet.

Yes.

My dad was tall.

And your mother?

About your height. She held it against me.

Why?

Givin me this name.

Thumbelina is a lovely name.

It never fit me.

Through the doorway I could see a table with a white cloth and silver candlesticks and silver forks and a big silver bowl full of green apples. That where you eat?

For fancy dinners, yes. If it's just Victor and myself, we eat in here.

What's a typical dinner for you two?

She blinked. You don't have to worry, Thumbelina. I don't expect your daughter to look like me—

I held up my hand to stop her. I wasn't in the mood to talk about it. Any chance I could see some of your pottery stuff? Mrs. Conn told me you got a pottery wheel.

Are you interested in pottery?

I am interested in beautiful things.

I don't know if you can call my teapots beautiful.

We heard a door slam far away. Oh, that's Victor. Honey? she called, and darted into the hall. I had the feelin the heat I was applyin was gettin to her. He came in and shook my hand and said, Nice to meet you, and we all took our drinks (the doctor got him a beer) and we went into the room with the fireplace. The kind of thing my mom drooled over in magazines. But my mom would never have a white rug on the floor, too easy to get dirty. You have got to be really rich to have a white rug on the floor. The chairs and couches had bright-colored pillows that filled up all the places where you are supposed to sit. Victor took his pipe off the mantel and then sat in the armchair. He had a bald head that had seen some sun lately, and brown eyes and a nose like a beak you see on birds around the park, although don't get the impression that he looked mean.

Fran sat me down on the couch. She took the wicker chair to my left. I looked down at my tall-girl shoes that lay like black rowboats in the white carpet. I was shiverin a little from cold and from nerves.

I was telling Thumbelina that I want her to see an OB friend of mine, Dr. Beedlan, honey.

Is that all right with you, Thumbelina? Victor smiled at me.

I got a doctor I like just fine.

She has a doctor she likes just fine. Victor smiled at his wife.

Fran Christofoletti sorted her hair with her fingers. Thumbelina. She smiled. Don't you want the best health care that you can get? Regardless of whether you decide to keep your baby or give it up, don't you want the best care for it?

I will think about it, I said, compromisin to shut her up.

Thumbelina is a lovely name, Victor said.

Don't give it to her.

He took his pipe from his mouth. Oh? Why?

If you're lookin for a name, I would suggest Angel. For my mom, who was Angelica. You want to see a picture of her? I pulled out the one that I had shown Mrs. Conn and passed it over.

Oh, my. You do look alike.

Not really. You think so? The sun loved her head.

Your noses and your cheekbones.

Naw, I said, smilin. Really?

They handed it back. Do you have one of your baby's father?

No, but brown hair and black eyes pretty much sums him up.

What do you think of the name Caroline? Fran said.

Or Ariel? Do you like that, Thumbelina? I'm a big Sylvia Plath fan, the Mister said.

She doesn't know who Sylvia Plath is, do you, dear?

A poet, Thumbelina.

A melancholy, *morose* poet who killed herself. I prefer a lighter name like Whitby.

Whitney?

No, Whitby. It's a little town on the east coast of England. Victor and I had our honeymoon there.

Her husband smiled. That'll set her apart from the crowd.

What did I hear you say?

Mr. Christofoletti took his pipe out of his mouth. I said that naming her Whitby would set her apart from the crowd.

How dare you even think of doin that.

Victor didn't mean it in a bad way, Thumbelina. He just meant—

I don't want her standin out in any crowd. You hear me? I want her smack in the middle of the crowd. You give her a normal name.

The doorbell rang. The husband and wife looked at each other, then at me. Mr. Christofoletti got up to answer it. Soon as he was out of the room the doctor came over and sat down next to me. I felt that she wanted to hug me, but was worried about crossin a boundary, so she just patted my leg.

I know it's scary, giving your baby up to people you don't know. You want the best for it.

Beads collected in her lap from her long necklace.

We have a lot of love to give, Thumbelina. We've worked a lot of years to get to this point where we're comfortable, and now we want nothing more than to have a child. We don't care what the child looks like. If it's a boy or girl, tall or short, brunette or blond.

She's goin to look like me, ma'am.

Then we'd be very happy parents indeed.

I got to think this over. I got to think. I can't make a quick decision on this.

{224}

She gently pressed my arm. Of course, dear. Take your time. Shall I give you my beeper number if you have any other questions? There is so much I'd like to tell you about us. We have a lot of friends. We're very active in the neighborhood.

What neighborhood, I said, turnin my head. Far below I saw Mrs. Conn's white Lexus.

There's a lot of houses tucked in the trees. And we have more than all that. We have values.

My mom used to collect those. Coupons for double off.

She smiled at my stupid joke. Old-fashioned values. Victor and I don't believe in divorce, your baby will always have a father and mother. That is very important, Thumbelina.

I bent down to take my shoe off and poked my hand in it like I was lookin for a rock. I was usin my mom's trick of hidin my eyes with my hair. Water dripped onto the rug. Why couldn't I go back in time to bein a baby and have somebody adopt me that could love me like I had the feelin this lady and her husband could love my baby? Why did you have to be new to the planet for people to want you?

Mrs. Conn came into the room, savin me. She came in on Victor's arm. She seemed to know him. She sat down for a couple minutes and they talked about this and that. We all agreed on another appointment in a couple weeks.

You don't have to come up with an opinion now, dear, she said as we merged onto the highway.

An opinion is easy, Mrs. Conn.

Oh? her eyebrows said. Did you like them?

Of course I like em.

You look a little uncertain.

{225}

No, I'm uncertain about whether to make em parents or not, not about whether I liked em. Big difference.

If they're right, you'll know it.

She's awful skinny.

So are you.

They spent more money on the furniture in that house than my mom made all her life at the beauty shop and they are goin to expect too much from my baby.

Mrs. Conn shot me a glance. Your mother is a beautician?

That lady doesn't look like she'd get her hands dirty if you paid her.

She's a doctor. Of course she gets her hands dirty.

She wants a blond baby.

She said that?

I can tell.

Oh, come on, now, Thumbelina.

She colors her hair. I am the daughter of a beautician, don't forget.

Every woman in America colors her hair, dear.

My mom didn't.

Naturally blonde, was she?

Her father's hair is dark brown.

Hmm.

That'll foul things up.

A brown-haired little girl will be just fine.

Fran might hold it against her.

Thumbelina—

I guess she'd be all that the lady can get, though, right? So she'd appreciate her. But what if they adopt another kid in a few years and like it better?

Mrs. Conn looked at me as long as she could, tryin to search somethin out in my face. She turned back to the road. There are no guarantees in life, Thumbelina. I can tell you've been hurt, and that it is difficult for you to trust. But if it's any comfort to you, I've got . . . unusual couples that will never have a chance of adopting a Caucasian baby because of their lifestyle. I've been going to China for two years now, to bring babies back for them, and not one of them has contacted me to tell me they're unhappy.

What's wrong with their lifestyle?

That's not the point—

Mrs. Conn?

They're lesbian couples.

You mean there isn't any man involved?

That's right.

Can you find me ladies like that?

She kept her eyes on the road, but I could tell by the silence that she was surprised. Are you sure you want lesbians raising your baby?

I'd like to meet some.

Well, let's take this slow. Let's meet the Christofolettis again first, or you'll get overwhelmed.

I clicked on the radio. It was a Simon & Garfunkel song. My mom used to have one of their records.

Dear? She spoke loudly to be heard. It's absolutely essential that you meet a wide variety of couples and make an informed decision. You've got plenty of time. You aren't due for nine weeks.

I turned down the la la la's. That's not what you told me when I called you the first time. You said I didn't have much time to waste.

She winked. I wanted you as my client.

Dr. K.'s right about lawyers, I muttered.

When she pulled into Heddinger Circle the windows of the house were dark.

The bank has her workin late, I explained.

But Saturday is still on? Mrs. Conn said.

They got this rule where if one of their customers stands in line more than five minutes, they pay em five bucks. People cheat. She keeps a clock on her desk.

The lawyer unsnapped her belt and leaned over and hugged me. I hugged her back, but just a little. I had to be careful. I might never let go.

On Saturday it was me who opened the door. Mrs. Leffer sucked in her stomach and said, Get that, Thumbelina? from where she sat in the velvet armchair in the livin room. She needed the sides of it touchin her to feel secure because she was afraid of such a successful lady. Mrs. Conn sat on the couch with her legs crossed. I brought em coffee. She wore a checkered skirt that showed her pretty nice legs and a jacket that matched with a cream blouse tied in a big bow at her neck which is not graceful like my mom's neck, but that's not her fault. After I got the ball rollin I went outside and sat on the back step and eyed the sky and when I got bored I watched Roy kick the ball on the other side of the Cyclone fence.

I nearly fell over when the orange head rounded the corner.

Don't I know you from somewhere?

Howdy. She was about to step over me and slide open the door but I hollered, You can't go in there!

Why not?

An important meeting is goin on.

I left my suitcases behind, she said.

I dragged her back. Well, you got to wait.

She flopped down beside me. I threw up this mornin.

The adoption lawyer is here, Myrna, behave, OK?

Goin to keep an eye on it this time. He bought me all these maternity clothes. He's bein really cool, makin me give up smokin.

He don't have anything to feel guilty about, does he?

The door slid open behind our backs. Here you are, Thumbelina.

Mrs. Conn, this is Myrna, my friend. They shook hands. Myrna's green eyes traveled up and down Mrs. Conn's pretty legs and took in the quality of her outfit and the red highlights in her loopy curls which were pulled back in a black velvet bow.

Mrs. Leffer's face was pink underneath her silver ringlets. I knew she'd been sneakin stuff into her coffee in the kitchen. It got pinker when she saw Myrna. I left em to sort out the suitcases and followed Mrs. Conn around the house to her Lexus. She said not to worry, she'd call me about the lesbians.

I woke up in the night and for a second I thought I heard Myrna breathin above me and I stopped my own breathin and listened.

Myrn? I whispered.

I got up and felt around up there but it was all mattress. I crawled back into my own bed.

I was afraid of sleepin on my stomach and suffocatin her. I was afraid that the part of me that hates him would make me roll over on her. I did not shut my eyes. I hummed Johnny Cash songs and looked at the moon that was also passin the night awake.

I find it very very easy to be true I find my heart it all belongs to you yes I'll admit that I'm a fool for you because you're mine I walk the line

~ ~ ~

I TOOK the bus to Beeson Avenue and went into the shoppin plaza where I'd got my stuff to make orange tulips. This time I had my eye on the pots of flowers in the home improvement center. Yeah, I said to the lady in the green apron who asked if she could help me. Which do you think is more respectful, these or these? What is it for? she said. A situation, I said, where I need to show respect. Well, I am personally a fan of red, she said, and nodded at the bitty red flowers. I said thanks. And hauled the huge purple plant up to the checkout. I said to the guy, Is it too early? For what? he said. For plantin, I said. Don't I have to wait till spring? He said, Look outside. It's come early.

Whatshisface was singin come on baby light my fire as I came up the front porch. I wondered if I should knock, in case they were kissin or somethin. I banged the wood. No answer. Did it again. No answer. Figured oh well. She was layin on the foldout couch with Stan the man. They were on their backs. Stan was snorin, Myrna was shootin smoke at the ceiling from a little white cig. I sat down in the arm-chair she had recently bought and crossed my legs.

Well? I said after a minute.

Well, what?

Aren't you goin to offer me nothin to drink?

There's a half case of Coors in there. She fluttered her hand toward the kitchen. Get me one, will you?

I brought back one beer for her and sat back down.

You on the wagon?

I'm with child. I put my nose in the air.

Oh, God. You hear that? She whacked Stan. She's with fuckin child. Well, so am I. She swigged the beer. Stan continued snorin. Well? She propped herself on her elbow so she could down beer and also look at me. How's the search shapin up?

You could have spent one night at Mrs. Leffer's.

Not this again.

It wouldn't kill you to show some appreciation to her.

You didn't come all the way over here to say that, so get to your point.

I sighed. I needed her advice too bad to argue.

I met the so-called perfect couple.

Her eyes snapped alert. What's perfect about em?

They're rich.

Myrna blew pot at the ceiling and chuckled. What's the problem then?

Who said there was a problem?

You look worried.

It's natural under the circumstances, don't you think?

And you like the man all right?

He's all right, I said.

Her green eyes glittered. I figured that would be the snag.

There's no snag, Myrna.

You're afraid he might hurt her.

Myrna, I'm not in the mood.

You're easy to read as a McDonald's sign. You're thinkin he might hurt her. Don't tell me you're not thinkin it, I just said it for you to bring it out in the open because you shut everything away in your dark, dumb head.

You really have got the ability to piss me off, Myrna.

I shoved myself out of the armchair. In the kitchen I got a cold beer. It was sour and good and I poured it down my sore throat and stared out the window at Black Bean's rock, rememberin.

She was hollerin for me. I took my time comin back. I leaned my shoulder up against the doorjamb. Her livin room was a pigsty. Clothes were draped over all the new furniture she had bought, includin a long steel lamp growin like graceful grass out of the floor.

Interestin decoratin, Myrna.

I'm goin to finish the remodelin that my sister started. Those green walls in the kitchen are goin.

I think a softer yellow would be nice in the bathroom.

So what else is perfect about em, besides their money?

What if he does hurt her, Myrna?

Myrna sighed. Did he seem like the type?

I shrugged. Who can tell.

I guess it's not the kind of question you can come right out and ask.

No, it's not. Not without givin somethin away.

Her eyes narrowed. You mean like implyin that you've had experience with the kind of man you're afraid he might be?

Stan snored on his back. Asleep he looked all right. Nice, fat, and old. She watched me watch him.

This doctor says my baby might be infected, Myrna. I might have passed it to her.

Her little tongue cleared beer off her lip. She waited.

He says if I keep takin AZT he might whack it out of her, though. I guess you can whack it out of a baby. Beats me why you can't whack it out of a girl. He says I got to have it through a needle when she's comin out of me. A needle. Man, the guy is deaf. But that's a seriously bad time for gettin infected, when the kid's bein born.

So if you do what the doctor says it could come out—
you know—all right?

Sounds like it.

She sighed. That means comin clean.

Yep.

Bye-bye to decent parents.

Yeah, that's the problem.

So what are you goin to do?

I got the strangest feelin, Myrna. I plopped down in the
armchair.

You goin to narrow it down for me?

I crossed my ankles. Well, you know how I got this
feelin that she's a girl—

You've mentioned it only about ten billion times.

I got a feelin that she's OK.

Yeah? Like you had the feelin it was my blood stoppin
to smell the roses? my friend snorted.

I coughed delicately. Nah. I believed you were pregnant. I was bein mean about that.

Well, fuck you.

I was jealous Myrn.

She shook her orange curls.

Man, do I have to spell it out for you? You get to keep your
baby. I'm never goin to know what it's like to be a mom.

You think I'll carry it all the way this time? she whispered, sittin up. Since you got the ability to know things?

Myrn. I shook my head. I don't know nothin. All I got
is a feelin.

She fell back against the sofa. The covers fell down off
her naked breasts. Then you don't need to tell that lawyer
nothin, do you?

I chewed my lip. Well, it's just a feelin.

Considerin for the sake of argument that your baby is a she—

She is, Myrn. Loud and clear.

She is goin to be a carbon copy of you.

Are you a carbon copy of your mom, Myrna?

Well, I got her knack of choosin men that sleep all day, I'll tell you that much.

She elbowed Stan till his eyes popped open. Don't you have to be at work or somethin, Stanley? The guy yawned, showin big teeth, and lifted the beer out of her hand. You shouldn't be drinkin this when you're pregnant.

He poured it down his hatch.

I'm not far enough along for it to matter, she muttered, tryin to grab it back.

I'm not takin the risk, honey, Stan said, and handed her the empty beer can and swung his legs out from under the covers and stood there completely naked, in front of me. His chest was black with hair, and hair curled up from his little carrot hangin worn out between his bony legs. He looked straight into my eyes as he passed.

Thumby? Under her mop of orange hair Myrna almost looked pretty. I felt sorry for her, suddenly, because I'd felt that somethin in Stan had loosened itself from the idea of havin a kid with her and was floatin away.

What, Myrna, I whispered.

Her green eyes did not blink. She felt it too. They sound exactly like what you want.

You think so.

What money can't buy, you don't need. Thumby?

What.

I just need him in my life till my kid comes, she said softly. After that I'm lettin him go.

I let that hang in the air between us and did not touch it, for fear of her claimin it back.

She lay back down in the crumpled sheets. All I could see was her nose. That ceiling must have fielded a lot of starin in its day from girls like her.

I picked up my pot of flowers and walked through the kitchen. Bein out in the cold cleared my head. I rolled the rock off my dog and the dirt came up easily in my fingers. I set the roots in deep. It felt good to leave somethin pretty there. I lit a cigarette and watched the towels in the alley flutter in the light breeze. I didn't go in to say good-bye to em. About three or four garbage cans down I just turned around and looked back at the purple spot I'd left in their backyard.

~ ~ ~

I'VE missed you.

Likewise.

You're taking your AZT?

Yeah.

Haven't been feeling too sick?

I'm all right.

How's the adoption business going?

All right.

How many have you met so far?

One.

That all?

I'm picky.

Don't be too picky.

You didn't tell Mrs. Conn.

Tell her what?

That I got. You know.

I can't tell her.

I am supposed to be meetin her doctor this afternoon. Goin to have to sweet talk her quite a bit to make up for this. She thinks I'm not gettin good health care from Dr. Miligiwamny. Not to mention what I'm gettin from you. She doesn't know I'm seein you. I'm surprised she hasn't asked me how I know you. She's not too nosy, like some people. I thought you were goin to call her and tell her all about me.

He took the heart thing off of my heart and took his hands off my stomach and said, You can sit up now.

He went over to the sink to wash his hands. His red laces dragged over the floor. I considered gettin down and tyin em for him.

Why didn't you tell her I got what I got, Dr. K.?

He ripped out a paper towel. Because I am bound by oath not to divulge information about my patients to any-one, lawyers included.

What if I pass it to my baby?

It doesn't matter. I am still bound by oath. But that *is* something I want to discuss with you. He sat down on the stool and crossed his skin and boner arms. You're taking your pills?

Every single one.

Optimally, you would have begun the treatments ear-lier.

Dr. K., she was swimmin inside me for weeks and weeks before I even knew she existed.

He fiddled with the knot on his bandanna. Any idea when you were actually infected?

You have got to be kiddin. I laced my hands together and hooked em over my knee.

Take a guess, sweetheart.

The bridge of his ex-wife's glasses was warped out of shape to fit over his nose. Are you askin me the first time I got poked by the queer? I was ... I don't know. That was a few years ago. We had moved out of Ravenhead where things were startin to happen. My mom caught me on his lap one day. We weren't, you know, doin nothin or anything. Just listenin to music.

What did she do?

Fixed it so I got my own bedroom.

Did she talk to you about it?

My mom didn't talk about anything but permin hair and gettin manicures and what we were havin for dinner. She wasn't a big talker by any means.

Hot tears fell onto my bare knees. He looked at the eye chart on the wall to give me privacy. Dr. K.'s bandanna was crumpled hard in his fist.

The worst thing about this whole dyin young thing is I won't ever know what it's like to get kissed. He never kissed me. He didn't like kissin. That was the main reason he didn't like Cary Grant movies. Too much kissin.

Dr. K. kept starin at the eye chart. I reached for my socks. It's not all it's cracked up to be, Thumbelina.

Comin from Mr. Four Wives Man who obviously can't stop believin in kissin.

That's enough, he said firmly. The reason I want the lawyer to know you have AIDS, Thumbelina, is not to meddle in your life, believe it or not. As I told you before, I am only thinking about the health of your child.

Can't you just do a little test on her when she comes out and tell me if she has it?

I'm afraid not. It takes time before we can do that effectively.

Hearin this irritated me greatly.

Dr. K.—I said tiredly, pullin my jeans on under my gown. Dr. K., I sighed, I can't risk it. She is goin to have every opportunity in life as long as I keep quiet.

You want the best for your child, he nodded.

Nice of you to agree with me, finally.

His skinny arm squeezed my shoulders and he kissed me, way too high. Won't be washin my forehead again.

Think of the parents, Thumbelina. Six months, two years, down the line, they discover their child is ill with something that could have been prevented. Is that fair?

Where'd you get a stupid idea that the world is fair, Dr. K.? And number two, what if she's fine? They'll just go on lovin her into their old age.

I can't force you to divulge the truth, but I am going to lean on you pretty hard.

I sighed. The guy up there wants me. I pointed at the ceiling. Not my baby.

He stopped scribblin on his note board.

She must be gettin lonely. Never could do without me for long.

A smile worked its way into the corner of his mouth and spread. Where do you get it from?

What?

Your optimism.

I can sing too.

This subject isn't closed, Thumbelina.

Thank you, February, for bringin spring.

march

THE SHOP MYRNA FOUND WAS ON THE TOP FLOOR OF
this art gallery near Bean Park. Our shoulders nearly
touched the walls as we climbed the stairs. The sign over
the door said exactly what she'd said. They cure many
things. The waitin room was so small we had to ration the
air. They made me take off all my clothes (I'm gettin used
to it) and lay down on the table. She'd told me it was some
kind of Chinese shop, so I was expectin a little guy with
slanty eyes, but this one was tall with wavy blond hair that
he obviously helps out with highlights because I am the
daughter of a beautician, don't forget. He took my wrist in

his hand and counted out loud. He made me stick out my tongue. White and wet, he said. Hmm.

I eyed him. Myrna was frownin at me from behind him, sayin with those green eyes, if you give him lip, Thumby, I'll knock your head in.

Everybody experiences AIDS in their bodies in a different way, the man said in his low voice that Myrna obviously thought was sexy by the way she was starin at him. The tongue is like a road map to reading a person's state of health, he said. I will choose acupoints based on what your body tells me. It is like creating a painting. Now, going by the state of your tongue—

Hocus pocus. I avoided Myrna's eyes.

It's white and wet.

Most people's tongues are wet, I said.

Thumbelina, Myrna muttered, warnin me with her eyes.

And this thick, whitish coating on it—

Dr. K. gave me medicine for it.

Who?

My AIDS doctor.

The guy stood back and his jaw unhinged. Is he a naturopath?

A what path?

He crossed his arms. You can't mix Western medicine with TCM. I don't allow it.

I'll give you double, Myrna said. If you would just get busy shovin the needles into her.

Hey, get some respect in your voice.

See, Myrna said. See how quick her moods swing?

She's definitely got a Qi and yin deficiency, the man said.

That's what I thought, Myrna said.

Her acupoints are L1, L7, L9, B13, and L20. Close your eyes.

Amazinly I closed em. Hot oil trickled down my shoulders and my back. I stiffened, feelin his hands rubbin it into my skin, but Myrna was there so I knew he wouldn't do nothin fancy. I started to relax. The tightness slipped out of my back. I didn't know I had fallen asleep until Myrna shook my shoulder. Come on, Thumby.

Where is he? He didn't do the needles yet.

Yeah, he did.

He did?

Had em pokin out of you everywhere, man.

It was just me and her in the room. The candles were blown out and the lights were on.

How do you feel? she asked, handin me my clothes.

Tired.

Thumby, I just paid one hundred bucks for this. Can't you at least pretend you feel good? Just to make me happy? Tears loaded up her gorgeous eyes.

I'm sorry, Myrna. My selfishness drained out of me. I feel spectacular.

When I got home there was a message on the notepad in Mrs. Leffer's fat handwritin that said, *Call C. Conn.* Her bedroom door was closed. She was in there a lot lately. Roy was kickin the ball in the street. I watched him out the slidin door. It was gettin lighter in the evenings now. His black hair flung up into the air as he ran after the ball. He was so little in his striped T-shirt. Somewhere in this city was his mom, livin and breathin.

I punched out the number on her push-button phone. I've got another couple for you to meet, Thumbelina.

I want to see Fran Christofoletti.

Fran and Victor?

Is that what I said, Mrs. Conn? Gettin poked with needles had made me feel more tired than ever. I sank into a plastic foam chair at the dinner table. I want to see her alone, Mrs. Conn, man to man.

Silence while she thought this over. Right. I will see what I can do.

Tell her I'm lookin forward to seein her teapots.

~ ~ ~

IT TOOK most of March before that day came. My long feet hit each one of those steps like they meant it and my classy dress fluttered all around my legs. The pink clip held back a slab of yellow hair. I looked good in the mirror hangin on Mrs. Leffer's bedroom door. Never would of guessed I was dyin.

Fran took me into the kitchen and picked up the tray of coffee and cookies and I followed her butt in expensive black pants down steep stairs with carpet that killed any sound. We were in a room that was sunk into the ground up to the window. The walls were the yellow I suggested Myrna paint her bathroom. Bushes scraped the window. In the middle of the room sat a barrel-shaped machine with a box of controls attached to the side.

This is my kiln, she said. I dry my pottery in it.

She set the tray down on a round table and pulled out two of the four chairs, but I was already over at the long table against the wall. It was crammed with teapots. They were shaped like everything. Pigs, sunflowers, gingerbread houses, with different-shaped spouts to pour your tea.

You sell these things?

I won't be quitting my day job soon. She smiled.

They're pretty weird lookin.

She smiled like a sunny day out of her. Some people seem to think they are nice.

I lifted up a red beach bucket with a yellow shovel restin against the rim that you poured the water out of. How much?

Two hundred dollars.

I nearly dropped it.

Can you boil water in it?

Yes, of course you can. Would you like it?

Naw. I set it back down carefully.

What about that one? She nodded at this brown pot with a horse's neck for a spout and two holes for water in the nostrils. Candace said you were fond of horses.

Naw. Thanks anyway.

Oh, go on. Have it.

I could recognize a bribe a mile off. Naw, thanks. I don't drink tea. I ambled over to the chairs. I kind of came here to talk to you, Mrs.—Fran.

She poured coffee for us.

I assumed it was decaf, after our conversation the other day. I slurped it up. I was nervous as heck suddenly. I thunked the mug down.

I am goin to sit here and watch you eat one of those cookies, Fran, if it's the last thing I do.

Her hand jerked back from her coffee mug, which was light blue as her eyes. Excuse me?

I smiled at her. You don't eat nothin. Are you afraid of gettin *f, a, t*?

She sighed. Well. Maybe a little. I was a fat child.

No kiddin. Were you unpopular?

Popular girls don't go on to med school, dear. She patted my hand. I didn't become beautiful until I began my residency at the age of twenty-six.

{243}

What made you beautiful then?

Colored my hair. Too much work to eat, so that I lost thirty pounds, a credit card to buy pretty clothes. She lifted her coffee mug. You're a very perceptive young woman.

With two extra eyes, it's easy, I shrugged.

That's the loveliest pair I've ever seen. Ever thought of contact lenses?

A narrow tree trunk grew past the window. Her face was bright, butter-colored. What color would you say my eyes are?

She squinted at em. A particular shade of blue, definitely.

You sure?

Well, when you turn your head that way, there's a bit of green.

Turquoise?

Yes. Exactly.

I blinked, feelin the water risin. My mom said I was vain for knowin the color of my eyes.

Oh, Thumbelina. She fumbled her hands in her lap. A woman should know her assets. Tell me about your mother.

The cookies were oatmeal raisin today. I nibbled one because I was nervous. Give me a startin point.

Is she happy that you're pregnant?

Well, to be honest—I put down the cookie and coughed into my hands—it all goes back to Ravenhead Apartments. Uh—I turned it over in my head, where to go next. Fran, ma'am, I didn't really come here to see your teapots. I got to tell you somethin. With your patients, do you have to keep stuff confidential that they tell you?

You're not my patient. She swept her bangs out of her eyes.

You got your heart thing around?

{244}

My stethoscope? I have one upstairs in my briefcase. Would you mind goin and gettin it?

So she went upstairs and came back down with the thing in her hand. I lifted my shirt. Will you please listen to my heart and tell me if it sounds normal? She warmed it in her hands before she put it on my skin. She put it all over my back.

Her thin, dark eyebrows touched gently above her delicate nose. I hear an echo in your chest that worries me, Thumbelina.

Great. I smiled at her. So now I'm your patient and you're worried and what I tell you has got to stay in this room. OK?

Does this have to do with your child?

Everything in my life has to do with my child, ma'am. I am goin to tell you how it started growin in me. I have to go back to the days when we lived in Ravenhead Apartments. That was the apartments where Del and me bounced down the front steps in cardboard boxes. I was seven, eight then but I didn't go to school that much. He was goin to marry me. He had a big head and fat elbows but I liked him so I said, OK Del, I'll marry you. Once I fell out of the box and hit my head and he was so afraid I was goin to be retarded. He took me to the grass and made me lie down till I stopped cryin. But him and his daddy moved out in the middle of the night because they were behind on their rent.

She had refilled my mug, but my hand was rattlin so bad I didn't get it halfway to my lips before most of it was on the table and drippin onto my classy dress.

Took her a few minutes to get a cloth and dry me up. I used that time to take deep breaths and calm down.

I slept on the couch at Ravenhead, I explained. There was only one bedroom. She'd be out workin late and Lester would come in when I was takin a bath and sit on the toilet. How was your day? Fine, I'd go, pullin the shower curtain across. He'd wait a minute, then pull one side and stick his head in. Give me the soap. I can do it, Lester. Let me help you, Thumbelina, and his big hands would suds my back. Sometimes he'd squeeze the shampoo on my hair and take my head in his hands. It was quite a bit smaller in those days. Sometimes when I was starin into the dark in the livin room he would show up. I'd hear him breathin above me. His knees would crack as he bent down. My blanket would roll back. His hand would go up and down my arm, over to my stomach. He'd ask me, Do you love me more than her? In my head I'd be countin. Get to five hundred and he'd clear out. But I'd make myself count slow, no point in cheatin. She'd come home and he'd be under his own covers. She'd come in and kiss me where I lay on the couch, kiss my eyelids which would be coverin my eyes. Sometimes she'd elbow me until I woke up and she'd whisper details about her date in my ear. When I was young she told me all about the guys. When I got older she stopped tellin me because I would glare at her in the mornin while I ate cereal from the box. That's another regret I got. Judgin her.

She got wind of somethin because all of a sudden we moved out of that apartment over to these other apartments next to the park. Bean Park. All of a sudden I had my own room. She said the old neighborhood was goin to pot. It was. Lester's van window was busted twice and we'd wake up late at night from people yellin in the alley. Havin my own room was, when I look back on it, like a invitation to him, privacy to do it now. That's when it really started and the dresser didn't stop him.

I forced myself to look Fran in the eye. I was amazed to see her so sad.

You got such a pretty face and a pretty house and pretty life, don't be sad, Mrs. Christofoletti. In a lot of ways Lester was good to me. He just needed love. My mom took from him, his lovers took from him, he needed somebody to give. He needed waterin like a plant. I know, because I got that same need. Sometimes late at night he'd go back to her and I'd get up and go to the bathtub and fill it with water so hot my skin scalded and I would lean back and stare at the corner of the ceiling where mold had survived Lester's sponge. My knees would turn cold up in the air all alone. The bass would be thumpin, other side of the wall. She couldn't fall asleep without her tunes. What did he tell her? I was thirsty? How could she believe it? How come she didn't worry about me? How come she didn't think about me—

I stopped. I had said too much.

I watched her twist her weddin ring. No wonder you have ambivalent feelings about being pregnant, Thumbelina. No wonder you're putting it up for adoption.

Her voice was low and sweet.

There is more, I muttered.

Yes, I'm listening.

Lester belonged to the other half.

Pardon me?

My mom was a hairstylist, a beautician, hair technician, whatever day of the week it was, she had a different name for herself. She wore tight jeans and little high heels. She had the window chair. Betty was a good business lady, trust me. Men used to come in who didn't need their hair cut at all. She'd go out with them quite a bit, but never seriously. She only liked guys who she couldn't have. Like Lester is a prime example because he belonged to the other half.

I gave her a minute to figure it out but she still looked confused.

He liked other *men*. Liked women too. But when he was down in the dumps, he went after men.

(What was I sayin? But I couldn't stop myself.)

Oh, my God, Fran said. Her delicate hand with the whoppin big ring covered her mouth.

I didn't mean to shock you.

No, she said, please, go on.

He had one boyfriend in particular named Marcus who was some kind of writer and had this big house on the water which he inherited when his old mom passed on. Marcus was my mom's worst nightmare. Lester was always over there when he wasn't drivin his truck. He was the reason my mom had all these other boyfriends, like Donny, who also came in to get his hair trimmed, but my mom didn't want to date no Mexican guy. She did for a couple weeks, though, just to make Lester jealous. It did make him jealous. Donny was sexy as they come.

I gulped down my coffee. Lester looked good too. Most queers do. They take care of themselves. I sat back in the chair and took a deep breath into my body.

Is that everything you have to tell me? She was ruinin the polish on her thumbnail with her teeth.

Are you goin to hold this against my little fish?

I had suspected that the circumstances of your pregnancy were troubled, Thumbelina, but—oh, my—

There is a tiny bit more to the story.

The lady shut her eyes, then opened them. How bad does it get?

Lester didn't take precautions.

Her eyes were glued to me.

He didn't protect himself. You know what I mean? I mean for sex, and stuff.

Oh, God—

He has—

You're joking.

I looked at her.

She gripped the edge of the table. The veins stood out like blue worms on the backs of her hands. He has AIDS?

I cringed. I rubbed my stomach protectively. Don't say it too many times, it's an ugly word for my girl to be hearin.

Oh, Thumbelina, she breathed. Why are you telling me all this now?

I took off my glasses. The disappointment in her face killed me.

And you? Have you been tested, Thumbelina?

Don't worry about me.

And your mother, what about your mother?

I sat forward, wonderin who this girl was that was blabbin because it sure wasn't me. She's dead. I'm sorry I didn't tell you sooner.

Not—of AIDS?

I put my glasses back on. She is dead because she could not face losin him, I whispered, because that meant losin herself. I slipped off my shoe and started fiddlin with my toes. I had to do somethin with my hands. They were shakin again. I got to be careful, I said softly. She is dead and she deserves respect. I don't know for sure what she knew. There is knowin and there is knowin.

When did she die?

You mean how, don't you? She slid across Washington Avenue and went down that long grassy slope into Bean

Park. You couldn't see it at the funeral, the gash on her head, they fixed it up. They found her in the duck pond early in the mornin.

In a car?

Donny's Corvette.

This wasn't last summer?

You heard about it?

Of course. There was an inquest.

Yeah, well, they said it was a accident.

Are you telling me you think it was more than that?

I fiddled with my toes. My mom was a complicated lady.

Oh, Thumbelina. She touched my wrist. Her eyes were damp. What you've been through, Thumbelina.

I guess I've had a sad life, accordin to some people.

Ding dong went the doorbell. She looked at me and I looked at her.

I think I understand why you're being so honest with me, she said sadly. You don't like me. You don't want me to adopt your baby.

Are you tryin to tell me that you're still interested?

Victor and I, we'd have to think this over—

You don't want her.

Don't put words in my mouth. We'd have to have her tested—

It'll be I don't know how long—Dr. K. won't give me nothin specific—before you believe what I already know, I snapped. How are you goin to treat her in the meantime?

Her light blue eyes did not blink. This is serious news, Thumbelina, you've got to let me talk to my husband—

Aw, you'd probably take it out on her anyway, I muttered, pushin back my chair. But I didn't get up. I can see her doin somethin to piss you off. Daughters do piss off their moms, you know. She won't do the dishes and you tell her she better, she is lucky to have a roof over her head because her mom had AIDS and if you didn't take her nobody else would. Man—

Thumbelina, I wouldn't say—

It's goin to be a darkness in her life, I said quietly. Not knowin why she was put up for adoption. Was her mother just havin too much fun bein young? Didn't her mother want her? Does her mother have other kids? One day she'll search for me. She won't ever find me.

Find you for what, dear? Mrs. Conn said, comin down the stairs behind the maid. Is everything all right?

I eyed Fran who was eyein her hands which she had spread wide on the tabletop.

My heart was jackhammerin in my chest, but I forced my voice to be calm. Fran is givin me a teapot, Mrs. Conn. That horse one. You think it's OK if I take it?

She laughed, bringin brightness and light into the room. Of course you may have it, Thumbelina. It's the least of what you deserve.

~ ~ ~

DR. K. pushed his strong fingers into my neck. Does that hurt?

Hurt? Well, could you be more specific?

Does it hurt, Thumbelina?

Well, you're pushin awful hard, what do you expect?

I am hardly touching your neck, he said gently. He moved away from me, he crossed his arms over his red and purple tie-dye. I am going to send you over for a chest X-ray.

What for? I feel good. No cough. What I need is somethin for my ulcer.

{251}

Your what?

I got a ulcer, Dr. K. Like my mom. I inherited it from her.

I was sittin on the table in the paper gown, pickin at a wart on my knee. Yep. I know I got a ulcer.

He balled up his bandanna and stuffed it into his back pocket like it was a wallet. And what makes you so certain of that?

I can't eat.

You can't eat because of the infection in your throat.

My throat is fine.

You're allergic to the new medication.

I take as many of the pills as you give me. Give me somethin for my ulcer, please.

Dr. K. sighed. He started puttin his hands all over me. Had no idea what he was lookin for.

Dr. K., are you listenin to me?

Are you listening to me?

I am tired of listenin to you.

Do you want a new doctor?

I keep a close watch on this heart of mine, I sang softly. I keep my eyes wide open all the time, I keep the ends out for the ties that bind, because you're mine, I walk the line.

Get dressed, I'm sending you across the street for that X-ray.

What kind of trouble do you see in my chest?

I don't know yet. I don't know where the trouble is, yet.

A man with skin the color of Mrs. Leffer's beauty bark said, How you doin, hot lips? as I thumped across the porch and went down them clinic stairs. There was a long line at the radiology clinic. I deserve a medal for waitin.

I went back to the clinic and waited on a plastic chair and finally some guy with a white coat a lot shorter than Dr. K.'s came up the steps with my X-rays and gave em to the lady behind the desk who buzzed Dr. K. I sat in his office in my clothes. He looked at em a long time without sayin anything. Hmm, he said. Hmm.

My heart thumped. What?

His eyes were tryin to hold back information but I saw it seepin out around the edges of his eyeballs.

What? What's wrong?

You've got a string of swollen lymph nodes down the center of your chest, Thumbelina. He pointed at the X-rays. This one here, the one that's gotten bigger, it troubles me. It might be a lymphoma.

A what?

Cancer.

I keep a close watch on this heart of mine! I shouted.

I opened the door.

He grabbed my arm. I know this is rough news, sweetheart. It's common in AIDS patients. Because your immune system is so worn down—

Get your hands off me! I hollered.

His body blocked the door.

Why in the hell don't you get out of my way!

That's enough, Thumbelina.

Don't tell me a bunch of downer news when I got to be strong to find parents for my fish! I shouted.

Tears rolled out of my eyes. He shut the door firmly and stood with his back against it. Go on, let it all out, Thumbelina, it's about time.

When I was done cryin he passed over a red-and-green-checkered flannel hanky. I sopped my eyes.

You are immunocompromised, Thumbelina, he said in

a calm, soothin voice like you hear on the radio late at night. Your body can't protect itself. Your CD4 count is falling. Do you remember what the CD4 cells do?

Fight off infection, Dr. K.

I have to get you biopsied. If it is an opportunistic infection, looking at it under a microscope is the only way to tell what the best kind of treatment for it will be. He halted talkin for a second. I'd like to put you in the hospital for the biopsy.

I lifted my eyes. You got to be kiddin.

Do I look like I'm laughing, sweetheart?

I can't go into no hospital. I'm on a hunt for parents, don't you listen?

If you have cancer you need immediate treatment.

First I got to find parents.

Thumbelina, he said sharply. You don't want to wear out first!

Am I wearin out, Dr. K.? Give it to me straight. How much time do I got left?

He sighed. All I'm asking is that you let me help you to take care of yourself—

The phone rang. He pulled it out of his pocket. K. here, he said. He listened. He mumbled somethin. Then he folded the phone over and put it back in his pocket.

A couple minutes passed. He was starin at his boots. I was starin at him.

All right, he said finally. I'll make you a deal.

Kept starin at him.

I'll let you walk out of here today if you agree to come back in two days for a biopsy. We'll talk about the hospital then.

Two days isn't enough time to find parents, I snorted.

Oh, and sweetheart? He stopped in the doorway.

What, Dr. K.

Don't blow me off this time.

I don't blow you off.

You've missed several appointments. It hurts my feelings, especially when it's an attractive young lady pulling the no-show.

I'm busy, Dr. K.

So am I, Thumbelina, so am I. He pulled the door closed on his wrinkled back.

~ ~ ~

MRS. CONN called. Do you want the good news or the good news? She laughed.

I thought it over. How about the bad news.

What bad news?

You have bad news, Mrs. Conn, it's OK, I'm expectin it.

Oh, Thumbelina, you pessimist! Fran Christofoletti called me. She told me you two had a wonderful talk. She says you're an amazing girl.

And I suppose she still wants to adopt my baby.

As a matter of fact, she is still interested, yes.

Yeah right.

Don't you like her?

She wants my baby?

Why wouldn't she?

What did she tell you?

What do you mean?

Did she mention specifics?

About what?

I sat down in the chair just as my knees gave out. Relief had turned me to water.

I always thought I was good at readin people, Mrs. Conn. I always thought I was.

You like her, then?

A lot.

What about Victor?

Cross em off your list, Mrs. Conn.

Dead silence for about a year. What, Thumbelina?

I sighed. Your ears are workin.

Thumbelina, you're acting rashly.

Maybe.

Thumbelina—

What's the good news, Mrs. Conn.

Thumbelina, I—

Mrs. Conn, the good news?

She was quiet awhile. I waited. All right. All right. I respect your opinion. It is, after all, your baby. I've got another couple for you to meet. The DeVries.

I wrapped my arm in the phone cord. Lesbians?

No, a man and woman.

When am I goin to meet lesbians?

The DeVries are childless, like the Christofolettis. Late thirties. We can meet them Sunday afternoon. They go to church. They're Presbyterians.

Is that all right?

It is.

I can't wait to meet em.

That's the spirit!

I put my hand over my eyes. I am not a very talkative person, Mrs. Conn, so warn em.

Not according to Fran, she said quietly. She said that you talked and talked. What did you talk about, Thumbelina?

I probably bored the life out of her.

No, she thinks you are quite remarkable. She really does want you to keep her in mind, as a possible . . . you know.

{256}

Thank you for sayin that. I'll see you Sunday, Mrs. Conn.

After I hung up, tears plunked onto Mrs. Leffer's plastic tablecloth for quite a while.

I am sittin on the back step with my back against the glass. I am smokin a cigarette. Roy is down in his room smearin glue on airplanes.

She is a good lady. I'm not goin to forget her. Just gettin it out of darkness into the light of her pottery room was amazin.

I have never been able to take no for a answer, and my baby's goin to be the same way. She is goin to hound her mom night and day as soon as she can talk.

Why did my real mom give me up? my baby is goin to say.

She was too young, Fran (for example) would reply.

You met her?

Oh, yes.

What was she like?

Secretive.

What kind of secrets was she keepin?

Fran could hold her off for the first six, seven years, but by the time my girl turns fourteen Fran would crack. She was dyin, honey, that's why she gave you up. She loved you very much, but she was dyin. Thinkin that will comfort my baby.

Dyin of what? my offspring will say.

Nothin, Fran will say, realizin her mistake too late.

Dyin of what? my kid will say, stampin her foot.

Nothin.

Of what? Dyin of what?

A big sigh. A disease, sweetie pie.

{257}

What kind of disease?

And they'd go back and forth till she finished crackin.

What? My baby would cover her ears with her hands. My momma had *what?* But that's what *queers* get!

Why did I tell Fran anyway. I've kept it to myself this long. I could of told Myrna if I had to tell somebody. Could of gone to Bean Park and poured it in the ear of a tree.

I am not workin my butt off to get her a pretty house and a pretty life to have it end like that. Fran would regret tellin her, of course she would, nothin would be the same between em again. My girl would feel so dirty in the middle of all that Christofoletti beauty. But Fran has that kind of heart. She thinks gettin everything out in the open is for the best.

I used to think that way too. I rubbed my mom's face in the truth because I thought it was the right thing to do. That's how she ended up in the duck pond.

March, I don't got the energy to make you stay. So long.

april

with a knock on my door. Thumbelina?

No answer.

Thumbelina?

What, Mrs. Leffer, I muttered.

It's after eleven. You're goin to be late for that lawyer.

Yeah, yeah. I rolled over.

She came in and her old legs cracked as she crouched down and put her head by my head. What's wrong?

I'm not in a very good mood this mornin.

It's just depression from bein pregnant, dear. I had it too.

I didn't answer.

Soon as you find the right parents, you'll bounce back. She touched my shoulder. You want some orange juice?

No.

Well. I have to get to church. I have to go.

Don't forget Roy, Mrs. Leffer. I squinted up at her.

She just looked at me. Her watery blue eyes were sad. You can always call her if you're not up to it.

I took a bath and washed my hair. I sat on the toilet and aimed the hair dryer at my head. I felt dizzy. My throat ached. I felt somethin else. I felt a strong pressure push down inside my stomach. Naw, I thought. No way in hell. That's weeks off. The little man in my blood went around and passed the hat for some energy and I got my act together and got up to answer the doorbell.

It was Mrs. Conn. Her eyes went up and down me. You've got just a few wrinkles in that dress, dear.

I looked down at the navy dress. It looks all right to me.

Here, whip it off and let me iron it.

Mrs. Conn. Come on, man.

I've got a good feeling about the DeVries, dear. We want to make a good impression. Here, whip it off and let me iron it. And kindly don't refer to me as man.

You want some coffee then? I said, haulin out my manners along with the iron.

No, no. No time.

So I went down the hall and put on sweatpants and a sweatshirt while she ironed my dress. I put it back on in the bathroom and rolled on some lipstick. I looked all right, anyway.

Mrs. Conn herself wore a black-and-white-checked coat and black pants and black boots with skinny heels and square toes. She had a gold necklace on her white neck and her fingernails were light pink.

Everything about this situation was very regular. It was a small house. It was brown. It was on a street not a lake. Valerie DeVries opened the door before we knocked. She wore a blue dress and had black hair to her shoulders and she had a face warm as a fire and she was delicate and had white teeth because she was smilin. I said, Thank you, God, and sat down in the livin room which was warm and comfortable like a livin room should be.

The guy was all right too. He had glasses thick as mine so that was nice, but he does not have the nose to hold em, so they were always hangin. He does not push em up with his thumb like Dr. K., he squinches his nose. He is tall. (Comin from me remember.) He does computers at Microsoft. When he shook my hand I got a nice feelin so I said, Thank you, God, again. Then I sat down again.

The couch was brown with red wobbles all over it. There were paintings of Indians on the walls. Michael DeVries had strawberry red hair, not orange like Myrna's.

Computers are the wave of the future, I said, smoothin out my dress. (Heard it somewhere.)

He looked at Valerie DeVries, his wife, and she looked at him. Then they looked at Mrs. Conn. Michael worked his glasses up his nose. Valerie winked at the lawyer and said, Come on in the kitchen and help me with the cake.

So it was just me and Mike. He said, Why don't you come on in the den and I'll show you my computer. I said, Well, I'm kind of comfortable right here. I liked the room. It was cozy. I felt another pressure in my stomach and sent a silent message: Knock it off it isn't funny.

Thumbelina is a real nice name.

Thanks. Michael isn't bad either.

Were you named for that little girl in the fairy tale?

Yep.

Oh?

Somebody gave her a book of fairy tales in the hospital. She had a lot of time to kill. Her water broke and then I guess I changed my mind about comin. I took forever.

He grinned. Are you close to your mom?

I once thought I was.

How does she feel about you doing this?

She doesn't know.

You don't live with her.

It wasn't a question. I answered it anyway.

Nope.

Then he changed the subject, earnin big points.

I'm Dutch and Irish. Valerie's Italian.

Thought she might be Indian.

She's got a sliver of Yakima in her. You're very perceptive.

Well, the decoration gave it away, I said.

What's your background?

I got no idea.

You're so fair. I bet you're Swedish or Norwegian.

My mother comes from Texas originally but grew up in Sacramento, I offered.

Oh? He put one shoe on top of the other and leaned forward. I've done some work for the firm in central California.

You got a bathroom, Michael?

Up the stairs.

Thanks, Michael.

(It was cool callin these big shots by their first name.)

It was what you call a split-level. The stairs were rust-colored carpet. At the top was a landing like a football field and a bunch of doors which I didn't have no problem stickin my big nose into.

The first door was just a room full of boxes and old furniture. The next one must of been their bedroom, because it had a dresser so shiny I could see my reflection in it and a green bedspread and cream-colored carpet. The next room was what you call a waitin room. White walls and a white crib in the corner with little toys hangin over it to get a baby's attention, and white stuffed animals sittin on the windowsill. I thought of her playin in there. How old would she be? Two? Three? Sittin on her knees on the floor all alone in her white tights and pretty pink dress that Valerie would of bought her, pettin her stuffed animals. I closed the door to keep from cryin.

In the bathroom I lifted the toilet lid and coughed up my scrambled eggs and thought about the need for two sinks in your bathroom. At first I thought it was the ketchup I'd squirted all over them. Then I knew it wasn't. I crouched over the toilet bowl and thought about dyin like it was a person comin over to visit me. It was goin to come. Because you aren't supposed to bleed out your mouth, only your hole. It was two years ago when I saw blood in the toilet for the first time. I didn't tell my mom. I just wadded up toilet paper and put it in my underwear and took out some of my money and went to the 7-Eleven and got what I needed. I got used to havin it every month. It was supposed to mean I was a woman.

I rested my cheek on the fluffy pink toilet-seat cover and drifted off.

One time when we were still livin in Ravenhead me and my mom went to the fair. We went on the Ferris wheel and the bumper cars and the Hammer and the Corkscrew and we ate cotton candy and hamburgers that fell out of the bun and we went to look at the championship pies and pumpkins. And we went through all the animal pens, that was so great, especially the Clydesdale horses that got feet as big around as your head and could kill you if they stepped on you, but they are careful not to step on humans, the man said, because they are gentle as a kitten.

That was a real good day. I figured there'd be lots of other days like it. Didn't appreciate it enough. I should of held her hand tighter. Ate two hamburgers instead of one. Gone on all the rides twice. The problem is you don't ever enjoy nothin enough when you're doin it because you think you will have so many more times just like it.

I got up and wiped my mouth on one of the pink towels and turned it inside out so you couldn't see the stain. I can't breathe without leavin a stain.

Her birthday fell on a Friday last August. I'd been waitin at least one, two weeks by then. I rode the bus from ViewCrest to Betty's apartment and I looked out the window and I worried about it. Worried about it while I helped her put up pink and gold streamers for the surprise party. The ladies from the beauty shop knew how hard it was for my mom to turn thirty-three. They were goin all out for her. Chee Chee baked the double-layer chocolate cake. Even Daphne, the lady who craved the window chair, got her a present. We stacked them presents on the table by the cake and when Donny's Corvette pulled up and they came gigglin up the front walk everybody yelled, Surprise! Everybody went ooh and aah when they saw her lift swan earrings cut from ivory out of the green tissue paper. Oh, Thumby, she breathed, and started to cry. Chee Chee gave her a pair of gold scissors. Donny gave her a box

{264}

of good chocolates and a ankle bracelet with an orange flower on it, because she didn't waste no time lettin her boyfriends know her favorite things. Everybody had fun. Everybody bein the same people that went to her funeral. You're twelve, right? Donny said, and when I opened my mouth to claim fourteen my mom's little heel spiked my foot.

Yep. If two years made a difference to her, fine with me.

Everything was goin all right till Lester arrived.

Where is she?

Why the hell Betty didn't have her front door locked is one of those things I wonder about.

Go on out of here, Lester, you aren't invited, my mom hollered, with meanwhile Donny's arm around her neck.

Lester wore his black leather nylon trench coat and red sweatpants and blue terry-cloth slippers. He yanked my mom away from the other man.

Now, look here—Donny started. No. *You* look here. Lester pulled out his pistol. I am takin this girl home now! I got to talk to her! I got to talk to you, Angelica! He waved the pistol around like it was his report card or somethin. I had the feelin it wasn't loaded. He was drunk, we all could see that. Nobody screamed, case it set him off.

I got to talk to her. I got to talk to her.

Then he dropped her arm and ran back out the door. Chee Chee ran over and slid the bolt across. Everybody else just kind of stood there, hands in our pockets, recoverin slow.

You OK, Angelica? everybody said. You OK? Of course I'm OK, she said, brushin everybody off. Who was that? Donny asked her. Nobody, she said. Donny had brown skin and a cool car but his brain was pretty regular and asked pretty regular questions. Who was that? he said again, turnin to me. Your daddy? Insult me a little more, why don't you, I said. But Lester had left his mark on my mom and she pulled loose from Donny and said, Betty, hon, give us a ride home, will you?

You aren't gettin near him, Angelica.

He won't touch me, Betty.

I'll drive you, Donny said.

No, no, honey, that'll rile him further. Well, then, we will just take the bus, come on, Thumby.

I knew we were takin the bus like we were flyin. I did not budge.

Thumby? You deaf, hon?

And Donny blinked his long-eyelashed eyes at her. You live with that guy? he said.

Pretty hard to believe, isn't it? I said, glarin at my mom. She just ignored me.

When we got home our apartment was dark. We climbed up to the second floor and she fumbled around with the key. I had her presents in my arms.

She flashed the livin room light on and off to let Betty know we were OK.

You want a nightcap, Thumby? she said, and turned on the kitchen light. He was sittin in the chair by the window.

We eyed him.

Hello, girls.

Hello, Lester. There were empty beer bottles everywhere.

Have a nice time?

Till you showed up, I said.

Honey? she whispered, and put her little hand on his shoulder. It wasn't what it looked like.

Lester didn't answer which surprised me so much my eyes fell out of my head to the floor and I saw the paper layin under the table. I reached under the chair and picked it up and my eyes slowly traveled over it.

Your four-eyed daughter don't miss much, Lester said softly.

You want your whiskey hot, Thumby?

This is from the doctor. I looked up at him.

Show it to your mother. He rubbed his eyes and leaned back in the chair.

The doctor? What doctor, honey? my mom said, pourin whiskey into three glasses.

The doctor at the clinic, I said. Here, read it. I held it out.

I don't have my glasses on, Thumby. She was at the sink, fillin the kettle.

It tells you why my breath has been so bad lately, Angelica.

She spooned sugar into the whiskeys and stirred.

I got a disease, Angelica.

It was a lovely party, honey. I got all kinds of presents. A pair of earrings from Thumby.

Angelica. You might be infected.

The decorations were beautiful. All those candles everywhere and the streamers and balloons. Did you help Betty do that, Thumbelina?

Lester's knees showed below the hem of his bathrobe. His legs had gotten skinnier since I'd seen em last. His hair hung in his eyes. My mom hadn't given him a haircut in a long time.

You'll have to be tested, Angelica.

Balloons and streamers. Thumby, when did you get the time to do that?

I watched her move the spoon around and around in the glasses. I wanted to yell at her and smash her head into the cupboard.

He started to cough. Please, baby, please, I need you right now, baby. Help me.

The kettle whistled and she poured in the hot water, stirred the glasses some more, and put them down in front of us.

I'm tired, she said.

Her high heels lay under the chair where she'd kicked em. I picked em up the next day and wrapped em in newspaper to take with me. She went down the hall in her nylons. He went after her goin baby baby baby. She came into the kitchen about a hour later. I was sittin in the chair, my arms wrapped around my knees. I had the radio on the country station. I was hummin to myself.

She wore a denim skirt up to her nice-lookin thighs and slippers and her jeans jacket.

Reach me down a couple of those bottles, will you, Thumby?

So I got up and got em down from the top of the fridge for her and she shoved em in her big straw overnight bag.

Donny's comin by. I got to clear my head.

Can I come?

You stay and keep an eye on him.

It is too late now for us to leave him, Mom.

She ran lipstick around her lips, usin the pot lid. Don't wait up for me.

What are you doin, Momma?

Goin over to my boyfriend's for some peace and quiet, if you don't mind.

What about the piece of paper.

Thumbelina, will you quit pesterin me, for God's sake? I'll be back in the mornin.

Mom?

What.

I'm late.

For what? She blinked at me.

For you know what.

Her little chin fell loose from her teeth. Oh, God. Thumby, I can't deal with this—

My legs moved me fast. I blocked her escape route. No. We are goin to talk about it *now*. Sit. My skinny finger pointed at the chair. She sat, her eyes huge and blue.

You want to know who the father is?

Who, Thumby?

You know who, Mother.

She protected her head with her hands. I was not sure if she was cryin, but her shoulders shook. I did not touch her. You hate him that much that you'll make up stories about him? she said, her voice muffled. He's been good to you. He's goin through tough times right now, we got to stand by him.

I am tellin you the truth, Mom.

She took a deep breath and flicked her lighter, suckin on a cigarette.

I went over and started pickin up beer bottles. I couldn't stand lookin at her.

Donny honked. She picked up her straw bag and her purse and said, Bye, Thumby, and waited a minute. I did not open my mouth. I did not look at her.

She left Donny's little studio apartment at dawn, accordin to him, pretty nearly sober. How do you know she was sober? I asked him at the funeral. You think I'd let her drive my car if she wasn't? he said sadly. That car was my baby. They say she sat at the top of the hill for a while, emptyin the bottle of Smirnoff that I had got down for her from the top of the fridge. The next mornin it was floatin near the strands of yellow hair. Two joggers goin by saw

{269}

this sight. The duck pond is only eight feet deep. It hides nothin. She was dressed in her denim skirt and her turquoise ring. The swan earrings hung from her ears. But she was not there. She left without me.

When I got back down to the livin room they were eatin cake. Where've you been? Valerie got up and I saw that she was tall and her black hair swung gracefully, and she took my arm and tugged me over to the couch. She sat down beside me. Her perfume smelled like wet dirt and some kind of flower that probably had a pretty name. Mrs. Conn sat on my other side. Michael had his legs crossed at his bare ankles and the plate balanced on his knee.

I had to go to the bathroom, I said to the room.

Doing a little snooping, I hope, Valerie smiled. I certainly would in your shoes. Is there anything about us you'd like to know? And meanwhile she's hackin me off a piece of chocolate cake, icin drippin off in big gobs. I probably would of thought it looked pretty delicious if you were askin me last summer. The plate was pure white with a band of gold around the edge. I thought about me and my mom's orange and green plastic plates from the gas station. About them summer evenings, sittin in the kitchen eatin our potato salad and burritos with our legs under us, listenin to Johnny Cash and Waylon Jennings tapes. My mom used to say, One of these days, Thumby, I'm goin to get some decent china. This stuff isn't fit to feed a dog on. I didn't know what that meant. I figured it must be somethin that would break when you dropped it. Now I was eatin off it.

The coffee cup was the same pattern. Hot and bitter, I felt the coffee burn all the way down my throat to my little fish in my stomach.

I looked out the window. Thought about her ridin her

tricycle up and down that path. She'd have to wash her hands before dinner. There'd be the kind of music on the stereo that don't have any words. There'd be a couple different forks she'd have to figure out. There'd be bedtime prayers and new shoes for church on Sunday and she wouldn't be peein in em in the back of her closet, either.

I put down the cake plate and got up real slow. I smoothed down my classy dress which I'd wrinkled up pretty bad upstairs in the toilet. Beggars can't be chosen, my mom used to say.

I looked around at the three pairs of eyes, settled on Valerie's brown ones.

Do you want her?

Her fork stopped in the air, fully loaded.

Do we *want* her? Michael shouted. What kind of question is that?

I ignored him. Valerie's fork unloaded onto the rug. Yes, she whispered. Yes, Thumbelina, we want your child.

Then you got her, Valerie, on one condition. You got to love her like she is your own.

Water glittered in her brown, Indian eyes.

No. I am talkin like you carried her in your guts for nine months and got *attached* to her—

Whack! went her tail against my stomach. I doubled over, gaspin. She was mad. I had ignored her and she was mad.

Thumbelina? Mrs. Conn said.

Are you all right? Michael said.

Her tail slapped me again. I started coughin.

Thumbelina, what is it, dear? Mrs. Conn stroked my head.

I sat up. It's just my—I sucked in air—ulcer. It does this all the . . . time.

{271}

Are you having contractions? Valerie said who has got the eyes of a hawk.

Oh, God, Michael said. We'd better call an ambulance.

Oh, she has all the time in the world, Mrs. Conn said calmly, her water hasn't broken—

And just then water dribbled down my legs.

I was starin at my black suede slippers. My long toes crammed into em.

Mrs. Conn shouted orders. Because she knew like I knew that now my baby could arrive any minute.

Call the ambulance.

No, I'll take her in my car.

Which hospital?

The closest one—

Who's her doctor?

I'll call my own—

The emergency room?

Mrs. Conn firmly lifted me by my arm. Come on, dear, into the backseat. Michael, help me get her into my car.

Next thing you know I'm lyin on her backseat with my naked knees in the air, starin out the window at the ashy sky. She nearly jolted me off the seat as she shot up the driveway.

You OK back there?

I'm all right.

Thumbelina, you could be bleeding to death and I believe that would be your reply.

She talked to herself the whole way there, cursin red lights and slow drivers. Come *on,* she hissed, come *oooon.*

When we got to the hospital she ran in and came back with a brown-bearded man, the doctor.

How long have you been having them?

This is my first one.

Contraction?

Baby.

He pulled his face away. A bunch of hands tugged at me and hauled me off the seat and onto this high bed which rickety-racked up the sidewalk and through the double doors.

I felt so wide open I thought she was comin right there. I thought, Oh, man, I'm goin to see her, I'm actually goin to see her!

Then everything halted down. She wouldn't move.

Changed her mind about joining us, the beard said, who seemed to be the one goin to bring her out of me.

Where's Dr. Miligiwamny? I asked, their faces starin down at me.

I'm the one on call. He patted my arm. She's definitely changed her mind about joining us.

She's not comin today, I said. I'm ready to go.

I'm afraid you're not going anywhere, the beard said, pushin me back down and smilin.

I was just about to say, Oh yeah? when it felt like a train had rammed itself through my body and I roared the news out to the whole hospital.

She was movin again.

They say the memory of the pain fades. They are right in a way. I remember that it hurt but I don't remember the details. I was screamin and sweatin and screamin at her to get the hell out of me, when I felt her slip out of me in this one long feel of relief, like I had passed out all my wet guts into the world.

They were afraid that she was dead, arrivin so quiet. That her brain might be damaged. She was blue and did not respond when they shook her gently. This is what Mrs. Conn told me later when the fog cleared from my head, when she came to get my official permission for adoption.

I want to see her, Candace.

Dear heart, it is about time you called me that.

I repeated myself.

It will just make it harder for you.

What color hair?

She fiddled with the curtains. She doesn't have any yet.

What color eyes?

They haven't opened. She rattled the papers and put a pen in my hand. Sign, dear heart. Sign.

I signed my big Thumbelina all down the pages.

~ ~ ~

I CARRIED her around this world for eight months and one week. She was the most beautiful thing I ever made. I had to see her.

It was halfway through April. The sun filled the backyard of Mrs. Leffer's house where I lay in the lawn chair, sippin a Coke. Clouds like kernels of popcorn drifted across the sky. Mrs. Leffer was off makin money at the bank, Roy was at school. I was sittin there by myself, for the first time in months she was not bumpin her head inside me.

When Myrna appeared in front of me I blinked. Is that you or your ghost?

You like it?

The white wig, she meant, that hit her butt. She twirled around so that it swung out around her, I saw bits of orange underneath.

You like it? she repeated.

It's a little bright.

She plopped down in the other lawn chair, crossin her bare ankles. I thought of the day last August when I first met her, and wondered if that was why she had come. To bring our friendship around to the startin point so that we could both move on.

You missed it, Myrn.

She poked a menthol between her red lips. Missed what?

I patted my flat stomach. It's all over.

She leaned over and picked up my Coke. Jesus, Thumby. Of course I didn't miss it. I saw her. I was there.

I blinked at her.

A couple times. I stood outside the glass. I saw the blackboard that said DELIVERIES and Skyler with a X through the box. I picked her out easy from all the other babies. Number one, bein early she was the littlest of the bunch, and number two, aw, she looks just like you.

My eyes roamed her freckled face. I wanted to ask her why she didn't come see me, visit me when I needed her, but I thought that if I waited maybe she would tell me.

She sleeps like you do, all hunched up with her mouth open.

Does she really look like me?

Don't make me repeat myself, I'm in a rotten mood.

I eyed the remarkable blue sky a minute to calm down. Then I heaved myself up. Do you want a Coke or somethin to drink? (Seein as she was polishin off mine.)

She lit another stick. I just didn't have it in me to be congratulatin you and all in that hospital, Thumby, sorry, I guess that means I'm not much of a friend.

I kept my eyes on her.

Oh, hell, do I have to spell it out? I miscarried again. Eleven weeks along.

She pinged her cigarette across the muddy yard. It hit a pole in the Cyclone fence. A car rolled down the street, the tires smooth on the warm pavement.

I lowered myself back down in the lawn chair and held my chin in my big bony hands. I just sat like that, feelin her sadness wash over me. For once in my life, I did not give her no pep talk, I did not say nothin. My body was goin to have to communicate everything I was feelin because I could not say a word.

I can't stay long, she sighed, layin her head back so that her short white neck was exposed to the love of the sun.

Shine on her hard, old sun.

I saw em, Thumby. Sleepin in chairs in the lobby. The red-haired man and the pretty brunette. Nice choice.

I didn't answer.

Her eyelashes covered her green eyes. I can't believe your kid got out of you in one piece. The way you treated it. Remember when you were goin to kill it and I was goin to help you?

Shame and regret made it hard to talk. It's done, Myrna, I said quietly. It's over. She is safe now.

I hacked into my hands.

Her eyes flung wide open. You goin to the doctor?

It doesn't really matter now, Myrna.

She shaded her eyes. I could use that Coke now.

OK.

I can't stay long.

You mentioned that.

But I didn't move to go and get it and she didn't ask me to hurry it up, we just sat there, her behind her eyelids, the menthol wastin away between her little fingers, me roamin over her with my eyes. On her collarbone was a mole I had noticed often because her shirts don't very often cover it. I had never liked the look of it, but I included it with the other details to remember about her, like her delicate front teeth, white as bone, and them loose orange curls scattered across her freckled forehead that I have blabbed so much about, tryin to understand her.

The clouds drifted, enjoyin their freedom in the sky.

Then her horn tooted from the driveway and I jolted, rememberin all I had facin me today. I eyed her from nearly six feet above her. I got to go, Myrna. Yeah yeah, she said, but her voice was too bright, like high beams blindin you. I tried to think of somethin to say to end it. I knew we were endin it. Nothin great came to mind. She got up. We held each other. For once in my life I held on and held on, it was her who pushed me away. Somebody's honkin for you, she whispered. I would of liked to wrap them green eyes in newspaper and take em with me like my mom's high heels.

Have a few butterflies, dear? Mrs. Conn asked as we glided up the street.

I rolled down the window. The clouds lazy-boned away the day above us. Try a whole pack, Mrs. Conn.

She squeezed my knee which was available through the hole in my jeans. My comfy soft jeans, since I didn't have nobody to impress no more.

It's going to be fine. They are wonderful people.

You already sold me. You can relax now.

We didn't talk much on the drive over. There was nothin really to say. We rolled down the driveway and Mrs. Conn pulled up the parkin brake. Reminded me of other parkin brakes. Better turn your wheels the other way, I said, in case you roll. (Old habits die hard.)

Besides my jeans I had on my red sweatshirt and my mom's coat. I had washed my hair and applied lipstick. I was glad to see Valerie's smile, appreciatin my efforts, when she opened the door. The good warm smell of roast turkey welcomed me. I didn't get no sick feelings. Amazin. Instead my stomach stood up and said, Hi, how you doin, food?

Valerie DeVries hugged me and Mike shook my hand and they took me into the livin room where this little car seat sat in the middle of the rug. It was vibratin softly.

In that thing she lay.

Movement soothes her, Valerie said, scoopin her up and settin her in my arms.

I was holdin my flesh and blood. I could not take my eyes off her. Her eyelashes were long and yellow and yellow hair sprouted on her head, like it had been workin hard, expectin me. Water dropped out of my eyes onto her cheeks and her lashes parted, as if that was the cue she'd been waitin for. I was starin into my own eyes.

Hi, those eyes smiled, it's about time you came to hold me.

I got light-headed. I pressed my butt into the couch. I sucked in air. I slid my hand under her paper-thin head. I couldn't take my eyes off her.

Evenings are her cranky time, Valerie was sayin to me, the only thing that soothes her then is to be patted hard on the back in time with music. She favors Paul Simon's funkier stuff. *Rhythm of the Saints* and *Graceland*.

Try some Johnny Cash, I whispered. I was doin all I could to hold the tears from floodin over her. I was afraid they'd pull her away from me if I drenched her.

And meanwhile my eyes raced over her: a fat upper lip. It worked on her. Big hands. Good for catchin a softball. I pushed the yellow socks off her long feet and saw that the knuckles of her big toes had knotty, tree potential, like my mom's. It was only then, after takin stock of everything she'd took from us, that I allowed myself to believe that she had passed on everything he offered. I looked into them eyes again that are the color of a turquoise ring in Highland Cemetery. I saw her spirit. I saw her strength. When God said, What do you want to inherit from him? she stamped her foot on the ground and said, You must be jokin. I saw that she knew me, and we shook hands with our eyes. She had come here to live. To live.

Valerie put her arm around my shoulders. She did not know why I was cryin but she did not have to know.

Come on in and have some lunch. We've got cold cuts and curry soup, if you like curry, and lentil soup if you don't, and homemade bread, and for dessert we've got angel food cake.

Think I'll just keep on holdin her here, if you don't mind, Valerie.

Can you hold her and eat at the same time?

I'm not really too hungry.

We sat around the kitchen table like a family. They spooned up soup and tore off chunks of bread and told me that my little fish was still jaundiced because of bein premature and that they had to take off all her clothes and put her in the crib naked under the bilirubin lights.

We pump the heat up in our bedroom so high we can't sleep in there, they said. We've been pulling the couch out in the living room and sleeping there. She has to be completely naked, you see, to get the light on her skin. Oh, she hates it. She cries and cries.

I hugged her harder.

Valerie touched my arm. Gently, Thumbelina. Gently.

I held my little fish and once in a while put a piece of ham in my mouth while Michael and Valerie ate and watched me. We chatted about this, that, and the other thing, and they watched me watch her. I couldn't believe how nice they were, lettin me hold their baby. I asked em if it stressed em out. They said no. I knew they were lyin. I asked em, Could I feed her?

Well, of course, but you have to wait until she is hungry.

Valerie showed me the cans of formula in her cupboard and how you have to boil the water in the pot and then let the bottle of formula sit in the hot water for a few minutes, till a drop on your wrist feels like bathtub water.

When it was time Valerie fixed the bottle and I slid the nipple between my little girl's fourteen-day-old lips.

When she stopped eatin (the bottle was empty) Valerie set the burp rag on my shoulder and I thumped her gently on the back in time with You Can Call Me Al.

Then Mrs. Conn came and it was time to go back to Mrs. Leffer's. It was time to put her back in the vibratin car seat.

Does she sleep in this? I asked.

Oh, no. We've got a crib in our room, but it's too far away to hear her cry. So I keep her in here until Michael and I go to bed.

I didn't kiss her good-bye, that would be like eatin one potato chip for fat people. I just pulled the blanket up to her tiny chin. I ran my finger down her cheek. She was the most beautiful thing I'd ever seen. I could stare at her all day. And she came out of me.

Valerie turned on the vibrations.

It was rainin lightly outside. I followed Mrs. Conn up the path that one day she will tricycle up and down till Valerie calls her in to dinner, and she will go in there and wash her hands and she will know which fork to use and there will be flowers on the table and she will look into Valerie's brown, part-Indian eyes and see how much she is loved. She will never know nothin about a girl named

Thumbelina who carried her around in her stomach for eight months and one week and gave her her yellow hair and big hands for catchin all the good things in life.

~ ~ ~

I WALKED up the clinic stairs today. My legs complained, Come on, Thumby, ease up, will you? as if I'd put em through ten miles, not a hundred feet from the bus stop. They complained walkin up the stairs behind Dr. K. to his office on top of the building. I sat on the couch and he leaned against his crowded desk. The curtains were open and I smiled at the four wives.

You missed your biopsy appointment, he said. You promised you'd come back.

I've been busy havin a baby.

His mouth got softer. He eyed my new flat stomach. Everything work out all right?

I didn't know if he was askin me if she arrived OK, with arms, legs, a head, everything where it should be, or if I got parents picked all right, or if I cracked and told em I was dyin. I didn't know what he was askin me and I didn't feel like diggin to find out.

She's in safe hands, Dr. K.

Good.

She is real pretty.

Takes after her mother, no doubt.

I looked at the four wives who were lookin over my head. You use lines like that on em?

He wiped his nose with his hanky. I'll reschedule you for that biopsy.

He came over and lifted my shirt and put his stethathing all over my chest and my back.

My heart's fine.

It's a tough one, no argument there. It's your lungs where I hear the footsteps of pneumonia.

I thought this over. Are they loud?

They are audible.

Oh.

I want you downstairs for a complete physical exam. There's a throat infection and a pneumonia in front of you. I will have to admit you through the emergency room. You are going into the hospital as soon as I can arrange it.

I let his energy wash over me in a wave. Don't you ever get tired, Dr. K.?

Pardon me?

Of workin so hard for me.

Do I work hard?

I unfolded my legs. My nose met his chin. The worst thing about dyin young is I am never goin to know what it's like bein kissed, Dr. K., I mumbled.

He backed up a step, and turned to the window.

You OK?

I'm fine. He kept his back to me.

Will you miss me?

He spoke to the window in a voice you would use to say, look it's rainin outside don't forget your umbrella. If you do have a lymphoma it is just another battle in what could prove to be a very long war, Thumbelina. But you have to be willing to face each battle. You sound as if you think it is all over.

He turned around, foldin his arms over his heart thing hangin from his neck. Pneumonia is also serious, but I'm not surprised. It's because your immune system is so shot. But we'll assess it and treat it. There are many things we can do to help you, but you must be hospitalized. I won't take no for an answer, Thumbelina.

You won't, huh, I laughed.

I am very serious, Thumbelina.

Of course you are.

Because that's what I do. I treat this disease in any way that I can.

I rested my elbows on my knees. You ought to eat more, Dr. K. You look skinnier and skinnier every time I see you.

He lifted the warped bridge of his glasses higher up his nose, and I wanted so bad to ask him which wife they belonged to, which one he still loved.

OK, Dr. K. I'll go in the hospital. She's as safe as I can make her without takin her with me.

What do you mean by that?

I undid the knot in my high-tops and pulled the laces tighter. You can't take nothin with you, Dr. K., not even your toothbrush.

But the thought crossed your mind?

I dropped my eyes. Lifted em. Our eyes met and went their own way. He cleared jelly out of his throat. The red laces swept the floor. I stood up to meet him. There was no room in my throat for air. His long arm circled my shoulders. He kissed me and thumped out of the room. I stood there, feelin the wetness dry on the side of my head. I left my disappointment in that room with the wives.

He was waitin for me at the bottom of the stairs. He said go out in the waitin room and wait for him. He wouldn't be long. He slipped through a door and I saw a lady with dark hair pulled up in a pink scarf sittin on the table, waitin for him. She was fat. Must of been a different disease from the one takin me. My long legs moved me through the hall in two seconds and through the room with the plastic chairs full of people and the lady behind the desk with the phone under her chin, and I went like a shootin star down them clinic stairs.

He would come out lookin for me and I would not be there. I would be gone from this city, like my mom. He would forget me. I was just his patient, nothin more.

A lot of the light has faded from this side of Tacoma, I've been talkin about April so long. The wind has picked up, and the swing moves underneath me. I shove my hands into the pockets of my mom's coat and I squeeze out one of her cherry cough drops. I hum a Johnny Cash song.

Hey porter hey porter can you tell me the time, how much longer will it be to cross that Mason Dixon line.

I get off the swing. Down through the cracks in the planks of the bridge the duck pond shivers in the wind. It's empty now, but they'll be comin back soon, ploppin out of the sky like big rocks, quackin, quackin, gettin reacquainted.

Over there is the wadin pool where we used to sit and read and get a suntan. They'll be fillin it soon. Some guy is whackin a basketball on the court, other side of the pine trees. I smell algae and more rain comin.

The chain-link fence pokes into my elbows as I lean and watch the sky darken. Soon the moon comes out, watchin me through the pine branches. The water is nearly invisible under darkness.

I hope they name her somethin with elbow room. That's my one, last request. Somethin she can fit. Not too big, not too small.

I tuck my yellow hair into the back pockets of my jeans and push the plastic button through the top hole in my mother's coat, liftin the fur collar up to my cheeks. I can feel the stitches she put in back in the days when things like havin a fur collar mattered to her.

Good-bye, old moon. Good-bye, sky, trees, swings. Good-bye, feet. Thanks for lettin me stare at you so much.

I hope she's not mad that it took me so long to come after her.

postscript

THUMBELINA IS ANDREA KOENIG'S FIRST PUBLISHED NOVEL. Although not autobiographical in a strict sense, Andrea Koenig writes with a deep understanding and sympathy for women, particularly teenagers, living in difficult circumstances. Andrea Koenig is passionate about this subject matter. She grew up the fourth of eight children in the small towns and rural spaces of western Washington State. Though private about the specific details of her upbringing, she acknowledges that her parents were deeply troubled. 'I was a lonely girl. Writing saved my life.' Uncertain how one made a living as a writer, however,

Andrea Koenig decided at the age of 13 to become an engineer, a practical career that would eliminate the poverty she had known as a child. She dropped out of university at twenty to move to Dublin, Ireland and play in a rock n' roll band. 'I was the guitarist and I could hardly keep a tune. That's an indication of our talent. I began writing my first novel in a pitiful little house on the south side of the Liffey when it became apparent to me that I had no future as a guitar player. The house was haunted, on top of it. Every night a ghost announced himself in my wardrobe with a peculiar rubbing sound.' She finished the novel, sans ghost, back in the States, and found herself an agent. She wrote two more novels in the next three years, but was unable to find a home for them, and 'broke, hungry, unbelievably tired,' she returned to university in Seattle, Washington in 1991. In spite of her studies and part-time jobs, she could not stop writing. 'It was spring break, I'd been back in school a few months, my room- mates were gone for the week. I sat down to work that morning, a Sunday, I think, and this gangly girl with hair the colour of pee was sitting on my computer. Waiting to have her story told. It took me six years to tell it, to write Thumbelina's complicated life truthfully, but I never doubted her. I was compelled. Obsessed.'

Just short of finishing the novel, Andrea Koenig received a Fulbright award to Northern Ireland. 'I brought Thumbelina with me. I wrote her in the mornings, in the afternoons I walked around Belfast with my tape recorder, interviewing women.' She finished the novel in February, 1997.

The storyline of Andrea Koenig's Thumbelina is tragic in the extreme. In fact, it is hard to think of a more 'tragic' plot. But the power of the novel lies in its warmth. It is a novel about the redemptive power of forgiveness. Though Thumbelina suffers greatly, she remains kind.

Considering her upbringing and the desperate circumstances in which her mother, Angelica, leaves her, it is almost inconceivable that Thumbelina would find the ability to forgive. But she does, and the reason we as readers can accept it and understand it is due to the strength of Koenig's characterisation.

As always in the best characterisation, we get to know and understand the characters through what they do and think, as well as what they say. When Thumbelina gives up on buying orange tulips for her mother's grave and makes them out of orange paper instead, the reader's heart aches. You can't help but empathise with Thumbelina. Her comment, 'you got to do everything yourself in this world', sums up her practical, naïve wisdom.

That same naïve wisdom colours her relationship with her mother. Angelica is cruel, selfish, blinkered, jealous, vindictive. Thumbelina knows all that but she can also see through to the weak, vulnerable, dependant woman underneath; the woman with tiny gnarled feet, the woman who relies on her to put on the hand brake for her on the steep hills of Tacoma, the woman she longs to care for, to have to herself. She insists that her mother wears slippers in her coffin – 'my mom's little feet *always* get cold'.

The rare times when she and her mother do get on are precious times indeed for Thumbelina and later, looking back, she wishes she had appreciated them even more. 'The problem is you don't ever enjoy nothin enough when you're doin it because you think you will have so many more times just like it.' Philosophical and deeply true, but heart-rending from the lips of a girl who has had so little to enjoy in her lifetime.

Thumbelina can see her new friend Myrna's faults too, but again her tolerance, her quirky, big-hearted outlook on life overrides any negative judgement. 'Myrna is not the kind of girl you should take into a church anyway. She is too squirrelly.'

The original *Thumbelina* is a fairy story in which a thumb-sized girl found in a tulip suffers a series of entrapments and rejections before finally meeting her fairy prince. The fairy Thumbelina is tiny and cute. Andrea Koenig's Thumbelina is tall and gawky. Both are pretty but neither know it because they find themselves in worlds in which they are unable to belong. The fairy Thumbelina is rejected by various insects as being too 'different'; the big Thumbelina feels similarly alienated by her size, her name, her awkwardness, her poverty, her inability to swim, her tarty mother. But what she wants more than anything in the world is to belong. The one occasion when she lets down her guard is when the potential adoptive parents to her unborn child suggest a name for the baby that would 'set her apart from the crowd'. Thumbelina replies heatedly, 'I don't want her standin out in any crowd . . . You give her a normal name'.

In her notes about the novel, Andrea Koenig says that it always seemed to be raining as she wrote it – 'Thus, it is quite wet in and around these pages.' Indeed, the imagery of water pervades the story. Angelica drowns in a pond and the assumption is that Thumbelina does too – we learn early on that she can't swim. The fairy Thumbelina can't swim either, she gets trapped on a lily in the middle of a pond by a frog who wants her for his wife. Andrea Koenig's Thumbelina is trapped by her love for her mother into months of (ultimately fatal) abuse at the hand of Lester, her mother's lover (a similarly evil frog). Thumbelina refers to her baby as the 'fish', and the various references to the wet weather act as a backdrop to Thumbelina's own emotions.

By the use of such symbolism and allegory and subtle allusions to the fairy story, Andrea Koenig has succeeded in creating a compelling mood and atmosphere against which the carefully structured month-by-month physical and emotional ordeal of Thumbelina is played out.

In the fairy story a swallow rescues tiny Thumbelina, flying her away from trouble to meet her tiny prince. Andrea Koenig's Thumbelina doesn't get a prince, but she finds a loving home for her baby, breaking the legacy of abuse and loneliness, and that is her redemption. The novel concludes with Thumbelina joining the mother she adores and forgives; her best friend, her worst enemy. 'She must be gettin lonely. Never could do without me for long.'

Author photograph © Gregory Breytburg

Andrea Koenig received a Fulbright award
to Northern Ireland in 1996 and her M.F.A.
in Creative Writing from Syracuse University
in 1998. *Thumbelina* is her first novel.
She lives in Syracuse, New York.